THE HOUSEWIFE ASSASSIN'S WHITE HOUSE KEEPING SEAL OF APPROVAL

JOSIE BROWN

A BOOK BY

SIGNAL
PRESS

Praise for Josie Brown's Novels

"This is a super sexy and fun read that you shouldn't miss! A kick ass woman that can literally kick ass as well as cook and clean. Donna gives a whole new meaning to "taking out the trash."
—Mary Jacobs, *Book Hounds Reviews*

"*The Housewife Assassin's Handbook* by Josie Brown is a fun, sexy and intriguing mystery. Donna Stone is a great heroine— housewives can lead all sorts of double lives, but as an assassin? Who would have seen that one coming? It's a fast-paced read, the gadgets are awesome, and I could just picture Donna fighting off Russian gangsters and skinheads all the while having a pie at home cooling on the windowsill. As a housewife myself, this book was a fantastic escape that had me dreaming "if only" the whole way through. The book doesn't take itself too seriously, which makes for the perfect combination of mystery and humour."
—*Curled Up with a Good Book and a Cup of Tea*

"*The Housewife Assassin's Handbook* is a hilarious, laugh-out-loud read. Donna is a fantastic character–practical, witty, and kick-ass tough. There's plenty of action–both in and out of the bedroom... I especially love the housekeeping tips at the start of each chapter–each with its own deadly twist! This book is perfect for relaxing in the bath with after a long day. I can't wait to read the next in the series. Highly Recommended!"
—*CrimeThrillerGirl.com*

"This was an addictive read–gritty but funny at the same time. I ended up reading it in just one evening and couldn't go to sleep until I knew what the outcome would be! It was action-packed and humorous from the start, and that continued throughout, I was pleased to discover that this is the first of a series and look forward to getting my hands on Book Two so I can see where life takes Donna and her family next!"

—Me, My Books, and I

"The two halves of Donna's life make sense. As you follow her story, there's no point where you think of her as "Assassin Donna" vs. "Mummy Donna', her attitude to life is even throughout. I really like how well this is done. And as for Jack. I'll have one of those, please?"

—The Northern Witch's Book Blog

Novels in The Housewife Assassin Series

The Housewife Assassin's Handbook

(Book 1)

The Housewife Assassin's Guide to Gracious Killing

(Book 2)

The Housewife Assassin's Killer Christmas Tips

(Book 3)

The Housewife Assassin's Relationship Survival Guide

(Book 4)

The Housewife Assassin's Vacation to Die For

(Book 5)

The Housewife Assassin's Recipes for Disaster

(Book 6)

The Housewife Assassin's Hollywood Scream Play

(Book 7)

The Housewife Assassin's Killer App

(Book 8)

The Housewife Assassin's Hostage Hosting Tips

(Book 9)

The Housewife Assassin's Garden of Deadly Delights

(Book 10)

The Housewife Assassin's Tips for

Weddings, Weapons, and Warfare

(Book 11)

Declaration of Independence

WE HOLD THESE TRUTHS TO BE SELF-EVIDENT, THAT ALL MEN ARE created equal..."

Okay, yeah...

But what about women?

Reality check: these are the times that try women's souls.

Especially those women in two-breadwinner households, where the salaries are barely enough to make the monthly payments, utilities, food bills, medical and countless other expenses;

Including those women who have been mommy-tracked.

Or if they are their family's sole breadwinner.

Trust me, I'm not just whining. (But only because it guarantees frown lines!) This isn't some ladies-night-out pity party. Don't women also deserve to be endowed (men: my head is UP HERE) by their (choose your own) Creator, with the same inalienable Rights to Life, Liberty, and the pursuit of Happiness?

It would help tremendously if women got raises that would make them equal—not 81.4 percent—to men in similar positions.

Let's take a vote on it! By the way, all those in favor will be rewarded with a generous serving of All-American apple pie by your appreciative housewife assassin—

Sans arsenic, unlike those who vote "no."

"Care for some dessert, Mr. Cathcart?"

My question, delivered in a husky whisper, has the desired effect: my target, Milo Cathcart—tech billionaire and founder and CEO of Thunder Cloud Cover—raises his eyes from his iPad to proffer his answer: a nod, accompanied by an appraising gaze at my cleavage, which, between my sheer, low-cut white blouse and my deep purple push-up bra, shows no pretense at playing peek-a-boo.

From Milo's smirk, I guess he reads me loud and clear.

Those who serve The One Percent are usually invisible to them. I guess I've succeeded in mitigating this dilemma.

My cover—as the concierge member of a three-person flight crew on a tricked-out Airbus ACJ319neo—demands it. For the past four hours and some forty-one thousand feet in the air, I've been fluffing pillows in between serving Champagne, shrimp, caviar, and Chateaubriand to Milo and his three security goons.

We are winging our way to Zurich, Switzerland. It is the closest airport to Davos, Switzerland—a posh mountain resort town. There, Milo will attend the World Economic Forum, where he plans on doing a lot of glad-handing and hobnobbing with three thousand other highfalutin' attendees. These include a gaggle of Heads of State (over fifty of them, on taxpayer dollars, no less) and a plethora of billionaires (around one hundred and twenty of them), all of whom have flown in on their own jets (in total, over three hundred aircraft, so almost two for every one of those rich sons of bitches), all with full security details in tow.

Attending this shindig isn't cheap: around $52,000 per person or $300,000 for you and your entourage of up to five.

Still, membership has its privileges. Ostensibly, one is there to discuss how to save Mother Earth from human destruction, particularly that which is wreaking havoc on the planet and our environment. In reality, this event is the perfect opportunity for these corporate titans to out-humble-brag each other as to who gave the most money to the most causes, and which acts of their supposedly conscious capitalism has had the most significant impact.

It is philanthrocapitalism at its most woke.

If it were true that those who acquire great wealth are also the best equipped to mitigate Mother Earth's most vexing problems, this massive shindig should put all worries behind us. Unfortunately, that is not the case. A Davos junket has one purpose only: to pick up a lucrative contract or two.

Milo's aim is to offer a few of the attending heads-of-state-slash-dictators the ultimate stealth weapon: a way to spy on, say, a more charismatic political opponent, activists inciting civil unrest, or perhaps leaders of their enemy countries.

His bag of tricks includes the ultimate electronic eavesdropping technology: a cellphone hack he's named Cyclops that quashes anyone's attempt to "go dark"—that is, communicate through texts and other direct messaging software, like those found on social media. These encrypted channels make it easy for criminals and terrorists to hide from law enforcement, but they are also used by law-abiding citizens who just like to shoot the shit, talk dirty to each other, or grouse about a boss, parent, or spouse, to a buddy.

No doubt about it, despots will be lining up at his door, assured that all bugs have already been worked out by the client who originally contracted and funded Milo's software: the good old U.S. of A.

In other words, Milo is a cybermercenary who's selling state secrets: most definitely, a treasonous no-no.

MI6 stumbled across Milo's plan and passed it on to Acme Industries, my soon-to-be-former employer that also happens to be a special ops contractor to several US intelligence agencies. This is my last Acme mission before I'm to be sworn in by the President of the United States, Bradley Edmonton, as his new Senior National Security Advisor: a.k.a., hard woman for any dirty job he sees fit for me to do.

I wouldn't be here except for the fact that Edmonton is blackmailing me with the threat of jailing my husband, Jack, as a traitor to his country for an unsanctioned hit on Congresswoman Elle Grisham. Elle was a Russian asset. Edmonton sanctioned the hit for a very good reason: when she died, she took with her proof that Edmonton was also a Russian spy, and has been for the past four decades, since his college days.

Of course, Edmonton would deny it, then have Jack tried as her murderer and a traitor, all but assuring he would die in prison.

I'm sure MI6 would have preferred the intel on Milo to go directly to the CIA. But our cousins across the pond are no fools. Since Bradley Edmonton took over as President of the United States, they've noticed a disconcertingly friendly shift in our country's diplomatic policy toward Russia. The recent ousting of the Director of Intelligence, Marcus Branham, also raised eyebrows.

His replacement is the former Acme Industries' CEO, Ryan Clancy. This has quelled some of the Free World's squeamishness. But you can't blame the Cousins for thinking, *better safe than sorry*, right?

Along with Marcus, Ryan, Jack, and former US President Lee Chiffray, I have vowed to rid the White House of its foreign saboteur.

Milo contemplates my offer to indulge any cravings he may have. "Dessert, eh? What's on the menu?"

We've been airborne for the past few hours, but this is the first time he's elected to speak to me—or anyone, for that matter. I'm surprised at his voice: a very deep bass with a Kentucky drawl.

I smile pretty and coo, "Can I tempt you with cherries jubilee?"

Laughing heartily, he eases back onto the jet's serpentine leather sofa. "That's a new twist on 'coffee, tea, or me.' But hey, I'm game."

No surprise there. In Silicon Valley's swinging sex party circuit, Milo's hardcore appetites are as renowned as his staying power, the latter being rare among members of the Three Commas Club. (Techie slang for billionaires.)

Despite this flirtatious tête-à-tête, I have no plans to personally validate this rumor firsthand. But I do need to infiltrate his private bedroom to gain access to his laptop.

I'll stand and deliver, but I'll be damned if I let him do the same.

Milo nods toward his security detail, who, between swigs of Scotch, have been shouting curses at the sixty-inch television monitor as the Israeli soccer team scrimmages with Portugal. Grabbing his champagne flute, he proclaims, "Feed these animals while I relax in the sauna. I'll buzz when I'm ready to take you up on your offer for...something sweet."

If I have any doubt as to what Milo is expecting, he makes himself clear when he grazes my breast with his champagne flute.

As he saunters to his private bedroom in the rear of the plane, he looks back to give me a lascivious smirk.

We land in four hours. I have my work cut out for me. Milo's goon squad is made up of former Israeli military intelligence operatives: Mossad, which means I can't screw up in my disarmament plan, or I'm a dead woman. Just one of these guys would prove a challenge. Facing off against all three might literally mean breaking a heel. But only because both of mine are tricked out with a few handy accoutrements: a stiletto in one, a small aerosol vial of the knock-out drug, Fentanyl, in the other.

I don't wear these Louboutins simply because they're *pretty*.

Not to worry! My Loubies are safe. Plan A for how I'll get around Milo and his goon squad is already in the works. Their drinks have been laced with Rohypnol. Hey, why not? It's an equal-opportunity knock-out drug. They can holler "Me too!..." all they want at their next bro-out.

I watch from the galley as the drug takes effect. The men are sluggish. They rub their eyes and slur their words. In a few minutes, they are as peaceful as sleeping newborns.

Right on schedule.

I presume Milo has passed out too, which will give me all the time I need to add an undetectable trojan virus to his laptop, allowing Acme and MI6 to monitor all of Milo's communications. Before we land in Zurich, Acme's tech-op extraordinaire, Arnie Locklear, will have hacked the computer's file containing Milo's software program. This will allow him to add a line of code that informs the targets on his clients' watchlists that they've been infected so that they can ditch their devices *pronto*.

Milo will then have a lot of explaining to do. No doubt, a tap with a poisoned umbrella tip is in his future.

I rap softly on his door. Hearing nothing, I open it slowly.

The sauna is positioned in the far corner of the bedroom. Steam rises from the large smooth river rocks piled high in the large ceramic pedestal dead center of the small glass enclosure. Milo is fully shrouded from view. But then, for just a moment, the thick mist shifts, allowing me to see him.

He is lying down on one of the sauna's long narrow benches. His eyes are closed.

Perfect.

Milo's laptop is on the bed. While waiting in the plane's galley, I'd scanned his thumbprint from the water glass served with his dinner, which I now use to unlock his computer.

I've just inserted a thumb drive holding the trojan when I hear the sauna door open.

What the heck?

At that moment, I see Milo's champagne flute on the nightstand.

It's full.

He didn't drink it.

I don't turn around. Instead, with one hand, I slip the laptop under a pillow. With the other, I unbutton my blouse.

By the time I turn around, he only has eyes for me.

Well, my purple balconette bra.

At the same time, I'm trying to avert my eyes from Milo's only appendage standing at full attention.

Oh, bother. No problem with shrinkage there.

Milo snickers. "Like what you see?" His taunt is accompanied by a gangsta motion: the double-handed chop to his crotch.

I wince. His third leg is as long as his voice is deep. No doubt, he's the life of every Three Commas Club orgy.

Instead, I chuckle, as if he's naughty, and I'm shy. "I

thought saunas are supposed to relax you. From what I can see, you are *anything* but that!"

He nods toward the steamy glass box. "Have you ever made love in a sauna?"

I shake my head.

"It's invigorating! Opens all your pores. Releases"—he circles one of my breasts with his index finger— "pheromones." The word, dripping with menace, makes me wince. "They smell…"

I murmur: "Heavenly?"

He mistakes that as an invitation to pull me into it with him.

"But—I'm dressed!" I jerk my arm away.

"Not for long." To make his point, Milo strips my blouse off my back as he yanks me into to the sauna, backing me up against the steaming pedestal. With all my might, I flip him around so that he's got his back to the pedestal instead. (Easy enough to do. He may be tall, but he's also scrawny. What is it with tech types? Don't they understand the importance of upper body definition?)

Milo grins while I lean into him, my lips working their way over his torso and chest. By the time they reach his mouth, his eyes are closed. My kiss is deep, mesmerizing him long enough for me to reach back with my right hand and twist off my right heel—the one holding the Fentanyl vial.

I pour it into the steam.

Yes, I'm taking the chance that I'll pass out too. But then I hold my breath, counting down from my all-time record for doing this—

Seventy-six seconds…seventy-five, seventy-four…

—But at the time, my bra wasn't being unhooked and yanked from me. Nor was I being tossed onto to a bench.

Triumphantly, Milo holds my bra over his head. Swinging

its straps like a lasso, he hoots, "To the victor goes the spoils!"

Fifty-one...fifty...forty-nine...

But to Milo's mind, the real prize lies between my thighs. He jerks my skirt high on my hips and then straddles me.

When I lock my legs around him, he assumes it's because I enjoy his rough sex play. *Wrong.* What he doesn't know is that it's the only way for me to grab hold of my left heel and release the tiny stiletto encased there. I then drop my arm after palming it, blade open—

Thirty-three...thirty-two...thirty-one...

He's using a hand to position himself to enter me.

Ain't gonna happen, pal.

Instinctively, I try to rise up—

But Milo shoves me down again. His adrenaline rush is offsetting the Fentanyl misting around us.

Twenty-six... twenty-five...twenty-four...

Suddenly, he places my bra around my throat and tightens it, like a garrote. Leering over me, he exclaims, "Hey, I'm going to take you for a walk on the wild side! Have you ever tried autoerotic asphyxiation? ...No? Whoa, great! I get to be your first!"

Like hell you will!

The last thing I need is to let go of the breath I'm holding.

Milo doesn't get to make the decision for me. In one quick motion, I stab the knife into his neck.

When Milo's dead weight falls forward on top of me, I gasp from the shock.

I can't move out from under him. My lungs fill with hot steam as I struggle to get up.

Worse yet, the Fentanyl must be kicking in because I'm fading...

Fast...

Three...two...

2

Modus Vivendi

In international diplomacy, "modus vivendi" is the term for a temporary agreement, made in writing and pending further negotiations, that spells out a more definitive arrangement to come.

We try to be diplomatic in our personal relationships as well. Many times, we put a few negotiable terms in writing—say, an email, or a text—but then circumstances may change what we hope is the final outcome.

Fair warning: few things need to be carved in stone.

Or into the other negotiator's skin for that, matter.

Still, it makes sense to carry a knife, just in case.

Someone stands over me. He wears a gas mask.

When Milo's dead body is shoved out of the way, it lands on the floor with a thunk.

Gently, the bra is untangled from my neck: not an easy task, since I flail as I gasp for air. It goes into his pocket. Is he trying to shame me, or is he keeping it as a souvenir?

As he picks me up and carries me out of the sauna, I reach up to pull off his mask:

He is the plane's co-pilot.

He is my husband, Jack.

But of course, he is.

"WHAT DO WE DO NOW?" I MUTTER. I'M STILL A BIT WOOZY.

Right now, I'm mainlining coffee to stay awake. We stand in the cockpit with Acme's top pilot, George Taylor, who is the captain of our flight.

He glances over at Jack. "Up to the boss."

Jack grimaces. He's not used to being called "boss." It wasn't a position he coveted. He'd much rather be out in the field.

Really, he'd rather be home, tossing a baseball to our son Jeff; or teaching our eldest, Mary, how to drive; or helping our youngest, Trisha, with her homework.

Instead, we are on this one last field trip together—maybe permanently—until we come up with a way to get out from under Edmonton's thumb.

Which starts with fooling the three former Mossad agents in the main cabin.

Before they wake up, we've got to come up with a great excuse as to why they can't see their boss.

By how Jack flexes his fists, he's still upset with himself that he took so long to check on Milo and me. Granted, it was only a few minutes from the time I entered the bedroom. Still, with the combination of the Fentanyl, the steam, and Milo's dead body weighing down my lungs, had he waited any longer, I may not have made it.

To assure Jack that all is well, I take one of his hands in

mine and hold it up my lips to kiss it. I know he's shaken off the fear of losing me when I look up to see him smiling again.

"We're beyond Iceland," I point out.

George gawks. "You mean, eject them while we're in flight?"

"What I mean is…" George was once a fighter pilot, for God's sake! I hope he's not going soft on us. I try to make my point clearer: "Why wait for them to wake up to take them out?"

"I can't let you do that," he warns me.

"Sometimes, it's necessary," I counter.

"Donna, what George is saying is that we can't just open a door and toss them out. You've been there, done that. Teddy Grodin. Remember? How did that work out for you?"

"In my defense, he leaped out under his own volition," I remind him.

Teddy was a CIA contractor-turned-traitor who, like Milo, hired the wrong private jet company—again, Acme Air, with me playing air hostess with the mostess—in an attempt to fly the friendly skies to financial freedom at the expense of Uncle Sam's national security. His plan for getting a refund on his one-way ticket to a life sentence was to grab a parachute before opening our airborne plane's cabin door.

Somewhere around fourteen thousand feet, he figured out the parachute was a fake.

Still, Jack's got a point. It's a nonstarter. Since we're currently cruising at forty-four thousand feet, we'd need to be wearing oxygen masks and tethered to steel cables so that we don't follow Milo and his guards out the door.

Not to mention, the turbulence would probably break the plane apart.

Since this sleek set of wings is our ride home, I must gracefully concede, despite my growing panic that we won't be able to hoodwink Milo's goon squad into thinking all is well until we somehow escort them off the plane before taking off again.

"Whatever we do, now we can take Milo's computer with us," I point out.

Jack nods. "You're right. It's golden! Arnie and the rest of Acme's tech team can mine it for other tricks Milo had in his arsenal." He pulls out his satellite phone, which is buzzing. "Speak of the devil." Jack taps the line to open it.

"Hi, Craigs!" Arnie says in unison with Emma Honeycutt —Acme's ComInt director, who also happens to be his wife.

Yep, Acme is one big happy family.

"Great timing, you two," Jack replies. "Donna can start transmission in a minute."

"First, I need to bring you into the loop on another pending issue." Emma sighs. "At the behest of Edmonton's Chief of Staff, Mario Martinez, Milo now has another meeting on his agenda—*with Leonid Volkov.*"

"*What?*" Jack and I exclaim in unison.

Volkov is one of the oligarchs entrenched in Vladimir Putin's inner circle of thieves and sycophants. He makes his bazillions in the production of vodka.

"Ostensibly, Leonid is here introducing some sustainably sourced, eco-friendly version of his rotgut potato swill," Arnie explains. "He calls it 'Earth, Wind, and Fire'—EWF for short."

Jack snorts. "Catchy."

Not.

"Has Mario been instructed by Edmonton to use Milo as a courier between Edmonton and Putin? And, if so, is Volkov delivering the message, or is Milo?" I wonder out loud.

"That's what *You Know Who* wants you to find out." Arnie murmurs.

He's referring to Branham. Despite having been pushed out of his position as Director of Intelligence by Edmonton, Branham still has enough friends there. To them, he is still the intelligence community's heart and soul. The biggest, and perhaps the final battle of the New Cold War is being fought on American soil, and Branham is still our general.

"You can say his name," I tease Arnie. "My God, he's not Voldemort! He's one of the good guys."

"Better safe than sorry," he counters. "Edmonton has ears everywhere. Or, in this case, Milo. I hear he's been testing his own version of an Intelligence Assistant—you know, like Apple's Siri or Amazon's Alexa."

"In any case, Branham thinks you guys should tag along," Emma adds.

I sigh. "Um...It's...not an option."

"Why not?" Arnie asks.

"Milo Me-Too'd Donna, and she Me-Too'd him right back —only permanently," Jack explains.

Arnie and Emma's groans are like a Greek chorus predicting tragedy—at my expense.

"Our thought exactly," Jack mutters.

I turn to Jack. "We can't let this opportunity slip by. It may give us the proof we need against Edmonton."

Jack shrugs. "Agreed. But how do we pull it off?"

"Jack, you'll have to take his place," Arnie replies. "With all the photos of Milo available, we can have Acme's Paris office whip up a latex mask and meet you when you land in Zurich."

"What about my voice?" Jack asks. "Milo's voice is—I mean *was*—as deep as Darth Vader's."

"As it happens, DARPA has created a real-time voice alteration app," Emma informs us. "It's an enhanced version of the ones that gamers use for online cosplay."

"How does the technology work, exactly?" I ask.

"Jack will download it from Acme's secure cloud onto his iPhone. Then he'll upload a file that mimics Milo's voice pattern. Milo gave enough interviews that the ComInt team can capture his tone and cadence," Emma explains. "A tiny flesh-colored microphone—one-tenth of an inch in diameter —will be embedded in Jack's mask, adjacent to his mouth. When Jack speaks, the app in his cell will pick up whatever he's saying. Instantaneously, it transmits Milo's voice through the mic."

"I tested it myself," Arnie assures us. "I used Mickey Mouse's voice. It had little Nicky in stitches!"

"Yeah—to the point where he now wants you to do it all the time." Emma's exasperated tone is merited. A toddler underfoot is one thing. Having a husband who sometimes reverts to teen antics must also be exhausting.

Arnie huffed, "I thought you liked it!"

"*Not in bed*, silly!"

"Too much information," Jack, George, and I shout.

The home-based members of our team are chastised enough to give it a rest. Finally, Arnie mutters, "In any event, Boss, just push the button and the voice alteration app does the rest. You'll sound just like the dearly departed. You can practice with your iPhone's mic until you get the mask."

"If it's our only option, so be it." Jack sighs. "They'll be expecting me to bring an interpreter. Coquette Rambert is in our Paris office. Since she speaks fluent Russian, she'll be perfect in the role. Give her a call, Emma. She can bring the mask."

Hmm…

Coquette was at my bachelorette party. There, I learned that Jack had recruited her to spy on her lover: a Russian general assigned to her native country, Latvia, who enjoyed torturing women and children for the whereabouts of rebel fighters: their husbands and fathers.

She wasn't shy in mentioning that Jack's way of persuading her to play femme fatale included some bedroom gymnastics. It was years before he and I had met, so no issues there—

At least, for me. By the way that Coquette licked her lips as she rhapsodized about the incident, who knows if she'll be hankering for a trip down memory lane?

"What if Volkov isn't the messenger? I mean...we don't know if Milo was supposed to hand off the intel or receive it," I argue.

Their silence speaks volumes.

"Coquette and I will just have to wing it until Arnie is done scouring Milo's computer for any intel on the meeting's purpose," Jack declares.

I guess that leaves me twiddling my thumbs while we're in Davos.

As if.

I guess my smirk has caught Jack's eye because he's got a perplexed look on his face. "Is something wrong?"

"Not at all!" I bat my eyes.

"Are you sure?" The question comes with a raised brow.

I shrug. Then a bit louder so that the speaker picks me up, I declare: "Arnie, I'm ready to transmit whenever you are. In fact, before we start, I think I'll make myself comfortable in the master bedroom."

Despite the dead body shriveling up in the blood-splattered sauna.

All in a day's work.

In comparison, the White House should be a piece of cake. Sure, political foes stab each other in the back, but that's just metaphorically speaking.

For the most part.

~

It takes a half-hour for the files to transmit to Arnie back at Acme Headquarters.

I hear a knock on the door just after the upload is completed. "May I come in?"

Involuntarily, I shiver. Although I know it's Jack, his voice is a dead ringer for Milo's deep twangy baritone.

As I get up to open the door, I divert my eyes from the sauna. At least the steam is hiding Milo's corpse.

I open the door to find Jack holding a single red rose. "So, what do you think? Does my voice pass muster?"

I raise a thumbs-up. "Sort of, like a ventriloquist with a dummy, right?"

Jack must detect the frost in my response because he pulls me with him toward the bed and into his lap.

"Why don't we play 'ventriloquist and his beautiful puppet?'" he asks playfully.

I shake my head. "Why don't you save that line for Coquette? I'm sure she'd gladly say yes—especially after hearing your new deep drawl."

"I knew it!" Jack exclaims. As he throws up his hands, I'm tossed off his lap and onto the bed. "All of a sudden, you're jealous? Care to tell me why?"

"Because… Let's just say that Coquette made it quite clear that you're the one who got away."

"That's *her* problem—not yours nor mine." He strokes my cheek. "Donna, please—don't project your fear of this mission onto Coquette, or anyone else."

My laugh is mirthless. "You're telling me not to be afraid? Sure, okay! But fair warning: *I'm not afraid for me, but for you.*

If Coquette makes one false move, you could be burned! For this mission, there is no one you can trust more than me."

"She's been in life-or-death situations, too. Remember? She's slept with the enemy too—and lived to watch him die."

"Have you forgotten that we're up against the most powerful man in the world?" I argue.

"One with many powerful enemies," Jack points out.

"And one very powerful ally," I counter.

Jack frowns at the thought of Putin. "We're a team—*in the field and at home.*"

"That's just it, Jack! We're in the field right now. This is the most important mission we've had. In fact, this may be our last mission together—if not forever, then for a long, long time." I hate that my voice is trembling. "I should be in there with you."

Jack takes my hands. "Mrs. Craig, if something goes wrong, you're the Cavalry. You're the one person I can count on to save me."

Jack is right. I'll have eyes and ears on them at all times.

His rational response deserves a kiss.

But Jack doesn't want to stop there.

I click his phone to OFF mode and toss it on the bedside table. What's left of Milo may still be in the room, but I'm making love to Jack.

THERE IS SOMETHING TO BE SAID FOR A MAN WHOSE LOVEMAKING is always a satisfying tango of sensations.

His eyes are deep pools of wanton desire. Mine widen with anticipation of the pleasure they promise me.

My scent hardens him. Inhaling his musk, I melt into his arms.

He savors the taste of me. I crave to have him inside me.

His touch—firm grasps, frantic pats, that first deep thrust —thrills me.

His sounds—lusty growls—are drowned out by my bliss-filled moans.

The last movement of any dance should leave the partners on an adrenaline rush before crashing into sated contentment.

We have no such luxury.

Not while one of Milo's guards raps on the bedroom door, exclaiming, "Boss?...*Boss!*... Did you hear? The pilot just made the announcement that we are on the final approach..."

THOUGH NAKED, JACK AND I SCRAMBLE OUT OF BED.

"The app!" I hiss.

He grabs his phone and turns it on again.

At the same time, I reach for the two plush terry robes hanging on hooks near the sauna. Tossing one at Jack, I whisper, "I'll answer the door. Sit on the bed with your back to the door. When I open it, tell him to clear out with the others and that you and I will meet them at the hotel."

"Got it," he says.

His eyes open wide.

Damn it—*he sounds like Mickey Mouse!*

"What the hell..." Jack's hiss sounds as it's filled with helium.

I slap my forehead. Better Mickey than Minnie, I guess...

Well, not really.

"Don't say anything!" I warn him. "I'll take care of this." I fling the door wide open—

And find myself facing the largest of the guards, a solid block of muscle and sinew named Ori.

Smirking, I purr, "We're...*busy.*"

Because I'm in no rush to tie my robe, Ori sees plenty of full-frontal Donna. As his eyes take in the sights, Jack growls, "You heard the lady!"

Thank goodness—*now* he sounds just like Milo!

Ori tries to look beyond me, but his male instinct forces his eyes onto my exposed breast instead.

I also turn to look at Jack. His back is to us, and the robe's hood is up over his head. He barks, "Put your eyes back in their sockets. Then, you and the rest of your numb-nuts crew can just hightail it over to the hotel and await my instructions!"

I'm sure the kiss I blow to Ori does little to assuage his terror about losing his job.

Like Milo, the guards have rooms at the InterContinental Davos. By the time they reach the hotel, Emma will have a thick envelope waiting for them at the front desk. Inside will be three coach tickets in their names on the next commercial jet back to the states, along with checks amounting to two months' severance pay.

The letter accompanying these items will be signed by Milo's in-house attorney on the company's letterhead. It will state that their services have been severed due to their negligence. It will remind them that, per their employment contracts, any indiscretion on their part pertaining to Milo will be prosecuted to the fullest extent of the law.

We leave George so that he can prep the plane for a speedy getaway.

We have less than thirty-six hours to be stateside, where we both start new jobs: Jack, as Acme's head, and me as Edmonton's bitch.

I mean that metaphorically.

I pray I'm right about that.

3

State of Emergency

SITUATIONS THAT MERIT THE TERM "STATE OF EMERGENCY" include natural disasters, civil unrest, or armed conflicts.

At these times, the US government feels justified to perform actions or impose policies not normally permitted, such as suspending certain rights and freedoms guaranteed under basic laws of our Constitution.

A relationship may also undergo a state of emergency. If so, you too should feel justified to impose certain policies, effective immediately.

For example, if your husband goes AWOL with his buddies too frequently, you can suspend his freedoms by flattening his tires. If he insists on leaving your bathroom a natural disaster area, feel free to increase his national debt by calling in a maid service that will perform the necessary HazMat duties. If his dour attitude incites you to riot, consider making his rest less than civil.

Locking him out of the bedroom will accomplish this goal quite nicely.

And if you find lipstick on his collar, armed conflict is certainly in order.

MILO IS STAYING ON THE PLANE WITH GEORGE, WHO HAS BEEN instructed to store the body in the plane's cargo hold. While we're in Davos, the cold weather on the ground will ensure that Milo stays nice and fresh.

Once we're airborne, the temperature at high altitude will be frigid enough for it to keep until we land and move it into refrigeration in Acme's lab.

During the WEF, the only way into Davos from the airport is either by helicopter (ten minutes) or by car (an hour). If the latter, a limousine is the chariot of choice.

Milo, however, had chosen to make his grand entrance in a two-seater sports car: something called a Koenigsegg CCXR Trevita.

Seeing it, Jack lets loose with a low whistle.

I chuckle. "I guess I'm supposed to be impressed."

He groans at my ignorance. "Hell yeah! It's not even two decades old and already a classic. Donna, trust me—*this is one of the most expensive cars ever made!*"

"How much?"

Jack shrugs. "Almost five mil."

"*What?*" I bend down in order to gawk through the sports car's low-slung window. "Is it gold-plated?"

"Something like that!" He circles the automobile. "It's got a twin-deck carbon fiber rear wing, carbon ceramic brakes, an Inconel exhaust system—not to mention the patented Koenigsegg 'Shimmering Diamond Weave' bodywork—"

I roll my eyes. "Sir, you are now speaking in tongues."

"Only two were ever made," Jack's reverential whisper draws a snort from me.

"Is that your way of saying that crashing it would bankrupt us—not to mention Acme?" I grab the key fob from his hand. "Then I guess I should drive."

He snatches it back. "Like hell, you will! Not in Switzerland in January. Not during gale-wind flurries, black ice, and snowbanks that come up to your shoulder—"

"Okay, all right! I get the message!" I tweak his nose. "Sheesh! Boys and their toys!"

We heave our duffel bags into the trunk. We've also taken Milo's computer along with some of Tech Boy Wonder's hipster duds, which make Jack look like a million dollars (yep, he's keeping them). We leap into the Trevita and it's over the black ice and through the woods, to the WEF we go…

THE INTERCONTINENTAL DAVOS IS NICKNAMED "THE GOLDEN Egg" for two reasons. First, the hand-over-fist money it makes during this one week of the year. And secondly, because it is indeed gold in hue and oval-shaped. The middle floors bow out cylindrically from the building's frame, leaving less square footage on the top floor, like an egg that is laying on its side.

Just a mile east of Lake Davos, the hotel is nestled in the crook of an elbow formed by two mountains.

We check in as Milo's advance team. No questions are asked. Milo's suite is on the very top floor of the hotel. It's humongous enough to claim dead-on views of the lake and the tallest mountain peak. A terrace runs the full length of the suite.

I assume Leonid Volkov has a similar set-up also on this floor.

Speaking of which, a fruit basket is waiting for Milo, courtesy of the gentleman from Moscow. Accompanying it is an invitation to an event he's throwing in less than an hour: some hoe-down where the VIP guests will be sampling "several naturally flavored eco-vodkas, along with an Earth-friendly smorgasbord of delicious hors d'oeuvres that include sustainably harvested Russian caviar served on fair-trade crackers made from GMO-free grains."

I snicker. "Volkov knows that caviar is a fancy word for fish eggs, right? Not exactly plant-based cuisine—"

The words are barely out of my mouth when there's a knock on the door.

Jack and I glance at the room's security monitor.

Coquette Rambert waves at the camera.

Despite being tall and slim, Coquette has a generous bosom which her skin-tight low-cut cocktail frock emphasizes to its full advantage. The color of the dress is an iridescent bottle green. Her glossy mahogany tresses flow below her shoulders. Any pretense that she's merely an interpreter begins and ends with her glasses.

"How adorable," I mutter. "Her dress matches the color of her eyes."

"Donna! *Please*—"

"I know, Jack. She's just the interpreter. Whereas I'm the *Cavalry*."

Which means, if the time comes, I ride in, guns blazing.

Appropriate enough. If anyone is going to be doing a reverse cowgirl with Jack, it's me.

"Speaking of which, if you want to stay close to the action, why not try passing yourself off as a waiter?" he suggests.

I huff, "I'm sure I can do better than that."

By the time Jack opens the door, I've wrapped my arm around his waist. He's too taken aback by this quick maneuver to do anything but look annoyed.

I take up the slack by cooing, "Ah! Coquette! Long time no see! Please come in. We've been dying to play catch-up..."

First, there are the air kisses, on both cheeks—

For me.

For Jack, Coquette brushes her lips against his, if barely.

"You haven't changed a bit since we last met!" She gazes into his eyes. "When was it again?"

Grrr...

"The day Jack and I married," I growl.

Jack winces. After collecting himself, he leads her to one of the suite's couches and then waits until I take my seat—on the couch opposite hers—before joining me there.

Good boy.

Coquette opens her valise and pulls out a makeup kit and a pair of scissors. Then, from the valise's hidden compartment, she unzips a flat black shirt box. "*Voila!*" She opens the box's lid, revealing the latex mask. Gently, she lifts it off its mold. "Time is of the essence. Shall we?"

Milo sits before us.

Jack's version of him is more muscular, and the hair is just a tad shorter. But, frankly, Milo never looked so good.

Thank goodness, the voice is lifelike.

Emma informs us that Arnie has yet to hack Edmonton's encrypted email to Milo. Jack and Coquette will have to wing it until he does. Thankfully, our Acme team can relay the intel directly through Jack's earpiece. Since I'll be wearing mine, I'll hear it too, just as my special contact lenses will allow me to see what Jack is transmitting through his pair. Emma and Arnie will also have video surveillance via Jack's lenses and Arnie's hack into the hotel's security feeds.

There are still a few minutes before Volkov's party. While Coquette coos and I stew, Jack takes a few minutes to watch videos of Milo: in news interviews, doing a Ted talk, and onstage at his Thunder Cloud Cover's annual sales shows.

IN THE MEANTIME, I'VE DECIDED I'M CRASHING THE PARTY. My little black dress is really silver: a metallic Ralph and Russo off-the-shoulder cocktail dress that clings to all the right places. I pair it with curved-heel pearl-encrusted sandals.

I join Coquette as she freshens her makeup in the adjacent powder room. Seeing me, she nods appraisingly.

As I stroke my upper lip with a gloss wand, I casually ask, "Dating anyone?"

Coquette's hand freezes so that she doesn't muss her perfect lashes with her mascara brush. "All the good ones are taken, *ma cherie*." Shrugging, she adds, "How is marriage treating my Jacques?"

Her Jacques? As if.

"We're still in the newlywed phase! He is…well, let me just say, 'passionate' is an understatement." My declaration sounds too loud, too insistent, too…

Worried. To make up for it, I attempt a blissful smile.

Big mistake. My gloss wand roams too far north of my upper lip, giving me a smeared leer worthy of the Batman's nemesis, Joker.

"*Est-ce vrai?*" Coquette's brow arches. "*Bien…!* Your declaration sings to my heart, as it rivals my own memories of true *amour,* my *cheri.* As George Sand once famously said: '*Il n'y a qu'un bonheur dans la vie, c'est d'aimer et d'être aimé.*"

I'm almost afraid to ask, but I must: "What does it mean?"

"'There is only one happiness in life: to love and be loved.'" Coquette lays her hand on my shoulder. "Jacques felt that about you the very first time he saw you. The love story you share is legendary in our industry, dear Donna. After this mission, we will drink a toast to it, for it is as rare as life is fleeting—especially for those who must lie and kill for their country." She wipes away a tear. "*Merde!* I am a mess! As if we have time for tears, eh?"

Suddenly, I feel silly to have felt so threatened by her. "I wish you luck in finding your own 'Jacques,' Coquette."

"Who knows? Maybe he is here tonight." She's all smiles again.

"And if so, we'll have another reason to raise a glass in good cheer," I vow.

"Filled with some *magnifique* Champagne," Coquette declares firmly. "Not vodka—especially not Volkov's piss! When I was with the general, I had enough of that to last a lifetime." She shudders. "It is time to go, I'm afraid." She gives me an appraising glance. "All the men in the room will be staring your way, which is good. Heaven knows, Jacques and I will need a diversion if we are to pull this off with no concrete intel as to what we are here to do."

She heads out to get Jack.

I'll give them enough lead time before making my entrance.

THE PARTY IS TAKING PLACE IN THE HOTEL'S BALLROOM, ON THE lobby level. Four stories tall, it doubles as an amphitheater.

A gigantic clear circular plexiglass tank is in the center of the room. It rises to the fourth-floor balcony. The tank's base is encircled with a much shorter pool, just chest-high.

The women swimming around the tank wear sequined fishtails and sheer bodysuits decorated with strategically placed glitter and colorful wigs sporting waist-length tendrils. The guests—both those on the ballroom floor and others who sit in the amphitheater's cantilevered second and third-floor balconies—are enthralled by these mermaids, who dive into the tank from the cordoned-off top balcony.

The mermaids flip, twist, and wave to guests as they swim all the way to the tank's bottom. When they resurface in the pool surrounding the base of the tank, they are holding bottles of flavored vodka. I assume there is a trap door between the two.

The guests sit close enough to beckon them over for a sample.

Despite four separate lines to get into this shindig, a formidable phalanx of guards check invitations against all guests' formal identification, causing the line to move slowly.

Recognizing "Milo," a guard quickly ushers Jack and Coquette out of the line and toward the event's host.

Leonid Volkov is as broad as he is tall. The scar that roams from his left cheek to his forehead isn't as off putting as his scowl, which borders on a sneer.

Through my ear buds, I hear Volkov's interpreter making the introductions. When Volkov shakes Coquette's hand, she flinches. He frowns at the affront.

We're trained to grin and bear it. She knows this all too well. I hope she doesn't blow it.

Volkov walks Jack and Coquette to a seating area on the far side of the tank.

Just then, Emma mutters into my ear: "Donna, Arnie

cracked Milo's email encryption! One email contains the message he's supposed to pass to Volkov. But we seem to be getting interference. It's coming from the voice altering app on Jack's phone. Can you write down the intel and pass it to Jack?"

"On it," I murmur.

Suddenly, I notice someone on the second-floor balcony, watching them.

It's Edmonton's Chief of Staff, Mario Martinez.

Does that mean Edmonton is also here?

If so, I can't afford to let either man see me.

I watch as Mario's eyes scan the thickening crowd. Just as he looks my way, I duck behind the entourage of an Oscar-winning actor renowned for his support of environmental causes.

I need not worry. Like every other guest, a ruckus in the line farthest from mine has caught Mario's attention. Three men are protesting a gatekeeper's assertion that the party is not open to everyone.

They aren't on the invitation list as they are Milo's former bodyguards.

They got their marching orders. Why aren't they long gone?

I duck out through the masses eager to party into the night.

THE FIRST THING I NEED TO DO IS FIND A PRIVATE PLACE TO WRITE down the intel needed to be relayed to Jack. The line for the powder room is too long, so I head for the one in the basement level lounge—

Only to discover I'm in Mermaid Central.

At least two dozen lithesome ladies are lounging around

in sheer bodysuits, awaiting the makeup artists to finish so that they too can take their turns in the colossal tank.

Unused costumes hang from nearby clothing racks. Stylists dart around with palettes of what I assume are waterproof paints, touching up the swimmers' faces.

Suddenly, a couple of swimmers come stumbling in. They lurch toward a nearby sink and retch into it.

"What's wrong with them?" I ask the closest mermaid.

She shrugs. "Didn't they tell you? We have to swim four floors down! It's easy to get the bends, or vertigo." She points to a bowl filled with medicinal capsules. "If we must take a break, they insist we take these pills to help us get through it."

"Who wants to take a break?" Another mermaid retorts. "We're paid by the pour!"

It's a crazy stunt. Unfortunately, so is what I have to do next.

First, I grab a bodysuit, a swim cap, a wig, a makeup palette, and a tail. Next, I swipe a pen from the check-in table along with a blank timecard. Finally, I pocket a few capsules before heading for one of the portable changing rooms.

EMMA READS ME MILO'S INTEL: A SERIES OF NUMBERS AND letters, twenty-one in all, in sets of four spaced by dashes.

I scribble it onto a scrap of paper, including the dashes in between:

38HA - POOR - LULU - WILL - HATE - U

"What do you make of it?" I ask.

"Beats me," Emma admits. "I've got the SigInt team trying to decipher it."

I can't let the paper get wet. I open one of the capsules, pour out the medicine, and replace it with the intel before twisting it shut again.

"Warn them I'll reach them from poolside, and that the intel is in the capsule," I tell her.

Emma sighs. "I hope they hear me! So far, I've been given no indication that they can."

I suit up quickly. Like the other women, I carry my tail over my shoulder before heading to the service elevator and our fourth-floor destination.

Following the moves of the other mermaids, I slip into my tail, which snaps at my waist. Then, sitting on the ledge of the tank, I hold my breath and shove off into the water.

4

The Tank

THE JOINT CHIEFS OF STAFF CONFERENCE ROOM LIES DEEP IN THE bowels of the Pentagon—a sanctum sanctorum, if you please—where those who lead our country's armed forces gather to discuss the gravest issues concerning our nation's security.

Its massive table can seat a battalion of generals. Its appointments are gold as if reflecting the stars that line the epaulets on these great soldiers' shoulders. Wall-sized monitors, skipping around the world via satellites, are aimed at the hot spots that might explode into a war at the whim of a despot.

Because this room's invincible security is akin to an armored vehicle, it is nicknamed "the Tank." But a fish tank is also an apt metaphor, considering how fast one must swim to survive in the murky waters of the military establishment.

Every housewife needs her own tank: a place she has designed with her world's best interest as its focus. A place where she has eyes and ears on her domain, where she is in complete control.

To put it bluntly: your home is your tank. Your family's issues are your hotspots.

As President Theodore Roosevelt so famously said, "Speak

softly and carry a big stick." Ergo, should any despot step into your domain, diplomacy is advisable as the first step in your negotiations toward a peaceful detente. Still, from the get-go, let the interloper know there are other options and you aren't afraid to use them.

THE GOOD NEWS: THE MERMAID TANK IS EQUIPPED WITH OXYGEN suction hoses that run vertically through the tank, ten feet apart.

The bad news: Jack sits in a chair with his back to the tank, so he may not even see me.

I dive toward my destination: Volkov's VIP couch by way of the trap door that takes me out of the tank and into the shallow pool.

Coquette, who is in a chair placed between Jack's and Volkov's couches, would be able to see me if she took a moment to look in the tank's direction. Unfortunately, she's too busy translating the conversation between Volkov and "Milo."

When I reach the pool's bottom, I grab one of the racked vodka bottles—one claiming to be lime-infused—before pushing the button that sucks me from one side to the other.

All this time, I've been holding my breath. I emerge, gasping for air.

Jack sits twenty feet away.

I'm not the only person swimming toward him. Another mermaid seems to have the same plan, which means I have to wriggle more quickly through the water.

Mario now sits on a sofa adjacent to Volkov's private party. He has his back to them, but he's close enough to listen in.

The other mermaid beats me by the tail of her finnie-fin-fin—

Which I grab to fling her out of the way.

The Volkov-Milo confab is intense enough that they miss our little sideshow. Good thing, too, because my competitor retaliates by dunking me under the water.

Oops, did my bottle slam into her kneecap? I guess so because she lets loose with an underwater gurgle worthy of Flipper.

Despite this, I'm able to make out Coquette's declaration: "Milo, Mr. Volkov wishes to know if you brought the item of importance to both your dear friends—"

My nemesis's dolphin imitation has distracted Jack. As he glances over, I exclaim, "Sir, would you like to try our lime-infused vodka?"

Proof he recognizes my voice is that his jaw drops open. Still, Jack takes the hint and holds out his glass.

I drop the capsule into it before pouring a generous shot into his glass.

Jack gulps it down. Oh my God! *Did he swallow the capsule?*

At that point, I realize Mario is crouching toward me from his sofa. His glass is extended. "I'd like to try some too." He's blocking my view of Jack. For all I know, my husband is choking on the damn thing.

So that I don't have to make eye contact with Mario, I keep my eyes on his glass instead—

But when Mario grabs my wrist, instinctively, my eyes go to his.

Oh, heck—he's squinting as if he's trying to place me.

"May I go first?" Coquette lays her hand on his.

His eyes shift over to her.

She smiles sweetly—

While I get jerked under the water. The miffed mermaid

kicks me out of the way and takes my place at the edge of the pool.

Fine with me. I paddle away on my back.

I watch as the mermaid pours a drink for Coquette and then for Mario. At the same time, "Milo" reaches out to shake Volkov's hand. The way Volkov cups his palm, I can tell he's holding something. By his nod at "Milo," my guess is that it's the paper with the numbers.

After taking a deep breath, I slip back into the large tank and swim to the top. After pulling myself over the tank's raised lip and onto the floor, I gaze down through the tank at Jack and Volkov.

Mission accomplished, they shake hands and part ways. I can breathe easy again.

But before stepping away, Volkov turns to Coquette. She frowns when he puts his hand on her shoulder and pulls her closer.

Chuckling, "Milo," wraps his arm around her waist as if to say, *hands off—she's mine.*

Volkov shrugs grudgingly. A nod to his interpreter signals the minion that the host is ready to mingle with his other guests.

I hope to get back to the suite before Jack and Coquette. I don't need to be teased about my mermaid costume—

Although I will consider hanging onto it. Jack and I rarely role-play in the tub. Who knows? Maybe he'll find it a turn-on.

I TAKE THE SERVICE ELEVATOR STRAIGHT UP TO THE SUITE. IT'S AT the far end of the curved hallway from our room.

When I turn the corner, I notice three men outside our door.

Although one is dressed as a hotel waiter, I'd recognize them anywhere:

They are Milo's guards.

The fake waiter—the one Jack shamed back at the plane—has just buzzed the room's doorbell. The other two look around furtively—

Just as I duck out of sight. I run back to the elevator.

The carpet is so thick that I can't hear footsteps behind me, but I'm taking no chances.

I leap into the elevator and frantically press the DOWN button to the mermaid holding pen.

Just as two of the men turn the corner, the door closes.

Did they see me? And if so, did they recognize me?

Milo's suite is on the penthouse floor. Still, if they run down the fire exit, it won't take long for them to reach the lobby.

I tap my earpiece to go live with Emma. "Warn Jack and Coquette that Milo's guards were at the suite, trying to ambush us, I suppose. They may have seen me get into the service elevator and be on their way downstairs, either by the elevators or the fire exits."

"A call came in from George just a moment ago with the same warning. One of the airport mechanics said they'd shown up at the terminal, asking if Milo had changed his previous flight plan for the return trip. They were told no."

"They must have headed back here to confront Milo over their dismissal," I reason.

"Arnie is searching the hotel's security feed now for their whereabouts," Emma assures me. "In the meantime, I'll let Coquette know about the situation, but the voice alteration app did a number on Jack's earbud. It scrambles all outside transmission!"

The service elevator reaches the mermaid lounge. Thank goodness, it's empty. The party is in full swing. Emma comes online with an update: "For some reason, I can't reach Coquette! We have eyes on Jack, but he's not with her. By the way, he's headed for the lobby."

"Warn him away from there," I implore her.

"I'll do my best," Emma promises, but she sounds doubtful.

"She must be on her way to her room," I reason. "What floor is she on?"

"We booked the closest empty room to Milo's suite. In fact, it's directly under it."

"Call the front desk and order an extra keycard for Mademoiselle Rambert. I'll pick it up as her. Keep trying to reach her and let her know to meet us there."

"Got it."

"By the way, Edmonton's Chief of Staff is here—Mario Martinez," I add. "Can you find out if Edmonton is scheduled to make a surprise appearance?"

"Not unless DARPA has built a transporter since we last spoke to our contacts there. Edmonton has got a fundraiser tonight in Florida. And tomorrow he's back in the Oval Office for a bill signing ceremony."

"Check and see why Martinez is not tending to his master."

"Will do," Emma promises.

Finally, the elevator has reached the basement level. In a jiffy, I've stripped off the bodysuit, dumping it on the floor next to my wig and my tail.

So much for the fun kind of role-playing.

From a locker, I steal a pair of jeans, a black turtleneck, a black lambskin coat, and sturdy boots. In return, I leave my silver dress and heels.

I hope whoever ends up with my designer goodies appreciates my taste.

∾

"I FOUND JACK," EMMA INFORMS ME. "HE'S IN THE LOBBY, waiting for an elevator."

"Good. I'm on my way up there." I head for the service elevator.

Darn it, it's been called from another level and is already ascending. I've got no choice but to take the fire exit up to the lobby.

I'm there when I hear footsteps. I pause, hoping that whoever it is will open the door to the lobby instead of following it to the underground level.

The steps pause, as if considering this option. If it's one of Milo's guards and he noticed I was wearing a mermaid wig, it would make sense for them to head to the lobby to see if I'd made it back into the tank. But if he knew the mermaid staging ground was in the basement, he'd head here.

By his footsteps, I know it's the latter.

I inch back down the stairwell to the fire exit door.

It creaks when I open it.

His steps are faster and closer.

I fling open the door—

But I don't run through it. Instead, I hide behind it.

And just in time, since he sees that it's open and he runs on in.

Gently, I shut the door behind him. It won't take him long to figure out I'm not in there. I'll need to brace the steel handle shut. Glancing around, I spot a ball-peen hammer attached to a fire extinguisher box by a slim chain. I try yanking the chain off the metal box, but it won't break. I hit the box with one high kick, but it doesn't budge.

So, I kick it again—

And then again—

Until the box flops off the wall. It's barely hanging by its bracket.

I reach for it, but, suddenly, the goon slams me against the wall.

I've missed locking him up by mere seconds.

It's Ori.

He's ready to pound his fist into my face, but I stop him with a kick to the groin. When Ori folds, I give the loosened box one more kick—

And, finally, it falls from the wall.

I grab it, and, with all my might, I swing it at the Ori's skull.

He drops to the floor like a ton of bricks.

I drag him into the mermaid staging room and close the door, shoving the ball peen hammer against the door handle so that it can't be opened from the inside.

No doubt, his buddies are still on the prowl for "Milo." I stumble up the stairs. I've got to reach Jack before they do.

5

Persona non Grata

THE DIPLOMATIC TERM FOR ONE WHO IS UNACCEPTABLE TO, OR *unwelcome by, a host government is* "persona non grata."

The origin of the term is Latin.

Surely there have been times when a particularly annoying acquaintance has shown up at your doorstep unannounced and uninvited. Consider these rules of engagement:

Should you be throwing an open house or other large gathering, resist the urge to bodily toss them out the door or to proclaim loudly, "Get the hell out!" as these overreactions will only have your other guests reflect on your lack of grace under pressure. Instead, do your best to ignore the party crasher.

However, if you are alone, act pleasantly surprised and still welcome him in.

In fact, invite him to see your new wine cellar.

In the basement. Where there are no windows or exterior doors, let alone a cache of wine.

One shove and a quick lock of the door will solve all problems —

At least, until you notice an "odorem suavissimum non

grata." *At that point, quicklime and a shovel are a hostess's best friends.*

As Emma indicated, I find Milo—that is, Jack—in the lobby. He's not the only one. Volkov's soirée is breaking up. The partygoers are moving on to the WEF's opening night banquet. There, celebrated environmentalists from all over the world will implore the captains of industries in the audience to pillage the earth's resources with great care.

Sadly, a lost cause unless mandated and enforced by law.

Jack has been buttonholed by a high-profile blowhard while waves of the entitled, there to see and be seen, wash around them. He pretends to be listening studiously as if what the man says really resonates with him, but his eyes shift to the elevator banks, waiting for the next one to open and whisk him skyward. I go to the front desk and ask for Coquette's extra keycard before starting over toward him, all the while keeping the elevator bank in my sightline.

I'm just a few feet away when one arrives with a ping. It opens, filled with WEF attendees. Another of Milo's guards is among them. He steps out, looking around the lobby.

I grab a luggage cart waiting for a bellman to take it upstairs. It's filled with numerous hanging suit bags. As I roll it toward Jack, I use the bags as a scrim obscuring me from Guard Number Two.

I wheel the rack up to Jack and say, "Sir, sorry, but you're needed upstairs immediately."

He takes the hint. Excusing himself from his many admirers, he walks with me to the open elevator.

We get in, but I leave the rack behind. I push the button to the fifth floor.

At that moment, Guard Number Two turns back around—

Just as the elevator doors close. He catches a glimpse of the back of a woman who is kissing a man whose face he cannot see.

～

RELUCTANTLY, I PULL OUT OF THE KISS. I HATE CUTTING IT SHORT, but duty calls.

At least I try to pull away, but Jack isn't having it. Finally, I say, "We've got company upstairs. Milo's guards are on the warpath. I detained the one you insulted—Ori—in the basement. Just now, we almost got spotted by one of his buddies in the lobby."

Jack rolls his eyes.

"I'll bet they left the third goon on Milo's doorstep," I continue. "That's okay. If so, we can hide out in Coquette's room until Arnie gives us the all clear." I show him the keycard. "Strangely enough, Emma can't reach Coquette. Hopefully, she's already in her room."

"Maybe." Jack sounds doubtful. "I left her at the party. She said she wanted to see if she could identify any of the Russians who may have been floating around the room."

"Well, I ID'd an American who is certainly of interest." I take a deep breath: "Mario Martinez."

Jack frowned. "Edmonton's Chief of Staff?"

"None other. Emma is getting back to me as to why he's here in Davos, considering his boss is elsewhere."

"Maybe he's playing messenger," Jack reasons.

"But wasn't that Milo's role?" I counter.

The elevator stops. We've reached Coquette's floor.

We start down the curved hall toward her door—

Which is open.

Someone is going inside:

Mario.

I grab Jack's arm and pull him back down the hall until the door closes behind Mario. If he sees me with "Milo," his first call will be to Edmonton, who would have reason to be suspicious.

"Did she let him in?" I wonder aloud.

"Hard to say. You shoved me out of the way. I missed what happened next," Jack admits. "How and why would she know him?"

"Great question," I murmur. "Mario made it a point to sit as close to you and Volkov as possible. When I was in the mermaid pool, Mario asked me for a shot of vodka. So did Coquette. He was mermaid-curious, but he didn't seem to recognize me. He didn't appear to know her either. In fact, she flirted with him so that I could swim away."

"If that's the case, then she may be in danger."

"So, how do we get in there?"

Jack looks down the hall at Coquette's door. "You and I can't—but 'Milo' can."

He's right.

"Wait here," he says as he trots down the hall.

WHILE JACK RINGS THE SUITE'S BELL, I DUCK OUT OF SIGHT.

No answer.

He rings again.

Still nothing.

He bangs on the door—

And finally, it opens. I'm too far away to see by whom, or to hear what's being said.

A moment later, Jack goes inside.

There is nothing I can do but wait.

And wait.

And wait some more. *What the hell is going on in there?*

Suddenly, Emma's voice crackles in my ear: "Donna, there is no footage of Coquette leaving the ballroom!"

"Can you access the ballroom footage?" I ask.

"It was turned off during the party," she explains. "Perhaps she's still in there."

"It would be highly unlikely because the party was breaking up. But I'll pop back down there and check anyway. If you get through to Jack, tell him where I went."

"Should he meet you there?"

"With the guards roaming the halls, I'd prefer he stay put. I'll meet him in Coquette's room. If she's not already in her room with Mario and 'Milo,' she may be headed back there. In any event, tell him to get rid of Mario as soon as possible."

GREAT NEWS: GUARD NUMBER TWO IS NO LONGER HAUNTING the lobby.

Bad news: Now that the WEF attendees are at the opening night banquet, the ballroom door is locked.

I take the elevator to the fourth floor.

Like the second and third floors, it opens up to a small lobby. Halls on both sides lead to the rooms on that floor, but there is also a closed double-door leading to the ballroom's balcony seating.

From it, I can scan the mermaid tank as well as the room, which appears to be empty. The ballroom's lights are off, so it's hard to tell. I flip on the flashlight on my cellphone and move its beam across the left side of the room.

No one.

I'm about to do the same to the right side when the beam hits the tank.

Coquette's rigid body floats slowly through its clear, motionless depths. Strands of hair fan out, like long blades of grass gently waving in a lazy breeze. Her eyes, opened wide, stare back at me. Her full lips are puckered into a grudging pout as though resigned to a fate she found disdainful.

Can't blame her in the least.

On the lobby level, the ballroom's service door opens. Someone flicks on the lights. For a second, I'm blinded. Still, I duck out of sight.

I hear the heavy footsteps of three people. I inch toward the balcony and look down.

Ori now has his head bandaged and walks funny. *Oopsy, my bad.*

When his eyes scan upward, I freeze. Can he see me?

"Chara!" Ori exclaims. In Hebrew, that literally means "shit."

Oh, hell....

One of his buddies points up at Coquette's floating body. In English he exclaims, "Let's get out of here!"

Although they didn't attend the vodka party, they saw "Milo" make his entrance with Coquette on his arm.

One more reason we need to dump "Milo" once and for all.

My guess is that his security detail will try to distance themselves from him and his involvement in any murder, especially with a decent severance package and airline tickets in hand.

Heck, if I were in their shoes, I'd get the hell out too.

I've got to get to Jack.

∼

I TAKE THE ELEVATOR TO MILO'S SUITE. NO ONE IS ON THE HALL or waiting outside.

Hastily, I enter. I pack up our duffels and Milo's computer. While doing so, I call Emma. "I found Coquette—dead, in the mermaid tank."

"Oh...*no!*"

"Have you been able to raise Jack?" I ask.

"I've tried, but he hasn't responded. At least we can hear him. Mario is still in Coquette's suite. Apparently, he knew Milo and is shooting the breeze with his old pal," Emma replies.

"Mario must have had a keycard to Coquette's room. If he took it from her, he's got to be her killer!" I exclaim.

"You're right! And eventually, someone will find Coquette's body. She'll be remembered as Milo's interpreter," Emma reasons. "You and Jack have to get out of there before they suspect 'Milo' of killing her. They may be knocking on his door at any moment!"

"But 'Milo' left without her! The security footage will show that."

Emma sighs. "No, it won't. When we realized Jack was leaving the ballroom, we erased all of the lobby and hall footage to cover his and your tracks. And none of the cameras in the ballroom were operational. Remember?"

Darn it, she's right. We won't have the proof we need that Mario killed Coquette.

Hotel security—or worse, Davos police—will be knocking on "Milo's" door any moment now.

"Listen, Emma, as soon as Jack turns off that damn voice-altering app, let him know that I'll be slipping into Coquette's room by way of the balcony."

Because the hotel's egg shape means that the enclosed

49

balcony below bows out slightly farther than our terrace, it shouldn't be so hard to fall onto it, right?

But I've forgotten one thing:

It is also bitterly cold.

Like pixie dust, snow flurries whip around me. Despite wearing a thermal neoprene bodysuit and special gloves that have a silicone grip, the slick, damp steel surface is slippery. I wear this suit, not because it makes me look svelte and gorgeous but because the airport is an hour away by car. If there's a manhunt for Milo, we may spend part of that time trekking through the woods.

Also, there is a full moon, which will make it easier for them to spot us.

I tie a duffel bag on the end of a rappelling cord and slide it down my terrace's slick steel exterior half-wall until it lands with a soft thud onto the one below. I do the same with the second bag.

Now it's my turn to drop.

If I miss Coquette's balcony, I'll crack like Humpty Dumpty.

I move to a corner of my terrace. After hooking the rappelling cord to its lip, I wrap it around my waist and climb over. Gripping the ledge, I ease myself down the rope until I can use my body as the necessary torque to swing into Coquette's balcony—

Only to land on one of the duffel bags.

I lose my footing and slap into the wall.

"What was that?" It's Mario's voice.

I fall to the floor and crawl to the farthest inside corner—

Just in time, too. Mario walks to the balcony door and looks out.

"Milo" chuckles. "They've been shooting off the avalanche cannons every hour," he drawls.

Although the curtain is open, are its gathered folds voluminous enough to shield me from Mario? I'm afraid to look...

Finally, I hear him say: "I'm sure someone else corralled Coquette with the same request I had for her—to act as my interpreter while I'm here." As his footsteps move away from the window, he adds, "Well, thanks for giving her my business card and asking her call me with her availability."

"Milo" warns him, "She's mine for the duration, so don't hold your breath."

I wait until I hear the front door close before standing up and tapping on the glass.

Jack comes over and lets me in. After a welcoming kiss, he exclaims, "First, a mermaid dive and now an exterior drop from the terrace above! Your entrances keep getting better!"

Shuddering at Milo's face looming over mine, I stifle the urge to wipe my mouth of Jack's kiss. "Take off that damn mask! Besides the fact that the transmitter is blocking incoming calls from Emma or me, I didn't like kissing Milo at all, then or now! I just dropped in to warn you that Coquette was murdered—perhaps from the gentleman caller who just left. Her body will be found soon, so we—that is, Donna and Jack—should skedaddle."

Jack frowns.

But before he has a chance to say something, Emma buzzes in. "George says the plane is ready whenever you get there."

"We're heading back now. But even so, the airport is an hour away," Jack replies.

"Well, you'd better hurry. Coquette's body has just been

found. They're trying to ID her now. In the meantime, hotel security has cordoned off the ballroom and called the local authorities."

"Damn it," Jack growls. "Someone will point out that she was Milo's interpreter. He'll be the first person they'll want to question."

"Well, hopefully, we'll be long gone. We've got to get to the garage, like, *now*."

ACCORDING TO EMMA, ARNIE IS STILL SCRAMBLING THE HOTEL'S security camera feeds until we are safely on the road. His interference allows us to head to the basement by way of the fire exits without being seen.

For cover, both Jack and I wear caps that fully cover our heads as well as lightly tinted glasses.

When we reach the parking lot, we're dismayed to see that it has an attendant. As we drive up, he gawks, he's so impressed by our wheels. A shame for us, since he'll be asked for a description of the driver.

That is, if he sees anything at all of Jack's face. Before he hands the attendant the parking ticket, I pull him in close for a kiss.

Still, Jack's gloved hand holds out the ticket and the cash, which includes a very healthy tip—enough to give the attendant a strong bout of amnesia.

I WAIT UNTIL WE'RE SURE THAT WE'RE ZIPPING ALONG WITHOUT anyone tailing us before asking Jack: "I'm dying to hear why Mario was there—both in Davos and in Coquette's room."

Jack shrugged. "He told 'Milo' that he was there to give a speech tomorrow on behalf of Edmonton's administration on the United States' economic outlook, and how it goes hand in hand with its environmental policy."

I snicker. "I'm glad I'm not driving this bucket, or it would have gone off the road. I guess it's easy enough to check and see if he's on the WEF's program."

"He wouldn't be on it. He claims he's filling in for the US Commerce Secretary, who is on the program, so we have to take him at his word."

"Even though we both know he was there to watch Milo hand off the intel?"

"Whatever quid pro quo Milo had with Edmonton, I guess following through with the brush pass pays Milo's debt," Jack points out. "Or it did until Coquette was murdered. Now that Milo has disappeared into thin air, he's the prime suspect in her death."

"Can we use that to our advantage?" I ask.

"Hell, yeah, we can. I've got one idea as to how. I'll wait until we can discuss it in person with our brain trust." By that, he means Ryan, Marcus, and Lee.

Hearing that, I smile. There was a time he referred to Lee as a headache. Or worse yet, a pain in the ass. "Did Mario explain how he got into Coquette's room?"

"He claimed she invited him up for a drink, but that she had to meet with someone first for a few minutes and suggested that he go on up."

"I guess that's supposed to explain why he had her keycard." I'm so disgusted that I'm shaking. "And because Artie scrambled the security camera feeds, we can't investigate Coquette's death and whether Mario had a role in it."

"If he did, he'll pay for it." Coming from Jack, it's not an idle threat.

"If Mario exterminated her, it was at Edmonton's behest," I remind him.

"Just one more reason we can't fail," Jack mutters. He revs the engine.

It doesn't seem as if the wheels are touching the road. Instead, we seem to be gliding at warp speed.

Jack is right. The sooner we get in the air, the sooner we take care of Edmonton.

We're already wheels up when Emma transmits the message we hoped we wouldn't hear: Milo is the prime suspect.

"There's an all-points bulletin out for Milo and his expensive set of wheels," she warns us.

"No problem. We ditched the car in a train station's underground parking garage," I explain. "Then we hot-wired another in the long-term parking section."

"What are the authorities doing with Coquette's remains?" Jack asks.

"The director of Acme's Paris office is on her way to claim her body," Emma replies.

"Did Coquette have any next of kin or a significant other?" I ask.

"None," Emma says.

"Supposedly, she stayed behind to meet up with someone," Jack insists. "Emma, I know there isn't any video footage. Still, there may be other clues. Her phone, say. Or her computer."

"I'll get Arnie on it," she promises. "Hey, um...so... Donna..." Emma's stutter is filled with hesitation.

"Time's a-wasting," I remind her. "Spit it out."

"What I'm trying to say is...what have you done with Milo's body?"

"Great question. The answer: nothing—*yet.*"

"You mean it's on the plane with you?" Emma exclaims. "Jeez! That must stink!"

Jack laughs. "Not in the cabin. George moved Milo's body into the plane's cargo hold to stay cold."

Emma lets loose with a low whistle. "Jeebus! It's like 'Weekend at Bernie's'!"

"You're telling me," I mutter. "Your illustrious boss is still ruminating on what to do with him. Rest assured, it'll be solved in a manner that is Acme-sanctioned."

Emma snickers. "Well, now, *that's* leaving things open to interpretation."

No argument there.

6

Homeland Security

HOMELAND SECURITY IS A NETWORK OF MILITARY AND POLICE *agencies that ensures our nation is safe, secure, and resilient against terrorism and other hazards to the American way of life.*

A smart housewife is also the first line of defense against home invasions! For example, should ants find their way into your pantry, you'd use environmentally safe deterrents. Perhaps you'll spray them with soapy water, or set out cucumber peel at the point of entry. By the way, mint—in leaves or tea bags—or lines of cayenne pepper or coffee grounds will also do the trick.

Bigger critters will undoubtedly need different deterrents. Should raccoons discover a way into your yard, just cut them off at the pass. Mend fences and vent covers, and plug all forms of entry —all eco-friendly.

Should you find yourself face-to-face with a human intruder, all bets are off. Cayenne in the eyes is an eco-friendly way to disarm a burglar, but it can leave a messy stain on your carpet. The same goes for coffee grounds.

In other words, it's okay to bring out the big artillery. A rock salt shell in the tail quarters will have them scurrying to a neighbor's abode instead.

And, yes, it is also environmentally friendly.

"MOM…*MOM!* TELL TRISHA *TO LEAVE ME ALONE!*"

Jeff's bellow rouses me from a sound sleep.

And yet, Jack sleeps through it. Go figure. Along with all the excitement, I guess the detour we made to Ecuador tuckered him out. It was a necessary stop since we had to make it look as if Milo went on the lam. Ecuador doesn't have an extradition treaty with the US, so it was added to our flight's itinerary. It will be assumed that Milo has retired to a jungle paradise and is living on his Bitcoin stash.

Jack and I arrived home at three in the morning to find Janie Chiffray was bunking in the spare twin bed in the room of our younger daughter, Trisha. The two girls were chattering away like a couple of magpies. Janie's Secret Service agent, Porter Crosby, who was sitting in a chair outside their bedroom, rolled his eyes. Sixtyish and a confirmed bachelor, this probably wasn't how he saw his later years in the Secret Service playing out. And yet, he's just as loyal to Janie as his now-deceased colleague, Lurch Muldoon, was to her mother: the late former First Lady, Babette Chiffray.

We implored the girls to try to sleep. We also told Porter to get some shut-eye, too. No army is going to get past any of us, we assured him, let alone our Acme-modified state-of-the-art security system and our two dogs—Rin Tin Tin and Lassie. Reluctantly, Porter headed for the great room's fold-out couch.

Jeff's shout has me grabbing my robe from the foot of the bed and stumbling to my feet. I guess I shouldn't be too upset with him. I'll have to rouse Jack anyway. The sooner, the better, since we have to meet Lee in an hour at Lion's Lair—the former POTUS's secure compound at the top of our planned community, Hilldale.

The supposedly responsible adult—my aunt, Phyllis—is not much of a chaperone, especially when she has turned off her hearing aids. And besides, she's snoring away in the guest room, which is the farthest room in the house.

I peek out my door. Jeff is doing the same. His hair is tousled, and one cheek is rosy from being pressed against his pillow as he slept. Jeff is scowling. Seeing me, he points at the subjects of his ire.

Trisha is tiptoeing down the hallway with Janie. They are tossing something back and forth—

Oh. My. God.

I hiss, "Girls! Is that... *Jeff's jockstrap?*"

The girls stare at me sheepishly, then burst into a fit of giggles.

I hold out my arm. "Give it to me—*now!*"

Trisha's act of contrition starts with a slow trot back in my direction. She rounds it out with a pout and eyes cast downward.

Before she hands it over, Jeff snatches it out of her hand, slamming the door behind him.

Trisha snickers until she sees my face. She mumbles, "Sorry..." as she shrugs.

I have to ask: "What possessed you?"

Janie exclaims, "Mrs. Craig, it's part of Riley Trent's scavenger hunt!"

Which begs my next question: "What the heck is a Riley Trent?"

Trisha rolls her eyes as if I've been living in a cave.

A fish tank, but close enough.

"Only the most popular girl in our school," she replies. "She has a couple of openings in her posse—"

Janie chimes in: "And everyone wants to be in it! It's *really* cut-throat—"

"So, to choose who's *really* worthy, she came up with the idea of the *scavenger hunt!*" Trisha butts in. "It's...BRILLIANT! Don't you think so, Mom?"

I've never heard my baby girl call anything "brilliant." Or, for that matter, emphasize so many words in one sentence. I guess this Riley kid's affectations are worming their way into Trisha's speech patterns.

Should I be worried?

I shake it off. "So, I take it stealing your brother's jock-strap was Riley's idea?"

The girls exchange blushes. "Well, sort of," Janie admits. "Stealing an intimate item from a male is worth ten points—"

"Speaking of which," Trisha sighs. "Mom, do you think Dad would miss it if I took...well, like, an old—"

"Trisha Marie Craig! If your next word is 'jockstrap'—"

"No! *NO WAY!*" Adamantly, Trisha shakes her head. "But, maybe... a tee-shirt or something?"

I sigh. "I'm sure he won't miss it."

"*YES!*" She hugs me tightly. "I'll take a dirty one out of the clothes hamper!" Triumphantly, Trisha slaps palms with Janie.

"You're both on the Hilldale Middle School girls' soccer team. And you've both made the debate team and the honor roll too. Am I right?"

The girls nod.

"Isn't all of that enough to impress Riley?"

Trisha frowns. "You don't understand!"

"Sure, I do. For some reason, you feel this girl's approval is worth running around in circles for."

"It is, Mrs. Craig! Trust us on that!" Janie's voice trembles with sincerity.

"Okay, sure. I get that you *think* so." I shrug. "So, tell me, what other items are on this Riley person's scavenger list?"

"We don't know until she sends us a text after the last period of each day, for the next two weeks," Janie explains.

"Fair warning, ladies: don't do anything stupid or illegal. Joining her club isn't worth a broken bone—or a stint in Juvie, for that matter."

The girls grimace.

Uh oh.

I hated middle school when I was in it. I don't hate it any less now. "Okay, listen. Your dad is still asleep, as is your sister and your brother—"

"Not anymore," Janie snickers.

"Thanks to you!" Jeff yells from his room.

"Can everyone please just *SHUT UP?*" My oldest, Mary, yells from her bedroom.

I nod toward their rooms, and then mine. "*Please—be quieter!* It's too early for any shenanigans!"

Trisha rolls her eyes. "What do you mean, 'early?' It's already ten!" The girls race off downstairs, like a cattle stampede.

I sigh as I go back to my bedroom.

Jack's head is under a pillow. When he feels me beside him, he turns over to spoon me. "Home sweet home," he murmurs.

True, that.

TODAY, BREAKFAST AT THE CRAIG HOUSE MEANS PULLING OUT the extra leaf on the kitchen banquette to accommodate not just Aunt Phyllis and the rest of the family, but also Janie and Porter.

We only need a few minutes to get up the hill, which is good because in forty minutes, we're to meet at Lion's Lair with Lee, Marcus, and Ryan to recap of our mission.

Mary slices strawberries and cantaloupe as Jeff scrambles eggs while I flip pancakes and Jack stands over enough sizzling bacon to feed our small army.

While keeping one eye on the food, I've got the other on Aunt Phyllis' flirtations with the trim, white-haired Porter. The fact that he's a few years her junior doesn't seem to faze her—

Or him, for that matter. If the way he chuckles at whatever she's cooing in his ear is any indication.

Hmmm…

"Did you find your sleeping arrangements comfortable?" I ask him.

Realizing that my pointed stare is aimed at him, Porter almost chokes down his coffee. He sits up straight. "Yes!… Um…very nice," he assures me.

He winks at Phyllis.

She winks back.

I glance over at the great room's sleeper sofa. It's not open. Does that mean Porter found a comfier place to lay his head?

Yikes.

Jack must be just as intrigued because suddenly he's not paying attention to the bacon. As smoke fills the kitchen, I reach for the frying pan—

As does Jack. Unfortunately, neither of us is wearing an oven mitt, which is why we're cursing in stereo.

Moving between us, Jeff scoops up the bacon with a set of wide tongs and tosses it on the thick paper plate laid out for the strips of sizzling pork.

He then sidles to the pancake griddle, saving eight golden brown flapjacks from blackening.

This whole time Trisha and Janie have been watching with eyes as large as saucers. Noting their stares, Jeff snaps, "Yo, girls—*this isn't a diner!* Grab this stuff and put it on the table —*now*."

Awed by his forceful command, they leap up. Janie cradles the large bowl of scrambled eggs while Trisha takes the platter of pancakes.

Jeff frowns at the bacon, pronouncing it "charred, but not totally burned." Still, he takes the plate back to the table.

All this time, Mary has been at the cutting board, slicing a melon.

Make that *pulverizing* a melon. Some of the pieces are diced so small that they've liquified into pulp.

I put my hand on her shoulder. "Sweetie, I think these pieces are small enough, don't you?"

"Oh!... Yeah, I guess." Mary stares down at her handiwork. "My mind is...elsewhere."

My guess: it's in Berkeley, California with Evan Martin, her boyfriend, who also happens to be my ward.

Sighing, I point out, "It's just a few more weeks before you get word from Berkeley as to whether you're accepted or not."

She shrugs. "I know. But the wait is *so nerve-wracking*!" She picks up a strawberry and starts slicing again—

Into slivers so thin that you can see through them. If she keeps this up, the rest of the food will get cold before the fruit is ready to be served.

Before she slices off a finger too, I scoop up the bowl of whole strawberries. "Don't cut these, dear. We can just... um...pop them into our mouths."

Listlessly, she nods. "Mom, is there any way you can get out of taking this new job?"

Suddenly, all conversation in the room comes to a standstill. In the past week, this is the umpteenth time this question has been broached by every one of my children. Sadly, no matter how many times they ask, our new reality can't be altered. For the foreseeable future, I'll be working in DC.

Their persistence is appreciated as much as it is heartbreaking.

For that matter, my husband is just as upset. But he'll live with it because he knows what's at stake:

His freedom.

I force a smile onto my lips. "It's a temporary assignment. I'll be home...soon."

"Like what? A few weeks?" Trisha's question brims with hope.

"Trisha, how many times have we already gone over this? *I really can't say.* But I'll fly home every weekend. I promise. And I'll call you every night so that we can talk." I put an arm around both my girls. "If you miss hearing my voice, please —just call me. Because I'll be missing you too."

Mary leans in to kiss my cheek.

She knows I'm speaking to her, first and foremost.

The rest of the talk around the breakfast table is covert at best. Between bites of her pancakes, Aunt Phyllis tosses double-entendres at Porter. He returns them with a few of his own.

At the same time, Trisha and Janie giggle and whisper into each other's ears. Jeff's response to their sidelong glances is a disgusted glare. Because our focus is on our upcoming meeting, Jack and I skip any side discussions altogether. Not that any topics to be covered could be shared with anyone at the table anyway.

And Mary is lost in her own world.

A mother's greatest joy is her children's happiness. When one is sad for reasons outside of our control, it breaks our hearts as well.

I wish I could get her mind off her worries.

PORTER KNOWS THAT WE'LL BE FOLLOWING HIM AND JANIE UP the hill. "The president suggests that you enter through the bunker," he declares.

"What's that?" Jack asks.

Porter chuckles. "You'll see. Just follow me."

"Maybe I should tag along too," Aunt Phyllis simpers.

Before Porter can answer, Janie makes her pitch for having Trisha ride up with them. "Her parents are meeting with Dad, anyway," she points out.

Despite any attempt to be stern, Porter's blink is his tell. He caves by acknowledging, "It is Saturday. And since he's tied up for the next hour anyway, I guess he won't mind."

I turn my head so that he doesn't see me smiling. Is he the only one who doesn't realize that she's got him wrapped around her little finger?

I pull Aunt Phyllis into the great room with me and point to the couch. "I take it that Porter never slept here."

"That old thing? Of course, he didn't! It's *so* lumpy—"

"So, he slept in your room?"

"It's close to Trisha's—and *far* more comfortable." Aunt Phyllis smiles supremely. "It was all very innocent, believe me."

I raise a brow. "Do you expect me to believe that Porter slept on the floor?"

"No, of course not! That would have been silly—"

"So, you invited him *into your bed*?" I hiss.

"Yes, of course." Aunt Phyllis puffs up indignantly.

"Aunt Phyllis! *Have you no shame?*"

"You think I...that *we...*" She rolls her eyes. "I slept in Evan's room, you silly goose—*over the garage.*"

Ah.

Oops.

"Oh...well...I'm sorry that I..."

She folds her hands under her chest. "That you inferred I was a slut?"

"I don't think I said anything of the kind!"

"You didn't have to! Your tone said it all." She raises her head with pride. "You know, you can't judge a book by its cover!"

Says the woman still wearing a short silky negligee and matching robe.

Mine, in fact.

I raise both hands to indicate a truce. "Well, it's good to know that nothing untoward happened between you two while you were chaperoning the children."

"You're darn tootin' nothing happened." Aunt Phyllis chuckles. "Now, tonight, when Porter is off duty...*all bets are off.*"

Watching my jaw drop, she adds, "Oh, don't you worry, miss! I'm taking him back to my place. He says it's been years since he's slept on a waterbed...not that we plan on doing much sleeping..."

TOO. MUCH. INFORMATION.

I grab the car keys and head for the door.

JACK AND I FOLLOW PORTER'S CAR OUT OF HILLDALE'S ORNATE gates, as he goes west for a mile. Suddenly, he veers onto a dirt lane I've never noticed before. Partially hidden by bushes and tall trees, the lane stops at a double gate built into an old ornate fence.

"Where the heck are we?" I murmur.

Jack laughs. "From what I can tell, we're on the far side of the hill which our little community is named after."

In other words, the hill crowned by Lion's Lair.

I realize he's right when the gate opens. Forty feet in front of us, the bushes slide to one side on yet another barrier, revealing a tunnel burrowed into the hillside.

LEE IS WAITING FOR US IN THE RECEPTION ROOM ON THE OTHER side of the tunnel. Two guards scan Janie, Trisha, and us with security wands before Lee greets us: a kiss for Janie, a hug for Trisha, and a handshake for Jack.

Lee holds out his hand to me, but I shrug before honoring him with a dismissively quick kiss on the cheek. "What a surprise, meeting you here like this—in…what did Porter call it? Oh, yes, the 'Bunker.' But it's really a tunnel, isn't it?"

Lee chuckles. "By your tone, I take it you're miffed that I never told you about it."

I shrug. "Of course, I'm 'miffed!' It would have helped tremendously to know you have a secret way in and out of this place—especially when we suspected you of being the Quorum's evil mastermind."

Jack is now laughing so hard that I fear he may choke.

I glare at him. "Admit it. You were thinking the exact same thing."

"Guilty as charged," Jack confesses. "But now that we

know he's one of the good guys, isn't it time you cut him some slack?"

I stare at him, then at Lee. "Am I witnessing the start of a —dare I say it—a *bromance*?"

Perplexed, they turn to each other, as if contemplating the theory.

And the day is just starting.

This meeting ought to be fun.

7

Freedom Fighters

In some international circles, claiming to be a freedom fighter bestows heroism for the acts of those who use violence against the ruling party because of policies its citizens find outrageous.

Depending on who the violence is directed at, another name for a freedom fighter is "terrorist."

So, how can you tell the difference?

Easy-peasy, when using housewifery as an example:

Your husband is a freedom fighter when he punches the neighbor in the nose because he pointed out, loudly, that: "your old ball and chain has packed on a few pounds."

However, the man you married is a terrorist if he cuts off your credit cards because of one bad-day out-of-control shopping spree.

Your children are freedom fighters when they exfiltrate a neighbor's neglected dog.

However, they are terrorists when they break into your costly make-up and decimate it while playing "dress-up."

I think you get the point: anytime your family rebels against your house rules, feel free to treat them as terrorists.

A few days in the dungeon is advisable, at which point they'll take the hint and be model citizens.

MARCUS BRANHAM AND RYAN CLANCY ARE ALREADY WAITING for us in Lee's downstairs office. Since the decision was made that nothing we discuss regarding this mission is ever to be put in writing, they listen as we replay the events of the past thirty-six hours:

About MI6's intel that Milo was going to use his WEF meetings to sell his DARPA-contracted cyberwar software to enemy nations, and that while downloading this valuable intel from his computer, I had to kill him before he asphyxiated me.

We also break the news that besides scrubbing his computer for intel, Acme is keeping Milo's body on ice.

This raises a few brows. "Why in heaven did you feel the need to do that?" Lee asks.

That's a question I've been wondering myself. I keep my mouth shut as Jack replies: "I'll explain after this recap. I have an idea for a course of action—with the approval of this brain trust, of course."

Lee's nod is his signal that I continue.

"We learned that some coded message was to be handed off between Milo and Putin's best buddy, Leonid Volkov, at his vodka party," I explain. "At first glance, it looks like a series of names, but our SigInt team is still trying to decrypt it."

"Who was making the brush pass?" Ryan asks this to determine if it was Volkov's way of getting intel to Edmonton, or vice versa.

"We didn't know until we broke the email's cipher—

which happened during Volkov's party," I reply. "As it turns out, Milo was to pass the intel to Volkov. I got it to Jack just in the nick of time."

"We deduce he was playing courier for Edmonton, and there was to be some quid pro quo for doing so," Jack adds.

"Edmonton's Chief of Staff, Mario Martinez, was also there," I inform them. "He watched the drop."

"'Milo' talked to him afterward," Jack says. "Mario explained that he was pinch-hitting for the Secretary of Commerce's keynote speech." He hesitates. Looking over at Ryan, he adds, "An Acme asset, Coquette Rambert, was used as 'Milo's' interpreter during his meeting with Volkov. She stayed behind at the party, as did Martinez. He was the last person to see her alive."

Hearing this, Ryan frowns. He was at Acme's inception. He helped build it from the ground up. He interviewed and oversaw the training of every agent and asset. Ryan took all the hard calls. If you were in the field, you never felt as if you'd been left out in the cold.

He was a father to all of us.

Suddenly, I'm hit with the enormity of Jack's position as the new head of Acme.

I do my best to shake off the sadness of Coquette's death and to focus on retribution for it. To this end, I declare: "Mario had a keycard that got him into Coquette's room."

"Was her card found on her?" Ryan asks.

Jack shakes his head. "Acme's Paris bureau chief says none was found in her clutch purse. I'd searched the room and none was there either."

"So, the inference is that Mario took it after he killed her, and entered her room with it," Lee mutters.

"He's the logical suspect, yes," I reply. "Mario is Edmonton's Chief of Staff. As such, he does POTUS's bidding. And he was somewhere he wasn't expected—twice: in Davos, not to mention Coquette's room. Why was he there? And what was he looking for while she was floating, dead, in a four-story tank of cold water?"

"Despite this, we're about to cut Mario a break," Jack interrupts. "Because Milo is taking the fall for him."

"How?" Marcus asks.

"And why?" Lee wonders aloud.

"I'll answer why first," Jack replies. "Because it's the quickest way to implicate Edmonton on the record. You see, the Swiss are already under the assumption that Milo killed Coquette and then took off for parts unknown. To drive that theory, we made sure the plane that left Switzerland with 'Milo' onboard could have easily been tracked to where we flew it: to Ecuador. Then it—along with 'Milo'—conveniently disappeared. This should concern Edmonton. Milo can use his knowledge about Edmonton's Russian connection as leverage: either to cut a deal or to blackmail Edmonton. And if Edmonton facilitated Milo's sale of our Defense Department's spyware, Milo can implicate him there too. This should have Edmonton looking over his shoulder."

As comprehension sinks in, the others nod.

Jack leans in, smiling. "Now, to answer the question of how 'Milo' is going to resurface."

Lee guffaws. "Last I'd heard, resurrections had yet to be accomplished."

"You're right, sort of," Jack concedes. "Acme's motto is to prepare for the inevitable. To that extent, we felt it wise to hold onto Milo's body for a full-body scan. Who knows? If Acme needs a few spare body parts—eyes, fingers, teeth, face, whatever—to access his secured assets, we'll have it. And in the unlikely event Edmonton insists on a face-to-face meeting"—Jack shrugs—"I've played Milo successfully. I'll do so again, especially if it means nailing him once and for all."

Ryan grimaces at this thought. "So, you're going back out into the field." It's a declaration, not a question.

"I'll have coverage in the office." Jack promises.

Ryan shrugs in disbelief.

Jack faces Branham. "Would you care to come on as a management consultant?"

Branham thinks for a moment. "I'd be honored!" He chuckles. "And my wife, Muriel, would love it. She's not used to having me underfoot."

"It's a gamble, but it may pay off," Ryan admits.

"And at the same time, Edmonton will be using Donna to carry out his own agenda," Lee murmurs.

"Don't remind me," I mutter. "Which brings up a very important question. Shouldn't I have eyes and ears on me at all times? It would certainly make it easier to prove that Edmonton is a Russian mole if I record every interaction and request he makes of me."

Marcus shakes his head. "That evidence may not be admissible in court. First of all, his lawyers would make the case that video and audio could be doctored to make him look and say something he never did."

"And depending on your own actions after Edmonton's requests are made, you may also put yourself in legal jeopardy," Jack points out.

I nod. "In other words, unless others can corroborate my evidence against him, all I can do is try to mitigate the damage Edmonton insists on me making."

"And report to us, as often as possible, his schemes," Jack replies.

"It's a necessary evil, Donna," Lee concedes. "Still, having you on the inside allows us to document Edmonton's unlawful acts. Then, when 'Milo' makes his move, we reel him in— hook, line, and sinker." He leans back in his chair. "Go get him, Craigs."

SINCE LEE INSISTS THAT TRISHA STAY UNTIL DINNER TIME, JACK and I take off. She'll be home before I'm due to take the red-eye to DC. Still, when I kiss her goodbye, I allow my lips to linger on her forehead. Who knows what life holds for us?

Our drive is made in silence as we ponder what lies ahead. This mission could blow up in our faces. We both know it. If Edmonton or his minion, Martinez, catches on about my surveillance, Jack will be arrested in no time.

Finally, Jack says, "I want to be at your swearing-in ceremony."

I grimace at the thought. "Edmonton will just love that! I'm sure he'll use it to taunt me."

"Let him. The cockier he gets, the quicker he'll slip up."

"If you say so."

"I do. In fact,"—Jack takes a deep breath—"I think the kids should come too."

A cold wave of shame washes through me. "No, Jack! I mean...it's all a big sham!"

"I'm not supposed to think so, and neither are the children." He reaches for my hand. "We've got to make it look real to Edmonton."

I groan. Finally, I mutter, "Okay, if you say so."

"I do." He lifts my hand to his lips and kisses it. "Let's play him, Donna. Before he plays us."

He's right. *Game on.*

8

Adversary

In military terms, an adversary is a person, or group, *acknowledged as being potentially hostile.*

If you run across someone who resembles this description, use of force may be called for.

How will you know if you're facing off with potential adversaries? Simple!

They will say or do something to make you feel uncomfortable— on purpose.

They will threaten you verbally in some way.

They will physically assault you.

They will try to kill you.

As you can see, "Adversary" is a broad term, describing varying degrees of threat. Your response should match it.

For example, a verbal slight is no reason to scratch out your adversary's eyes. Choose a few choice words instead that befit the occasion. (Case in point: "Ho-tart," if she casts aspersions on your ability to keep your main squeeze happy for all the right reasons.)

On the other hand, a physical assault should be met with some-

thing stronger than a firm reprimand. (There is a reason the Bible mentions "an eye for an eye," so aim high and accurately.)

And if there is a murder attempt on your life, don't take it sitting down.

Instead, stand tall—

And carry a big gun.

Say, a TAC 50.

∼

THE LYFT DRIVER WHO PICKS ME UP FROM THE PASSENGER LINE AT Dulles International Airport is a sullen fellow in his sixties. With a sharp nod, he lumbers out of the driver's seat to toss my two suitcases into the trunk of his decrepit Toyota Camry. Still, he's enough of a gentleman to open a passenger door for me before grunting what sounds like, "Get in," and slamming it shut behind me.

"The Watergate," I tell him.

Hearing the name of the infamous office, hotel, and condominium complex, he snorts, nods, and then turns up the volume on his radio, which is tuned to an all-talk station.

I'm dismayed that I'll be spending the next hour in morning midweek traffic with this taciturn fellow, and not just because a few coils have sprung through the back seat or because I detect the pungent scent of *Au de Day-Old Banana* coming from under the front seat. I am more dismayed that this Grumpy Gus has got his radio tuned to the AM channel where Larry Zorn, Hart Radio Network's number-one syndicated talk show host, espouses his Dark State conspiracy theories, seemingly twenty-four-seven.

This is what passes as entertainment these days.

I'd once had the great displeasure of being Larry's co-host. Thankfully, for only forty-eight hours, which was long enough for me to be propositioned, both on and off the air. My putdowns of Larry resonated with enough women that rumor has it there's a website devoted to them, as well as several #MeToo workshops that train women how to respond to lascivious oafs whose verbal assaults have moved beyond Cro-Magnon grunts.

I believe in giving back, so, yeah, this works for me.

Usually, political chatter doesn't bother me, but I've just come off a six-hour red-eye flight, and I'll only have until tonight to prepare for the arrival of my family. They were ecstatic at the news that they would attend my swearing-in ceremony. Mary leaped out of her slump when Jack informed her that he'd bought a ticket for Evan too. "His flight comes in a few minutes after ours, so we'll wait for him at Dulles," Jack told her.

She hugged him as if she wasn't going to let go.

Even early morning on a Sunday, it may take forty minutes to get to my short-stay furnished rental. Now that Larry has moved from his Dark State tirade to some prime POTUS ass-kissing, I've had enough. "Can you turn off the radio?"

Grumpy Gus doesn't hear me, so I tap his shoulder.

This gets his attention. He nods at me in the mirror.

In the sweetest voice possible, I coo, "I'd really appreciate it if we could make the trip in silence." As encouragement, I wave a ten-dollar bill at him.

He snaps it up, exclaiming, "Sorry! I had to turn up my hearing aid to catch your drift. Ha! I can't stand this idiot either. But I get a lot of hoopleheads as fares who think that gasbag in the White House hung the moon."

Interesting. "So...you don't care for Edmonton?"

He snorts. "Heck, no! He's there for the wealthy, not the average working stiff."

"What makes you say that?"

"Because I've seen it firsthand! I used to be a salaried limo driver. Now, look at me." He frowns. "The gig economy? Ha! Well, he can gig *this*!"

Grumpy Gus's one-finger salute gets him a honk from the car behind him. Apparently, the driver, a twenty-something in a '66 Pontiac GTO, has misinterpreted it as a call to arms. As if to make this point, the dude rams Gus' Camry from behind.

Grumpy Gus hits the gas pedal. In no time, we've crossed the two lanes of traffic on our right to take the next exit.

The angered driver does the same.

Grumpy Gus forgets the speed limit on this isolated two-lane blacktop. New housing construction, still in the framing stage, is on all sides.

Gus makes the decision to turn into one of these new subdivisions.

Angry Dude decides he's going to follow.

We're chased through a maze of streets until we notice a road sign warning us that we're about to enter a cul-de-sac.

This doesn't deter my driver. As he pulls the emergency brake, he cranks the steering wheel while locking the back wheels so that we're now facing in the opposite direction—

And nose to nose with Angry Dude. Wielding a tire iron, the guy gets out of the car—

But changes his mind about paying us a visit when draw down my Sig Sauer P229 on him.

He stops short, but he's still seething.

"You're too cute for road rage," I coo.

He's unsure how to respond. Like most hotheads, he is confounded by all the mixed messages coming his way. Should he pay attention to my flirtatious words or my gun?

Why am I not surprised when he goes into default mode and stares at my breasts?

I wave my hand to get him to look at my face. "Dude, back off, okay? Believe it or not, my driver's indiscretion wasn't meant for you. It was for something the Houston Astros' coach was bellyaching about on the radio. So, let's just call this what it is— a misunderstanding—and both go on our merry way. Okay?"

He contemplates that with a grunt and shrug. A moment later, he's driving off.

I get back into Grumpy Gus' car. His thumbs-up earns him the question: "What should I call you?"

"Henry."

"That was quite an impressive turn. You're a regular Tanner Faust."

He grins. "Rich folks who are targets for kidnappers see defensive driving as a desirable skill set for a chauffeur."

A man after my own heart, although I can't let him know that.

After all, I'm POTUS's new patsy…

Um, I mean, Senior National Security Advisor to the President.

I'd say that merits a chauffeur with a reliable set of wheels.

"While I'm in town, will you drive for me exclusively, Henry?"

"Can you afford my day rate?"

"I'll double your highest day rate as a Lyft driver."

That sets him chuckling. "You've just hired yourself a chauffeur, Ms.…."

"Craig. But I insist you call me Donna."

We shake on it. He hands me a business card with his cell number.

If I need a quick getaway, I have my wheelman.

~

HENRY GETS ME TO THE WATERGATE IN RECORD TIME, PROOF that he knows the streets of DC.

The Watergate's doorman—a tall, strapping guy named Barry—opens the door.

The lobby has a concierge desk. When I say my name, the concierge—a young, fresh-faced twenty-something— practically leaps to attention. She introduces herself as Poppy Southcott. After handing me her business card and a welcome packet, she insists I should call her with any request twenty-four-seven.

I join a few other tenants who are waiting for an elevator. Sprinkled with a few well-dressed couples are men and women wearing the DC version of power suits. I recognize a senator (male), a Congressperson (woman), and a political pundit. No one is talking.

By default, all ears tune in on the only person who sees nothing wrong with doing so: an elderly man in a wheelchair. He's flirting loudly with a woman dressed in a posh suit and carrying a poodle in her arms.

Eyes skyward, she murmurs, "Aren't you feisty today!" Her attempts to slap away his hand has the others pursing their lips to keep from snickering. Irritated, the man's care-giver—a wiry guy with a blond Afro and horn-rimmed glasses—shakes his head in resignation.

Two elevators arrive at once. Like Moses parting the Red Sea, everyone except the old man and his male nurse moves toward the farthest elevator. I'd go with the herd except for the fact that I'm hauling a suitcase and a valise.

One pinch on my butt and I understand the stampede.

Few people have the nerve to slap the face of a randy old codger.

So, when I do it, I leave Old Codger's male caregiver choking in a spasm of shocked guffaws.

To add irony to insult, they, too, get off on my floor. Apparently, Randy Old Codger owns the apartment next door.

As they pass me, he winks at me as his caregiver wheels him to his door.

MY TEMPORARY DIGS ARE THREE BEDROOMS AND THREE BATHS, with a reasonably decent kitchen. The furnishings are nicer than I'd expect: mid-century reproductions in embroidered fabrics and solid wood. The ornate mirrors in every room dress it up a bit.

The bathrooms, with polished marble surfaces, are state of the art. The owners did a great job in staging it for the most highly desired tenants: policy wonks, lobbyists, and visiting dignitaries.

The unit faces east, toward the White House. I double-check to make sure a Russian flag isn't flying over it.

Nope.

Not yet, anyway.

I've just gotten settled into a nice hot bath when I hear the doorbell buzzing. The family isn't due to land until early afternoon.

Who the hell could that be?

I toss on a robe and slippers before stepping out into the living room. By the time I get to the front door peephole, the taps are louder, more insistent.

A Secret Service agent is standing at my door. I also see

two others behind him, staring up and down the hall and mumbling into their headpieces.

Just what I need: a welcoming committee.

I crack open the door. Through the safety chain, I exclaim: "Tell me you're lost!"

Not even a hint of a smile. So much for levity. "Ms. Craig?"

"*Mrs.* Craig," I correct him.

He shrugs. "The President is here to see you, ma'am."

"I'm not receiving visitors today." Codeword: *the chain stays on.*

The frowns on all three agents deepen at the sound of the footsteps coming from the far end of the hall. Edmonton's pleasant baritone rings out: "Mrs. Craig, welcome to DC— and thank you for extending this opportunity to get a jump on the coming week."

Yes, I want to jump.

Or, perhaps, push.

From the eighteenth floor, the fall would be a doozy.

THE SECRET SERVICE DOES A QUICK AND THOROUGH SWEEP through the apartment.

When they discover my gun, Edmonton chuckles. "I'm sure it's registered, gentlemen. And considering that Mrs. Craig and I are old friends…"

He pauses so that the inference is clear: *the last thing I'll do is shoot him.*

Don't bet on it.

His nod toward the door, coupled with my demure smile, placates his security detail enough to do his bidding. They wait outside.

The door's closing click seems to reverberate through the room, but I know it's all in my imagination.

Edmonton is trying to get into my head.

I can't let him.

"WHY ARE YOU HERE?" I ASK.

He motions me to the plush L-shaped sectional sofa with an incomparable view of the White House through the floor-to-ceiling window.

"I'm sorry, but I was in the middle of—"

"Let me guess. You were bathing." His eyes sweep over me.

"I'm also expecting company."

He laughs. "If you mean Jack and the kids, we have plenty of time, Donna. The United flight carrying them is running late. And besides, you're the kind of woman who one suspects lives in a constant state of dishabille. It comes with the job, doesn't it?"

"You're keeping tabs on us." I dread the thought even though it makes sense.

His smile disappears. "Always. And don't forget it."

I let him sit down first before positioning myself far enough away to make my intentions clear: *hands off.* "Speak your mind, Bradley."

He frowns. "You should be nicer to me, Mrs. Craig."

"You're Putin's lapdog. Does that mean I'm supposed to be yours?"

His hand hits my face so hard that my neck snaps back. I feel a warm trickle of blood inching its way from my lip to my chin.

My instinct is to retaliate: to punch him in the throat and

watch him gasp for air. I long to take one of the brass book-ends on the sideboard behind me and beat his face to a bloody pulp.

But that will accomplish nothing.

Worse, it will ruin our one chance to take him down.

Instead, I sit perfectly still as Edmonton moves beside me. I flinch when he raises his hand again to my face. But then, very gently, he wipes away the blood with his index finger. He holds the finger to my lips and demands, "Open."

My lips are barely parted before his finger is in my mouth. "Suck it off," he commands me.

I close my lips on it.

My blood tastes sour. As Edmonton's finger taps my teeth and probes my tongue, I wonder how hard it would be to sever the joint just below the tip of his finger? *Tempting...*

But no. That would provide an intimate moment he'd never forget.

Edmonton puts his face next to mine. He still has his finger in my mouth. He uses it as a hook to turn my head so that he can kiss me.

I stand up, moving just out of reach. "I accepted this posi-tion for one reason: because you need a few tasks completed, and I want Jack cleared of any wrongdoing. So, why don't we get down to business? Describe these tasks, please! Am I to be your personal hit squad? Am I supposed to sabotage my own government on your behalf?"

Edmonton growls, "All of the above. Our pact was that you're at my beck and call."

"How many successes will I need to get out of our so-called pact?"

Edmonton chuckles. "I hadn't planned on putting a cap on your successes. I would imagine I'd be encouraged to test your mettle even further!"

My laugh is harsh, mirthless. "The more tasks I take on, the higher the chances are that, inevitably, I'll fail at one. I might as well walk away now."

He considers that with a nod. Finally, he says, "Five tasks."

"Sex won't be one of them, Bradley." My voice is firm. "Admit it, the last thing you want is an unwilling fuck."

He sighs. "Whoever said, 'power is the ultimate aphrodisiac' was wrong, especially when a man's youthful glow has dimmed and his flesh sags over his shrunken muscle. You see it in the dead eyes of those pitiful women who perform for money. Or worse,"—Edmonton reaches over to stroke my thigh—"freedom." Reluctantly, he drops his hand to his side. "Could you ever learn to tolerate it? Possibly. Should you fail at even one of your tasks, we shall see."

"I won't fail."

"Not at *any* of them?" To mock me, he clucks his tongue. "Donna dear, do I disgust you so much that you're willing to wager your first failure on Jack's life?"

Of course not. Edmonton knows it too.

Another reason I cannot fail.

There is a knock on the door.

"Come in," Edmonton shouts.

The lead agent of his Secret Service detail pokes his head through the door. "Incoming."

Edmonton rolls his eyes. He waits for the agent to shut the door before saying, "Apparently, your husband broke all speed records to get to your side." He rises. "I look forward to meeting your spawn tomorrow."

He knows better than to shake my hand. Instead, he heads for the door.

∾

"WE SAW THE PRESIDENT'S MOTORCADE," JEFF DECLARES.

We are still in a group hug. My children's kisses are still damp on my face. My smile hasn't wavered—

Until I hear the excitement in my son's voice.

"You can see the White House from the balcony," I inform him.

My children and Evan break away to see for themselves, but Jack keeps me firmly in his grip. "I already miss you," he murmurs.

His kiss proves it.

When we break from our embrace, we find ourselves alone. The kids have grabbed their bags and are claiming their rooms: Trisha and Mary will share the guest room with the queen bed, whereas Jeff and Evan grab the room with twin beds.

Still holding my hand, Jack declares, "I guess that leaves me bunking with you."

For some reason, I find that so funny that I laugh until I convulse—

When I stop, I wipe away my tears.

Not of joy, but of irony.

"HOW WAS YOUR TRIP?" SO THAT JACK DOESN'T SEE MY EYES ARE still damp, I face the closet as I toss on jeans and a sweater.

"Smooth as silk and faster than a speeding bullet, thanks to George." He flops onto the bed.

"Oh!... So you took the Acme jet?"

"Sure. I thought it's a perk of the office, right? Why not take advantage of it?"

"Yeah, right... 'office perk.'" As soon as I realize how sarcastic I sound, I wish I could bite my tongue.

Through the mirrored closet doors, I see Jack sit up. "Is everything okay?"

I shrug. Now is not the right time to tell Jack about my pact with Edmonton.

I hope he doesn't blow his stack and do something we'll both regret.

For that matter, when Edmonton's security detail swept through here, they may have planted bugs throughout the place.

I'm saved from answering when Mary knocks on the door, then shouts. "Hey, hurry up! We're famished! Evan claims that a great pizza place called Campano is around the block—and he insists on treating everyone!"

I'll search when the children have fallen asleep.

So that my family doesn't see me cry, I wipe away my last tear. "I'm just sad that we're going to be apart after tomorrow."

Jack goes to my side. Putting his arms around me, he whispers. "No matter what happens, we'll be together, always."

I can't help it: I yelp out a giggle.

Jack stares at me. "May I ask what's so funny?"

"I just hope they'll give us adjoining prison cells," I whisper back.

Before Jack can say another word, I take his arm in mine and head for the door.

9

The Oval Office

EVERYONE NEEDS A PLACE TO CONDUCT BUSINESS. THE PRESIDENT *of the United States is no exception.*

Interestingly, no president thought to create a workspace worthy of the office until Theodore Roosevelt. In 1902, he built the West Wing. However, it was President William Howard Taft who decided to make the office larger. To do so, he moved it to what had been a round-shaped secretarial office.

A further expansion kept the office's unique form to some extent, albeit elongating it to its current oval shape. It was finally completed in 1934 by President Franklin Delano Roosevelt. Since then, every subsequent president has sat in the Oval Office.

With the president as its occupant, many important events have taken place in "the Oval." International dignitaries have visited there, and groundbreaking legislation has become law there. In times of crisis, the president has addressed the nation from there. Winning sports teams, Nobel Laureates, rock stars, and even a Russian spy or two have been hosted there.

And, to put it politely, at least one President was known to be pleasured there.

Ah, to be a fly on its curved walls!
Or any sort of bug at all.
Especially an electronic one.

"You have quite a handsome family, Mrs. Craig," President Bradley Edmonton's compliment comes as he tousles Jeff's hair playfully.

That doesn't bug me as much as the way he licks his lips when his eyes fall upon Mary.

Ah, hell. I knew bringing my family here would be a big mistake.

Thankfully, Mary misses his lascivious stare. She seems awed by the portrait of George Washington hanging within reach.

Anxiously, I look over to Jack. Did he see Edmonton's wolfish gaze as well?

Unlikely. He is busy talking to Mario, who will soon be taking my family on a VIP White House tour after our obligatory photo with the president.

On the other hand, despite nodding to Trisha's chatter about how many times she's been Janie's guest at the White House, Evan bristles at Edmonton's unconscious leering at Mary.

When Evan's eyes meet mine, he mouths, *what the heck?*

I tap my index finger to my lips.

He gets the message: *Now is not the time or place.*

Edmonton's secretary, Mildred Bartlett, buzzes with the message that the White House photographer, Rodney Abbot, is now outside the door. Her voice is a robotic monotone. From what I know, she's been with POTUS since his first elected office. I'm sure she's seen and heard enough to chill even the sunniest outlook on our government in action.

It's quite a difference from the upbeat tone set by Eve Pettival, Lee's assistant. Not only is she sweet, young, and pretty, she's also knowledgeable of the ins and outs of the administration. I'm sure Edmonton would have liked it if she'd stayed on the job. Being a smart cookie, Eve left to join Lee as soon as she showed Mildred the ropes.

Lee is lucky to have Eve.

Rodney, green bean lean and wearing a bad toupee, greets us with a curt nod. "What say we put our revered president right in the center and the boys at either end?"

Dutifully, Jeff moves to the left of the group.

Reluctantly, Evan moves right.

"Mrs. Craig, you have the honor of standing to the president's left. Hubby can stand to *your* left. The younger lass… let's put her beside the taller boy."

Evan bristles at being called a boy. Still, showing his game face, when Trisha moves his way, he puts his arm around her.

"The older girl…go ahead and move next to our great president! Not to worry, he doesn't bite!" Rodney winks broadly, even as he motions Mary next to Edmonton.

If he touches her, I'll…

Edmonton's hands stay clasped behind his back.

Good.

"Okay, everyone…I'll count to zero, backward from three," Rodney barks. "Here we go! Three… Two… *One*…"

I feel a hand cupping my ass.

Shocked, I look back and down.

It's Edmonton's, no surprise there.

When I look up, I notice Jack is staring down at it too. Rage has reddened his face.

When our eyes meet, I shake my head ever so slightly as if to say, *please don't kill him.*

Leave that to me.

"Now, now, ladies and gents! All eyes to the front, please!" Rodney insists.

Jack's back stiffens. Once again, he faces the camera. His smile is cruel and tight.

As the camera clicks away, Edmonton gives me a pat.

The only way I can keep a grin on my face is to envision taking a chainsaw to his hand and then feeding it to my dogs...

Gee! Now, I'm practically laughing.

IMMEDIATELY, MARIO STARES AT HIS WATCH AND ANNOUNCES: "Craigs, you'll love the tour I've set up for you."

But his attempt to nudge my family out of the room is akin to herding cats. They have enveloped me in hugs and kisses, making me vow to text or call often. They promise to do the same.

Finally, they release me.

My girls' eyes glisten with tears as they wave goodbye.

Not Jack. He takes me in his arms. His kiss is passionate and filled with longing.

When we part, he winks but says nothing.

When the door closes behind him, Edmonton claps long and hard. "Such a rousing performance!" he exclaims. "Should you fail at your tasks, your conjugal visits will be just as touching, I'm sure. Shall we get to work, Mrs. Craig?"

EDMONTON TAKES HIS SEAT BEHIND THE MASSIVE DESK WHICH anchors the Oval. His usual smirk has been replaced by a grimace. Jack's show of affection has had the desired effect.

I sit in one of the three chairs opposite him.

"Get up!" he barks. "I'll tell you if and when you are allowed to sit."

Slowly, I rise.

"My next engagement is a press conference," Edmonton continues. "You're to attend as well. When I take the podium, you are to stand behind me, along with others in my administration. Make sure you are far enough to the left that you are out of view of the cameras in the room. Should you fail at your mission, I'd hate for your children's future successes to be tainted by some video reel of your shame."

I wince at the thought.

"Other than standing silently and smiling benignly, your role is to mesmerize my guest. Make sure he's panting to spend the night with you."

"Who is he?"

"Saudi Arabian Crown Prince Mohammed Ahmad al-Nayef. Currently, he is his nation's defense minister and one of three of the old man's nephews vying to replace him as he gasps his way to his final reward of seventy-two virgins. Your first task is to make sure al-Nayef doesn't live past tonight."

That name rings a bell...

And for a good reason: he was besties with Salem Rahman al-Sadah, Babette's lover. Salem was also the CEO of Graffias International, a business front for the now-defunct worldwide terrorist organization known as the Quorum.

A pertinent aside: al-Nayef was hanging out in Salem's suite while he tried to rape me on my wedding day.

Will he recognize me now? Doubtful. But still...

"Do you have a preference as to how the task is carried out?"

Edmonton shrugs. "Your methodology is your own, but as he's a White House guest from a strategically located nation, I'd prefer nothing messy."

"In other words, an accident or natural causes?"

"In such matters, I follow a 'don't ask, don't tell' policy. It keeps me out of legal jeopardy. You did the same in your dealings with our last president, or have you forgotten?" He swivels his chair so that he can gaze out the window.

I guess this is my way of being dismissed.

"May I ask?"

Edmonton sighs. "What is it?"

"I assume you had someone else in my position."

"Several, yes, throughout the years." He keeps his back to me.

"Where are they now?"

He chuckles. "I'm sure you hope I'll say that their accomplishments were rewarded with some lofty position in the halls of power, or perhaps their dream retirement, well-feathered with monetary rewards in keeping with their accomplishments. I'm sorry to disappoint you. Each was eliminated by their replacement."

"No doubt it was their replacement's first task," I murmur.

"Why, yes, now that you mention it—until you. Yet another way you break the mold, Mrs. Craig!" He dismisses me with a wave of his hand.

I WAIT IN THE ROOSEVELT ROOM WITH EDMONTON'S OTHER minions who are deemed necessary for the Oval office photo op with al-Nayef. Ryan is already in there, as are the directors of Defense, Interior, Commerce, and Energy.

I am the only woman present.

When we move into the Oval, a few chosen journalists are invited to join us.

At the very last minute, Mario rushes in. He sidles beside me.

Edmonton and al-Nayef stand as they shake hands for the cameras. Then they move to armchairs. Edmonton's opening remarks are sprinkled with effusive compliments regarding our country's "strategically important" relationship with Saudi Arabia. As much as catchphrases like "freedom" and "democracy" are red meat for his more enthusiastic constituents, they will also have Putin seeing red of a different sort.

The press is allowed a few questions. Most are softballs. I figure that the reporters are oblivious to Edmonton's real persona. Washington's "Silver Fox" has been in politics long enough to come off as the assured empathetic statesman and a polished off-the-cuff speaker.

He also has a tight-lipped administration team that runs like a well-oiled machine. Mildred tops that list. As for his cabinet, I'm guessing they were all picked for their positions because (a) his charismatic personality enthralls them and they truly believe he's the Real Deal; (b) like me, they are the real deal, but he holds some dirty secret over their heads; or (c) like Edmonton, they are Russian assets.

More than likely, they are a combination of all three.

When Edmonton is tossed a question he would prefer to ignore—such as Saudi Arabia's archaic views on the freedoms of women, both married and single—he expresses empathy first, but quickly segues to a related topic he knows will placate his base: reduced oil prices.

When the reporters are finally herded out of the room by Edmonton's sour-faced press secretary, Vanessa Logan, Ryan introduces the other intelligence officials before Mario gets the high sign from Edmonton to steer me in front of him.

Edmonton puts his hand on the small of my back then announces, "Saudi Arabian Crown Prince Mohammed Ahmad al-Nayef, I'd like to introduce you to Mrs. Donna Craig, my Senior National Security Advisor. After the state dinner tonight, Donna will be accompanying you back to your hotel to address some of the more intimate details best discussed outside the confines of today's meetings."

The prince catches on to Edmonton's not-so-subtle hint as to my actual role in their negotiations. His eyes light up before roaming over me.

"Not blonde." He shrugs. "But she will do."

For different reasons, his assessment is one we both regret.

I sit in on the negotiations, which include agreements on what financial and military aid the US will be giving Saudi Arabia to protect its oil fields. The final figure is almost a billion dollars, most of which will go toward munitions such as counter-artillery radar systems, sniper rifles, night-vision technology, and rocket-propelled grenade launchers.

In other words, everything his kingdom needs to keep the smaller oil-producing countries, Qatar and Yemen, under Saudi Arabia's thumb.

When we take a break, Ryan and I end up standing close, but angled in such a way that, at first glance, we don't appear to notice one another because we're too busy reading copies of the proposed negotiation.

Ryan's voice is low enough that I can barely hear him mutter, "This should make Vlad take notice."

"B.E. wants me to take out the trash," I whisper through gritted teeth.

Ryan grimaces. "Undoubtedly, it's a show of allegiance."

He means Edmonton's to Russia.

Or, perhaps mine to POTUS.

From his nod, I have my answer: *Do Edmonton's bidding.*

A FEW HOURS LATER, WE HAVE A SIGNED AGREEMENT.

The cameras are back for a photo op of Edmonton and al-Nayef's signature ceremony.

I am excused to get ready for the state dinner. Having brought a gown and higher heels with me, I change in my new office, which is really the study off the Oval Office. This has raised eyebrows since it has its own hall leading directly into the Oval.

Edmonton is doing everything he can to ruin my reputation.

I check my office for any concealed cameras. I find two and fry them in a glass of tonic water. Then I pull out one of my own, hidden in a frame that holds a picture of my family.

Despite the position Edmonton has put me in, I hold my head high. It helps to be dressed to the nines: in this case, a navy strapless Carolina Herrera ballgown. Its only embellishment is a spray of crystal in the form of a branch on the right side of my waist.

But I'm not entirely dressed until I put on my heels. The hollow left heel contains a needle filled with a fatal dose of aconite.

EDMONTON SITS AT THE HEAD OF THE DINNER TABLE. NOT surprisingly, he has seated me to the right of al-Nayef.

Although al-Nayef has seven wives, none have been invited to this function.

"Didn't you bring them stateside?" I ask.

He snickers. "My wives are here—*to shop* for anything their hearts desire. Beautiful robes, fragrant oils and perfumes, any bauble they want, every craving they desire, is theirs for the asking. In my country, women of royal blood are precious ornaments to be pampered and admired—and to bear my sons."

"Many of the princesses have gone to top-flight universities and have graduated with honors," I point out. "Surely they are assets to you outside the palace as well, as your goodwill ambassadors."

The prince's eyes narrow. "It is true that my wives have studied Western cultures while enrolled in the world's most prestigious universities. But they did so only to learn how they best may move within it with the grace and ease befitting their place as my wives. Unlike the women here, Arabian women acquiesce to the wishes of their husbands at all times. Obedience is rewarded. Those wives who have tested my patience do so only once. Even then, they pay dearly for making such a thoughtless misstep." He runs his finger down my arm to my palm. "Take what I say to heart, Donna Craig."

"Duly warned," I mutter.

As if to make his point, the prince thinks nothing of putting his hand in my lap. It roams through the folds of my dress in search of my thigh.

I pretend to feel nothing.

Stymied by the fullness of my gown's skirt, he hisses, "I cannot wait to rip this rag off you."

This so-called rag cost Acme five thousand hard-earned dollars!

Granted, Jack doesn't know it yet, but only because the bill hasn't hit my company charge card. Still...

Al-Nayef will pay dearly for the privilege.

10

Diplomatic Immunity

DIPLOMATIC IMMUNITY GIVES ONE WORKING IN A FOREIGN *government's diplomatic corps the privilege of exemption from specific laws of the country in which they are assigned.*

In other words, a "get out of jail free" card.

Or two. Maybe three more cards.

Not fair, wouldn't you agree? It would seem that if one is a representative of one's nation, one would be exemplary in learning and obeying the laws of your host country, and then following them to a tee.

In your family dynamic, a version of diplomatic immunity takes place whenever a child plays one parent against another. Say your youngest breaks your neighbor's window, and your husband laughs it off instead of insisting on the appropriate punishment. Or, say, your oldest breaks curfew and your hubby never backs you up on grounding her.

Should he keep giving your kids diplomatic immunity, take matters into your own hands. Start by locking the brats in their rooms where they can do no harm.

Feel free to do the same to your husband.

THE MOMENT THE MEAL HAS ENDED, CROWN PRINCE Mohammed Ahmad al-Nayef wastes no time in making his exit.

He knows I will do the same, but separately so that our assignation won't come to the attention of any journalists still hanging around the White House grounds or al-Nayef's hotel. It's the last thing the prince wants. His playboy antics have held him back from being the current Saudi king's first choice as his successor.

As I leave the table, one of the prince's attachés hands me a keycard. Sneering, he says, "This will get you into the garage of the Intercontinental Hotel. It also summons the elevator leading directly to the Royal Suite."

I take it and head out.

I HAVE HENRY STOP A FEW BLOCKS AWAY FROM THE PRINCE'S hotel. Apprised of my assignation, Acme has already looped all security camera footage to shield me from view.

Emma has also sent over floor plans: one of the prince's suite, and another of the hotel's fire exits.

I notice the suite has a large terrace—very handy, in case I need a different egress. Not that it would be easy in this gown. More akin to suicide, unless he makes good on his promise and rips the gown's skirt from its bodice.

Not to mention that rappelling the exterior of the hotel, naked, in late January, ain't exactly the desirable option.

Other than my gown-length matching coat, I hold a small hard-shell clutch. Inside is a lipstick, in case I need a touch-up of the lipstick I currently wear. Created by the geniuses in

Acme's science lab, this particular shade, called "Murder by Mauve," is, quite literally, the kiss of death. Because it induces a heart attack, it is yet another way to take down my target via natural causes.

When all else fails, my Sig Sauer is also in my clutch. Edmonton would grumble for its use in this extermination, but too bad. Beggars can't be choosers. And besides, al-Nayef's brothers also have a target on his head, so it wouldn't be too much of a stretch to lay the blame at their feet.

The suite's massive foyer is dark, except for candles leading to an enormous bedroom.

I follow it but stop at the doorway.

The prince, naked under his silk robe, stands at the foot of the bed. "Enter!" he commands me.

I do as asked until we are face to face.

"Take off that coat and turn around," he demands.

Again, I do his bidding.

Slowly, al-Nayef nudges the zipper of my dress down my back. When it reaches my spine, he rips the gown straight down on its seam. As it lands on the floor, he kicks it aside.

Next, he jerks the clutch from my hand and throws it away. It ricochets off the far wall and skitters across the bare wood floor, landing a few feet from us.

"Kneel face down on the bed."

I guess that is the end of what he considers foreplay.

I follow his command. To my dismay, he removes my heels, one at a time, and chucks them out of reach.

Yikes! This is not going the way I'd planned.

I flip around, lips puckered. "How about a kiss, my sweet prince?"

"The only thing your lips will touch is this, you whore bitch!" He leaps onto the bed. Kneeling on either side of my chest, he swings his cock toward my face.

All I need to do is kiss his skin, and he's a goner. But *there? No way. Not happening.*

There's an old saying: grab them by their balls, and their hearts and minds will follow. With a quick twist, I test this theory.

As he jumps back, his howl bounces off the walls.

I reach for my heel—

Only to discover it's not the one with the aconite prick.

I throw the shoe at the other prick—the one rampaging toward me now. Its heel hits al-Nayef's eye. He's cursing in Arabic, but I can guess what he's saying.

Frantically, I look around the room for the second shoe. Finally, I spot it under the dresser.

I scramble on my knees to it. I've just snatched it up when al-Nayef grabs me from behind. He shoves me up against the wall, flattening me with his forearm as he positions himself between my legs. "I warned you to obey. You will soon beg for my forgiveness, whore!"

I struggle, but he is too strong for me. I feel him arching onto his toes—

And then he slams into me. He gasps in my ear. With a moan, he falls to the floor.

I turn around to find a woman, dressed in a colorful flowing abaya, holding a gun in a two-handed defensive stance.

When I see that my clutch is open, I realize it is mine.

Her dark eyes glisten with anger.

"Thank you," I whisper.

"We wives are on the floor below. I heard a scream. I thought... He sometimes attacks our older daughters too. Their suite is closer to him. Just down the hall." Her hands tremble as they fall to her side. "He is...*an animal.*"

I go to her, but she raises the gun again.

I hold up my hands. "Please...We should go before anyone else comes to check on him!"

She stares at me as if I'm crazy. "Go...*where*? I am a prisoner! All of his wives are nothing more than his chattel. We live under the law of male guardianship. Our husbands control the destinies of their wives and daughters!"

"But he's dead now! Leave with me," I plead. "The others can too! You are in Washington! This is a safe haven! And you have diplomatic immunity!"

"And leave the rest of our children—our sons—in Saudi Arabia? That would be worse than death! Women in my country inherit nothing. Upon his death, we lose everything. We lose *them!*"

"From here, you can fight for them!" I argue. "You can make a public case for getting custody of your children."

"Even if we were to do so, it wouldn't matter. Your president will do anything to stay in our king's good graces, even if it means turning us over to him. That man has no soul." Agitated, she waves the gun wildly. "Ahmad's family will scorn our little ones. Worse yet, they will torture them, just as they will torture us when they learn of Ahmad's death. There is no place for us to go!"

Her eyes bore into me. They gleam from the heat of her anger before hardening with resolve as she raises the gun again—

And shoots herself in the head.

She crumples onto the floor.

Shit!... Shit!

I want to take my gun, but I know I should leave it. It can't be traced. And besides, their murder-suicide is my alibi.

Instead, I use the rag that was once my dress to wipe down the gun and its magazine. I then place it in her hand, pressing her fingers around it again.

I put on my coat and shoes, then take my purse. I stuff the scraps that were once my dress into my coat pockets.

I leave by way of the elevator.

Only when I'm safely in Henry's car do I call Arnie to report I'm clear of the hotel's security cameras.

"I IMAGINE YOU'VE HAD A HELL OF A DAY," JACK SAYS.

I hold the phone as close to my ear as possible so that I can pretend that my husband is sitting next to me and whispering in my ear.

Although it's only been thirteen hours, it seems like a million years since we last saw each other.

How time flies...

"Did you leave right after Mario took you on your tour?" I ask.

"Yes, although the kids would have liked to have stayed longer. If you're still in DC during spring break, as opposed to you coming here for those weekends, I promised them that we'd visit you instead."

I snicker. "Jack, I don't know if I'll ever get out of this *situation*, let alone this town, alive."

"You will," he insists. "Do you want to tell me about it?"

"As we figured, my tasks are pretty egregious. I feel our 'three amigos' should be apprised of the situation."

Despite his concern, Jack chuckles. "Ha! That's a great name for them! Okay, I'll connect us now."

About a minute later, I hear their acknowledgments.

I begin by telling them how Edmonton barged in on me at my apartment.

"Not surprising," Marcus declares. "He's showing you he's got total control over you, even in your personal space."

"You can say that again," I mutter.

Jack is silent.

My guess: he's stewing because I didn't say anything about this to him when he was here. But hey, look at it from my point of view! When was this conversation supposed to take place? In front of the kids at the restaurant? Or, perhaps I should have ruined our few hours of sleep, when we were entwined in each other's arms.

As mission partners, now is the time such intel should be divulged.

As lovers, there is no right time.

He knows this as well as me.

When I mention my negotiation with Edmonton—five tasks, and then Jack will be off the hook—you'd think he'd be appreciative, if not actually whooping with joy.

Again, crickets from Jack.

Whereas Ryan growls, "What makes you think he'll stop there—or for that matter, hold to his promise?"

Killjoy.

Irritably, I retort, "What choice do I have? I've got to stall until we've broken the coded message that Milo passed to Volkov."

"Let's face it. This first task was a lucky break: the job was done by someone else," Ryan points out. "Odds are, a second miracle won't happen."

Damn it, he is really harshing my mellow.

But hey, I'm a pro, so I let it slide off my back. To prove it if only to myself, I give them a play-by-play of al-Nayef's murder—not at my hand, but that of one of his desolate wives.

"I'm sorry for her, and for you for having to be there and see how her desperation played out," Lee murmurs.

"I guess I was right when I told you it was a test for you

and perhaps for Edmonton too," Ryan adds.

"Maybe," Marcus counters. "Because Prince al-Nayef was always a wild card, he was certainly our last choice as the King's successor. However, if our intel is correct, he wasn't the Russians' preferred choice either. How do we know Edmonton didn't send Donna to do Putin's bidding?"

"We don't," Ryan concedes.

"Something you said concerns me, Donna," Lee declares. "You're to do anything Edmonton asks? Setups, blackmail, exterminations...whatever?"

"Well...yes."

"Even...*sex*?" Lee is seething.

"I...I told him it was off the table."

"Thank God!" Lee exclaims.

He is jealous.

So, why isn't Jack? I mean, has he fallen asleep? My God, he was angry enough when Edmonton grabbed my bum at the photoshoot.

"Mr. Craig, are you still on the line?" My question drips with sarcasm.

"Oh, I'm here all right," Jack's reply is polite.

Too polite.

Miffed, I ask, "And what's your take on all this?"

"I think you're handling it as well as you can, under the circumstances. You're doing Edmonton's bidding under duress. If you find any of the requests egregious, you'll try for some kind of workaround. Or maybe you simply refuse."

And put you in danger? Never!

"Should such a time arise, we'll deal with it as best we can. Just send up the bat signal," Jack adds.

Some superhero he is...

I guess what irritates me most is that he's sounding like my boss as opposed to my husband.

So, that's where we stand now, eh?

"Yes, sir," I mutter. "And you're right, it's been a full day. Gentlemen, I bid you goodnight." I end the call.

Then I throw the phone at the wall. It hits with a loud *thunk*.

I hope Dirty Old Codger has turned off his hearing aid.

11

Whistleblower

THE ACT OF WHISTLEBLOWING IS A NOBLE ONE. IT TAKES GUTS TO *disclose evidence of an unauthorized disclosure vital to our national security. Protections to do so anonymously are the only way to encourage those who know of such egregious acts to come forward.*

If one is to blow a whistle, one begins by filing the complaint formally with the Office of the Inspector General of the Intelligence Community. This individual works under the auspices of the Office of the Director of National Intelligence.

In your domain, you should also encourage anonymous whistle-blowing without disciplinary consequences.

If your daughter breaks curfew to meet her boyfriend — yes, you want to know about it.

The same goes for any child who is sneaking a cig or a toke. All bad habits must be nipped in the bud!

Encouraging your children to apprise you of their siblings' indiscretions is not a bad thing. (Nor is rewarding them with a monetary tip for doing so.)

Especially if it's your husband who has been sneaking out of the house. (Heaven knows why, considering your connubial bliss…)

"Let me guess—he invited Wife Number Four to join you in a *ménage-à-trois*, so you had to kill her too. And then you made it look like a murder-suicide, knowing that the king will make your little mess disappear, especially since Ahmad was more of a liability than an asset. Ingenious!" Edmonton is practically drooling at the thought that his fantasy was just realized: sadistic sex times two. "Regale me with the details, Scheherazade! Despite half the Cabinet demanding face time, conjure up a titillating tale, and I'll grant you the next half hour." He motions me to sit.

"Time is one thing I don't have. Ergo, I'll leave my methodology to your imagination," I reply coolly. "I'd rather get on with my next task."

"So, my seductive manslayer is getting antsy, is she? Perhaps I should put DARPA on the task of embedding a video camera into your eye. That way, I can live vicariously through you." Edmonton sighs rhapsodically at the thought.

Little does he know Acme has beaten the government to it.

If only I could use them now. Unfortunately, it would be inadmissible in court.

"Speaking of which…" Edmonton comes from behind his desk to sit beside me. He whispers: "There is a whistleblower amongst us."

A trickle of dread rolls down my back. *Is he talking about Ryan?*

I try to look intrigued. "Do you know whom?"

He rolls his eyes. "Nothing gets by me. Haven't you figured that out already?"

I don't give him the satisfaction of answering his question.

"In fact, I may have been the impetus of the leak,"

Edmonton admits. "Let's rack it up to unfortunate timing. I was conversing with one of our young, eager-to-please White House interns—Olivia Quinn—when a crucial call came in. She overheard part of the conversation. Sadly, Olivia's extermination is now necessary. Albeit, she will be missed. As you can imagine, sampling the eye candy is one of the perks of my office."

So, my next victim is a woman, maybe a few years older than Mary.

"Has her complaint been formally filed?" I ask.

"My sources say she'll be submitting by tomorrow, so you have time to get our prey before the deed is done."

Our prey.

I want to gag—partially because of what he said, but mostly because he feels he has the right to stick his tongue down my throat.

As bile rises in me, I push him away.

"Let me guess... *You're jealous!*" Edmonton chortles at the thought.

"Frankly, I'm disgusted."

"At the fact that a mere child is an object of my affection?"

"Get real! It's... disgusting that you'd prey on someone forty years your junior!"

"So much for your feminist façade, Mrs... *Ms.* Craig." Edmonton rolls his eyes. "You're not only a sexist, you're also an ageist to boot!"

Angrily, I mutter, "If you weren't the most powerful man in the world, no one would look twice at you."

"True," he concedes. "But women do look at me. More to the point, they do anything I ask of them."

"Olivia?" I ask.

He shrugs. "It was only a matter of time. Sadly, now it is not to be."

"Which one is she?"

"Long legs. Silky red hair. And, if rumors are to be believed, a tongue flexible enough to tie a cherry stem into a knot..." Savoring the thought, he closes his eyes.

So, sampling the eye candy is merely a fantasy—and a point in Olivia's favor.

"What did she overhear?"

Annoyed, he mutters, "None of your business."

"Fair enough." Faking a pout, I stand up. "Don't get too used to me doing your wet work," I warn him. "After her, only three more tasks, and I'm done."

He shrugs.

Not a good sign.

Because of my White House security clearance, I'm able to access Olivia's personnel file.

From what I see, she is the typical White House intern: intelligent, ambitious, patriotic, and hardworking to a fault.

She hails from Wisconsin. Cheerleader, student body president, and National Honor Society in high school. Currently, Olivia is a senior at the University of Wisconsin-Madison, with two majors: Statistics and International Studies. After this final semester and a gap year spent interning, she is supposed to start law school at Georgetown in the fall.

She serves meals at the local homeless mission at least once a month. She's an avid jogger. According to her Facebook page, she's signed up for a charity 10k three weekends from now.

She shares a flat with two other girls in the Hay-Adams district. I won't be able to approach her there—

Approach her to say what? To *do* what?

I am certainly not going to kill her.

She is the All-American Girl Next Door. Everyone's daughter, sister, or best friend.

I'll figure it out when I run into her.

Literally—while she's out jogging tonight.

ARNIE DOES ME THE FAVOR OF HACKING INTO THE GPS SYSTEM on Olivia's cell phone to trace her after-work jogging route. We learn that her usual running trail is through Rock Creek Park.

Instead of chasing Olivia down, I have Henry drop me at the closest point where the road meets the trailhead before she usually flips around to turn back.

Within half an hour, I see Olivia coming my way. When she's just a few yards from me, she slows to a complete stop and bends at the waist, huffing to catch her breath.

I call out her name.

Olivia looks over. Her stare indicates she doesn't recognize me from the few times we've passed each other in the West Wing.

I pull out my White House security badge. "I'm Donna Craig, Senior White House National Security Advisor," I explain. "Olivia, because of your whistleblower complaint, your life may be in grave danger."

Perplexed, Olivia grimaces. "But... How did you know? I mean, I haven't even submitted it yet! I took it home with me to look it over tonight before doing so."

"Edmonton knows," I tell her.

"My God! I was told my name would be kept anonymous! I wouldn't have done it otherwise!" Her eyes widen with fear. "One of them warned this would happen!"

"Wait—you mean to say you told *two people*?"

Olivia hesitates, still not sure I'm on her side. I wonder what is racing through her mind. Is it the rumors about Edmonton and me?

Finally, she spits out: "*Yes.*"

"Who were they?"

"I...I don't want to say!"

"You're right. You don't have to tell me," I concede. "But your name was leaked to Edmonton by one of them. Otherwise, I wouldn't be warning you to get out of town!"

Olivia's jaw drops open. Trembling, she asks, "Should I go home to Wisconsin?"

I shake my head. "If you do, there is no guarantee that you—or for that matter, your loved ones—will be safe there. Olivia, you need to go to a safe house until your complaint is formally investigated by the Office of the Special Counsel and submitted to the Congressional Intelligence committees for their own investigations."

"You're scaring me!" Olivia exclaims. "Look, I know you're close to Edmonton. For all I know, you're here to kill me now!" She backs away. She's ready to flee.

"I swear I'm not! Maybe if you heard it from someone you trust..." I punch in a phone number for a video chat.

It is answered immediately. "President Chiffray, it's Donna Craig. Would you validate my position for someone whose life may be endangered?"

"Brilliant," Jack exclaims.

"Why, thank you, sir!" At that moment, Jack is speaking as my boss.

Later, when the conversation switches to phone sex, I'll have my husband back.

"So, the game plan is that Olivia is to stay with Lee until the investigation is initiated by the Intelligence Community's Inspector General, and make herself available, shielded, should she be called to testify?" Jack asks.

"Yes. I asked Olivia to send an email to the White House Human Resources Department, requesting to take unpaid leave to care for a sick relative. She sent a similar one to her roommates. She also sent an email home, explaining she'd been asked to go to Brussels on a special assignment for a House Subcommittee project on EU trade agreements. And finally, Olivia allowed me to take a picture of her on the ground, eyes shut. Emma doctored it so that Olivia looks as if she's dead. When I showed the picture to Edmonton, I told him that I sent all three emails from her personal account so that no one would become suspicious as to her disappearance. I also said I dumped her body in the Chesapeake with enough weights that it will never surface."

"Do you think he believed you?"

"Yes." I shiver as I remember his cackle. I almost gagged when he kissed Olivia's photo, as if saying goodbye to her.

"Did Olivia disclose to you what she'd overheard?"

"No. But Lee will get it out of her. He'll also ask her to divulge the name of the person who recommended that she keep the information to herself as well as the second person who persuaded her to file the complaint."

"So, you think he'll charm her the way he charms you?"

Ah...finally. "Is that jealousy I hear in your voice, Mr. Craig?"

"Perhaps," Jack admits. "Tell the truth: is my jealousy a bigger turn-on than naughty talk?"

"Not at all," I purr. No need to tell him the truth.

12

Intelligence Community

THE UNITED STATES INTELLIGENCE COMMUNITY (IC) IS MADE UP *of the country's various governmental agencies and organizations tasked with the monumental job of conducting covert intelligence activities. Their work, both separately and collaboratively, support our country's national security.*

They say it takes a village to raise a child. These days, it takes an intelligence community to keep eyes and ears on our children at all times.

Great news—you've created one of your own! It consists of other parents who have your back—those of your children—and the teachers who have their best interests at heart.

You may not want to believe your kids will do anything that can get them in trouble or cause them harm, but hey: shite happens. Since you can't be with your progeny at all times, these kind folks will shadow them so that you'll know when they have stepped out of line.

And you'll do the same for their children.

THE REST OF THE WEEK GOES BY WITHOUT A SUMMONS FROM Edmonton. In my capacity as his National Security liaison, I spend my days going from meeting to meeting chaired by the various IC agency department heads. Hearing about the ingenious field tactics of the fearless men and women who are the country's first line of defense in covert warfare is tremendously inspiring.

Because I'm new, I am scrutinized carefully. Ryan is also attending these meetings. When I'm introduced to those who don't already know me, his subtle phrasing regarding my own fieldwork makes his message clear: *she is one of us.*

Considering my proximity to Edmonton—physically and via his administration's grapevine—I am grateful for this. The Intelligence Community trusts Ryan. Now, they know to trust me too.

Half of these meetings are also attended by Mario. The first time he heard Ryan introduce me, his mouth lifted into a shadow of a smile.

Had he picked up on Ryan's coded message? My guess is yes.

I anticipate Edmonton will now do what he can to make my life even harder.

FRIDAY—BEFORE I'M TO FLY BACK HOME FOR THE WEEKEND—I'M called into Edmonton's office.

He stands and walks out from behind his desk. "I need you to pick up someone at Dulles." He hands me a photo.

It is a candid shot taken from a window at least one floor above the street level. From the writing on the canopies over the sidewalk storefronts, I realize that the man is in Russia.

He looks to be in his mid-forties: graying, paunchy, and slouching, he has world-weary eyes and a hardened grimace.

"His name is Tom Jamison. He's arriving on this evening's Aeroflot from Moscow. Jamison is CIA, but his cover is that of a journalist with *The Financial Times*."

"In that case, I'm sure he can find his way to wherever he needs to be without my help," I reply.

"Don't be a smart ass," Edmonton huffs. "I'm not asking you to play 'sexy Uber driver'"—the thought puts a leer on his face—"but only because Jamison already has a car service picking him up. You'll intercept him at the bar nearest Aeroflot's baggage claim area. It'll be where he'll head after walking through customs. Steal his wallet and see to it that he never makes it home. It should be easy enough to do. Jamison isn't the sharpest tool in the box, especially after a few vodkas. He's been in Moscow long enough to learn how to drink like a Russian, and Aeroflot pours generously, so he should already be pickled well before you sucker him into believing you're the whore of his dreams."

"Gee, thanks for the compliment. Pray tell, what is his crime?"

Edmonton slaps me. Seeing the anger flare in my eyes, he growls, "Haven't you learned yet? Your only role here is limited to what I tell you to do. Never question me again!"

I nod silently.

"Much better, Mrs. Craig." He lowers his hand. From the top of his desk, he picks up an official White House pouch marked POTUS. "For the wallet. Put it in here and personally deliver it to my desk. Now, leave my sight."

He doesn't have to ask twice.

∾

An hour before Tom Jamison's flight is due to land, I have Henry drive me to Dulles.

"You've got to be excited to go home and see your kids," Henry declares.

"Yep. Can't wait." My clipped tone puts a perplexed scowl on his face.

Believe me, no one is more upset than me right now. Not that he needs to know this, let alone why.

The news that I might not be home until late Saturday night—sent via a group text so that I can avoid a phone call in which I'd inevitably end up choked in tears— goes over worse than I'd anticipated.

Mary's response is a varied bunch of angry emojis.

Jeff texts:

DAMN IT, MOM! I KNEW THIS WOULD HAPPEN!!!!

Aunt Phyllis responds:

Porter and I had planned a little weekend getaway, so I guess that's a nonstarter.
Thanks for nuthin'.

I get no response at all from Trisha, leading me to believe she's the most upset of all.

Only Jack shows the empathy I'd hoped for:

Call when things are less hectic there.

In case someone is shadowing me, Henry drops me at the terminal of my scheduled flight. Unfortunately, it's the farthest from the international terminal.

On the way there, I stop by the car rental area. At the

nearest counter, I hand over one of my many fake driver's licenses and a credit card under the same alias.

The rental agent tells me that the only car left on the lot is a Smart Fortwo.

I roll my eyes. "You're kidding...right?"

"Nope, sorry. And it's a smoker's car," he warns me.

Agh!

"Forget it," I reply.

I'm about to walk over to a competitor when he adds, "You won't find another rental available at any of the other counters. This is the first decent weekend weather we've had in a long time. Everyone is sold out."

Oh well, it'll have to do.

Sighing, I hand him my credit card.

I hope the rest of my night doesn't play out this way.

I'VE DRESSED THE PART OF THE ROAD-WEARY WARRIORETTE: A sleek fitted berry-red Prada suit and Loubies to match. When I enter the international baggage claim area, I'm carrying the luggage I brought with me: a Louis Vuitton handbag and a small valise.

The bar closest to the baggage carousel used by Jamison's Aeroflot flight gate is called The Welcome Mat.

I position myself at the counter. When the bartender walks over, I tell him to pour me only water, served with a slice of lime on a swizzle stick, but to bill all the drinks I order as vodka tonics.

Then I wait.

"Um…Is this seat taken?" Tom Jamison points to the empty stool next to me. Up until the moment he'd spied the bar, it had held the valise and purse that was now beneath my barstool.

"All yours," I say with a smile. "And the great news is that the bartender is quick." I nod toward the tip jar beyond my highball glass. "You can thank me for that. I've been keeping him on a very short leash."

Tom chuckles. "Then let me pay for your next round. What's your poison?"

"Vodka tonic."

Tom waves to the bartender. The man hustles over. Tom orders a vodka straight and asks him to bring me another V&T.

In no time, we have our drinks. I let Tom tip the barkeep.

Then we tap our glasses.

Tom's drink is gone in one gulp. I do the same. Tom motions the bartender for another round.

It's there in a blink of an eye.

It is downed by us just as fast.

As I put down my glass, I say, "Thank you for hosting this impromptu party, Mr… I'm sorry, I didn't catch your name."

"Tom. Jamison."

I hold out my hand. "I'm Donna Craig."

Although Tom takes it, his mouth purses, as he tries to place the name. His eyes grow large when it comes to him—

Then he frowns. As would anyone in our industry, instinctively, he leans away. His hands go into a defensive position.

"If you're wondering if I'm the Acme operative, the answer is yes. One and the same," I assure him.

"Your reputation precedes you," Tom replies. "As did the word of your resignation there. Not to mention your latest position: as a gofer to our Commander in Chief."

Jeez! Well, I guess my rep in Spooklandia is trashed for good…

"Yeah, well, word travels fast in the IC," I murmur. "I'll bet you're wondering why I'm here."

Tom gazes down at his empty glass. With a sigh, he nudges it away. "I think I know. Tell me, Donna, how long do I have?"

"As long as you want," I vow. "I only have to make it *look* like an extermination. You're to go to a safe house until we make a case for Edmonton's treason through proper channels. The intel you've brought with you will help tremendously."

Tom's nod is barely perceptible. "How do *you* know about it?"

"You've been burned. Edmonton is on to you. Maybe he's got a mole in the Moscow office."

Hearing this, Tom turns a pale shade of gray. "No way! Our office is clean as a whistle. Everyone covers everyone else's back. The mole has got to be someone at GVR—within the Russian intelligence agency."

"What do you have that he wants so badly?"

Tom leans in and hisses: "It's the GVR's file on Edmonton."

"That's golden!" I murmur. "Where did you get it?"

Still preening from the compliment, Tom replies, "A source I'd cultivated in GVR's archive department handed it off to me. She directed me to take it as far up the ladder as possible."

Hearing this, I gawk.

"Believe me, I was just as shocked as you are now," Tom admits. "Frankly, I think the Russian people know that only a concerted effort will ever get them out from under Putin's thumb."

"You're right. It's a very brave thing for her to do. Have you read the file?"

Tom shakes his head. "It's encrypted. But she warned me it was incriminating and that I'd better deliver it directly to DNI Clancy. In the field, we know he's the only firewall we have for the protection of this sort of intel. Otherwise, it'll get buried."

"It'll go to him, but in a roundabout way," I explain. "In the meantime, I've got to get you to a safe house."

"Works for me. Let me grab my bag and then let's get the hell out of here."

"Sure—but first, kiss me, you fool!" I exclaim.

He gets it. It's best to put on a good show in case he's been shadowed.

Tom makes the ploy look real enough. Besides pulling me close and putting a hand on my breast, he grinds his open mouth into mine.

I play along until I feel I may pass out from the alcohol fumes on his breath.

Then, feigning a tipsiness befitting the number of drinks I've supposedly downed, I rise unsteadily to my feet. With my arm around Tom's shoulder, we stagger toward the Aeroflot baggage carousel.

And that's when I feel something strange on the backside of his collar. With some quick sleight-of-hand, I pull it out: A tiny disk, no bigger than a dime.

It's a GPS tracker.

Apparently, Tom is being shadowed stateside.

I'm stunned enough that I don't realize I'm in the way of a family rushing to catch one of the Departure Gate trams. When they bump into me, I drop the disk.

Shit! Shit!

I search the floor, but I can't find it anywhere.

Tom glances around, worried. "Shouldn't we get out of here?"

He's right.

If it was planted by the GVR so that Tom would be easier to shadow stateside, leaving it at Dulles may make his disappearance easier. On the other hand, if someone is already watching, we've got to hit the road and lose them there.

Will Edmonton be suspicious if its signal doesn't end up in Chesapeake Bay, where I'm telling him I dumped Tom's body?

I'll have to chance it. We take off running.

～

WITH LUGGAGE IN HAND, WE ENTER THE RENTAL CAR GARAGE and claim the smallest car I've ever driven, I swear.

Once we hit State Road 267, I drive around for an hour—speeding up periodically, making sudden and unexpected turns now and again, getting on and off the expressway, ducking through neighborhoods, and turning in and out of driveways.

My erratic driving—not to mention a full day of drinking—gives Tom motion sickness. *Eau de Puke* now permeates our tiny clown car.

The rest of the drive is made with the windows open. You'd think the frigid night air would have a sobering effect on Tom, or at least wake him up, but no.

Finally, when I'm sure we aren't being followed, I pull over and poke Tom. He opens his eyes with a snort.

"Time to introduce you to your safe house host," I exclaim.

I guess his grunt means yes because he then pulls down the passenger seat visor to see if he looks presentable. One hard squint is all it takes to realize it may be a good thing to wipe a spray of hardened spittle from the side of his mouth.

"Showtime!" he declares.

I tap out Lee's cell number: "Hey, um… Have room at the inn for one more?"

Lee chuckles. "That's what I get for owning the biggest house in town."

"Make that the West Coast," I remind him.

"Whom will I be hosting?"

I point my phone's camera at Tom.

Realizing who he's talking to, Tom sits at attention and exclaims, "Good evening, Mr. President!" Frankly, that's quite a feat to pull off, considering the copious amounts of booze, the long flight, and our drive through the seven circles of hell.

"Mr. President, Tom Jamison is lately of the CIA's Moscow Bureau, but was recently burned—by Edmonton, we believe. He's carrying some intel of importance to our national security."

"A patriot is always welcome here," Lee declares.

I turn to Tom. "Your intel will be safe with President Chiffray. But I'll need your wallet and whatever else is in it."

Tom pulls out the wallet. He hands it over except for one thing: an innocuous-looking credit card.

"Mr. President, can you call Jack and ask him to send the plane to Manassas? Edmonton may have a tail on us, but we'll definitely be there to meet it."

Lee looks puzzled. "Isn't that a call you'd want to make?"

"I'd prefer it came from you. But do mention that I'll call as soon as Tom is wheels up."

Truth is, the lost GPS disk worries me. What if, somehow, we're still being followed? I can't have someone reporting back to Edmonton that I let Tom get away, let alone that I helped him.

That will be the end of Jack, for sure.

As I circle back to I-66, heading west toward Manassas. Tom falls back asleep.

When we get there, I take a picture that makes him look like a corpse. Since he already looks like crap, it's not a stretch. I send it to Emma for a little Photoshop magic.

Tom is still cutting z's when the Acme plane skids onto the Manassas Regional Airport's tarmac and taxis to a stop.

I shake Tom awake. "Your ride is here."

He groans as he opens an eye. By the time he focuses on Acme's plane, George is standing in the doorway. George gives us a salute and then walks down the airstairs toward us.

I pop open the hatch so that Tom can grab his bag and we both get out.

George shakes Tom's hand, but I insist on a hug, declaring, "You're a sight for sore eyes."

I shake Tom's hand goodbye, but I kiss George's cheek.

As instructed, I put Tom's wallet in the official White House pouch.

I drive straight to Sixteen Hundred Pennsylvania Avenue. It's late enough that Edmonton may be at some function, and I can put it onto his desk and then slip back out—

No such luck. When I enter through the connecting door between our offices, he's sitting there.

Without a word, I hand him the pouch.

He nods but doesn't smile. "How did it go?"

"All's well that ends well." Do I sound chipper enough?

"You make it seem so easy, Mrs. Craig." His eyes narrow as he glares at me.

"Does that disappoint you?"

"I'd be lying if I said no." He leans back in his chair. "Finding someone who is just as unscrupulous as me is a novelty that I would normally welcome. But the ease in which you carry out your tasks takes all the fun out of our agreement. But no matter! Things will get interesting when you inevitably falter at one."

"Sorry to be a spoilsport, but I don't plan on it."

"Considering that you hold your husband's future in your skillful hands, you'd better pray you're right."

That's my cue to leave.

As much as I'd like to run out of here and never come back, I take my time as I sashay out of the room.

I WAIT UNTIL I'M HOME BEFORE MAKING THE MUCH-DREADED call to Jack.

"Well, you sure took long enough," he chides me.

"Did I wake you?" I ask.

"I don't sleep well when I can't feel you beside me."

Can I love this man any more than I already do? I don't think so.

"I feel exactly the same way," I whisper. "Look, before we talk business, let's start with the most important thing. How are the kids?"

"As you'd suspect, Mary is climbing the walls about Berkeley. It doesn't help that Babs got her acceptance email yesterday."

I groan in solidarity with Mary's apprehension. I'm sure she's devastated that one of her two best friends since elementary school may end up going to her first-pick school without her.

In the hope that I'll get the right answer, I venture to ask: "Are Trisha and Janie still enthralled with the illustrious Riley?"

"Sadly, yes. And since you brought it up—"

Oh no...

"—Riley's latest antic was to pit Trisha and Janie against each other."

"That was inevitable," I mutter. "Did they fall for it?"

"Unfortunately, yes. She was to judge who could pull off the best practical joke. I have to say both came up with doozies. Trisha's gag earned her a week's suspension."

"Oh, my God! What did she do?"

"She made Janie chocolate cupcakes, sort of. They were loaded with Ex-Lax."

My groan is even louder than before. "I assume Lee is livid."

"I guess he would be if Janie's trick hadn't been just as bad."

"I'm afraid to ask, but I guess I have to. What did she do?"

"She substituted a depilatory cream for Trisha's hair conditioner. Trisha's hair fell out in clumps. So, as it turns out, her suspension couldn't have been better timed." Jack sighs. "She wants to cut her hair short and not return to school, even after it grows back. Mary said she'd take her to your stylist. I said I'm game for that, but I knew you'd like to talk to her about all this silliness, and that you'd back me about attending her school again after her suspension."

"I'll call Trisha at ten o'clock your time." If I weren't so furious, I guess I'd be laughing. "It's been a hell of a day, dear husband, and so far, you're batting oh-for-two. Any good news to report?"

"Yes, in fact! Thanks to Jeff sinking the longest three-pointer in the history of the county, the Hilldale High School Wildcats B-Team is one step closer to a high ranking in next week's tournament."

"Let me guess! Jeff is mad at me for missing the game."

"He'll get over it if you show up next weekend."

"I'm doing my best," I insist. "Was Lee able to get Olivia to talk to him?"

"Does the Chiffray charm ever fail? Don't answer that, since we both know what you'll say."

"Quit stalling. What did Olivia say?"

"Turns out that when Olivia was little, her grandmother, a Russian immigrant, was her caregiver while her single mother worked full time. She taught the girl her language. Last week, Olivia was asked to substitute for Mildred while she went to a dental appointment. As usual the door to the Oval was open just a crack."

"Edmonton likes it that way. It allows him to shout at Mildred when he needs something."

"Well, this time Olivia heard his shouts—into his phone —*in Russian.*"

I can't believe my ears. "The call with his handlers went through the White House switchboard?"

"No. It must have been on a cell phone."

"Was he loud enough for her to make out what he was saying?"

"In between a few choice curses that made her blush, he claimed he'd followed through with all of Putin's requests, including al-Nayef's extermination, and it deserved the quid pro quo promised."

"Wow...So, we'll have confirmation of Edmonton ordering the hit!"

"As long as we can keep Olivia alive, yes," Jack replies.

"After Edmonton hung up, he realized the door hadn't been closed all the way. He'd forgotten that Olivia was sitting at Mildred's desk. She could tell he was concerned about the worried look on her face. Usually, she flirts back with him, but she couldn't pretend that what she heard didn't bother her. She was scared enough that she felt she had to report it to someone."

"Olivia told me she'd mentioned it to two others. Did she tell Lee who they were?"

"One was Mildred. When she came back from the dentist, she could see that Olivia was shaking with fear. The other was Mario."

"Which one told her to report it?"

"Mario. Mildred advised her against it, but Olivia still felt threatened by Mildred."

"I wonder which of them told Edmonton that she was going to report it?"

"Good question. For that matter, both would have reason to do so, if only to stay in Edmonton's good graces," Jack points out. "But it doesn't speak well of Mildred that she told Olivia not to report it. It shows she was most concerned with saving her boss's ass."

"The same could be said about Mario," I counter. "Encouraging Olivia might have made him seem empathetic, but we both know the submission process isn't all that simple. He may have been trying to put her mind at ease while buying time for Edmonton to order her elimination. That, with what we suspect about the role he played in Coquette's death, puts him on the top of my list of Edmonton enablers."

"With Olivia's complaint and whatever Tom hands over to us, we may be able to make our case to Congress without Milo's missing clue."

"Tom says he was handed Edmonton's GVR file, but it's encrypted."

"Emma and her team really have their hands full, but they're on it too," Jack mutters.

"In other words, still no luck in cracking Milo's missive to Volkov?"

"Nope. But they're working around the clock on it. Speaking of which, by now, you've got to have been up a full twenty-four hours. Why don't you get some shut-eye?"

"I'll try. If you were here to hold me, I'd sleep like a baby."

"I wish I were, my darling wife." The wistfulness in his voice brings tears to my eyes.

I guess that's why I make the decision not to mention my suspicion that Edmonton may soon be on to me.

If I'm lucky, I'm wrong about that.

In my dream, a phone is ringing...

Only, it's not a dream. It's beside my ear.

I reach for my cell phone, but I drop it on the floor. Groaning, I roll out of bed to find it.

What time is it anyway?

When I finally locate the phone, I realize I've slept the whole day away—

And that it's Edmonton who is calling me.

Oh...shit.

I pick up the phone to hear him laughing...

I'm wrong, it just sounds like laughter, but actually he's hysterical with anger.

Soon, I'm able to make out the phrases that aren't curses, but threats that promise to break me: body, spirit, and mind. Like "...lied to me, *straight to my face...*" and "...you'll never see him again…" and "…when I get done with you, you'll never see your children again either…"

Finally, I shout, "Bradley, I can't make sense of what you're saying to me!"

Silence.

It seems like an hour has passed before he says, with deadly calm, "Your husband's warrant is being written now. And since I cannot have the wife of a traitor in my administration, don't bother to come back here."

The phone goes dead.

I can't…

I won't…

But I know I must.

I call him back. "He got away from me, Bradley! I had Jamison in the back seat of my car. He was drunk—and I'd drugged him too. But somehow, he kicked out the back window when I stopped at a red light and ran off into the night!" I'm crying uncontrollably now. "Believe me, Bradley! I looked for him all night! *I swear*! But…I couldn't find him!"

Edmonton screams, "That's because his tracker is on its way to Orlando—*with a nice Italian family of five!*"

"I'm so, so, sorry, Bradley! But Jamison is a marked man! He has nowhere to hide! And I took his wallet as you asked—"

"The fucking wallet was empty!"

"NO! It wasn't, I swear!" My sobs come out as hiccups.

"In any regard, Mrs. Craig, you blew it." His words cut through me like a steel blade.

"Please! I'm begging you, Bradley! Don't take it out on Jack! Instead…You can…"

I know I'm talking, but my heart is beating so hard that I can't hear what I'm saying: *"Take it out on me!"*

Edmonton says nothing.

Is he still on the line?

Finally: "If you're willing to bend your rule to save his life—"

"I am! I swear, Bradley!"

"Then wait for me." The phone line goes dead.

I have to do it.

For Jack.

13

Unfriendly Act

THE TERM "UNFRIENDLY ACT" DESCRIBES AN EVENT IN WHICH ONE *government does something to another so egregious it leads to military action.*

This can run the gamut from a surgical strike to boots-on-the-ground warfare.

Let's say your neighbor comes onto your property and cuts down your tree because, as she claims, it blocks her view. Both her trespassing and her handiness with a buzz saw could be described as "unfriendly acts."

The same could be said when you shear her prize rose bushes to the ground.

To defuse escalating rounds of retaliation, invite her over to tea. When she realizes the homemade Baked Alaska you've just torched is an exact replica of her house, perhaps she'll agree to a ceasefire.

I DO EXACTLY AS EDMONTON COMMANDS: I WAIT FOR HIM.

And wait. And wait.

Around ten at night, there is a knock on the door. Standing in front of it is a man I've never seen before.

He is over seven feet tall and broad-shouldered. His well-cut suit bulges from his massive chest, arms, and legs. But he's enough of a dandy to sport a yellow rosebud, white gloves, and a bowler hat.

Bowler lugs a large rolling suitcase.

When I look out, he seems to know because he smiles and waves grandly.

I open the door.

In a high sing-song voice, he exclaims, "I'm here to set up for your special visitor!"

As I step aside so that he may come in, dread roils through me.

"Please, madame...the bedroom is which way?"

I take him to it.

Bowler looks around, bemused. "Minimal, to say the least." Shrugging, he opens his rolling case.

Inside is a portable bench. With a single touch, four cushioned planks fold open, one for each of the submissive's appendages. Each plank has two straps with buckles that will hold the submissive face down, kneeling doggy-style.

In this case, the sub is me.

A smaller bag is left in the case. Bowler puts it on the bed and opens it, taking out one item at a time. I don't like what I see: four silver cuffs attached to chains with large hooks at the other end.

A ball gag.

A blindfold.

Handcuffs.

A cat-o-nine-tails.

Nothing else.

Ouch.

"Your lingerie drawer—where is it?"

I walk to the dresser and open the top right drawer.

Bowler scrounges through the items: bras, panties, kimonos, teddies, thongs, merry widows, and such. Suddenly he gives a happy squeal. "Nice peignoir set! Saks Fifth Avenue, am I right?"

I nod. The peignoir is sheer, long, and white, with spaghetti straps and a matching long-sleeved robe.

He sighs longingly.

He's a big boy. A real bruiser. They wouldn't have had it in his size.

He tosses it at me. "Strip down and put it on."

I do as requested.

Bowler watches with a smirk on his face, scanning me top to toe. "Now, a complete turn, please."

Reluctantly, I do as he asks.

"Fine, fine, fine!" He claps as if delighted by some circus act. "Now, disrobe again."

I arch a brow. "Excuse me?"

"I said, *disrobe!* You know, take it off. Your gentleman caller would be displeased by it, as it does absolutely nothing for you."

"Is that so? Well, it just so happens that my husband thinks it's sexy as hell—"

Bowler smacks me across the face.

I fall to the floor. Slowly, I get up—

So slowly, in fact, that he doesn't expect my punch to his groin.

He doubles over, gasping. It takes him a very long minute

to straighten up. When he does, he knocks me against the wall.

At first, I'm too dazed to fight him as he picks me up and carries me to the torture bench. Even when my adrenaline surges again, my attempts to bite and kick him are for naught. He's got me in a single-hand front choke. As I gasp, he tells me what I already know: "You fight, and I take you out. You're expendable, darling. Don't test that theory."

Like hell, I am.

Bowler slams me onto the bench, face down, and holds me there while he straps me in: arms first, then my legs.

I choke when he crams the ball gag into my mouth.

He leaves me for a moment. When he comes back, he's holding my purse. From it, he takes the front door keycard. "Since you'll be otherwise engaged, your special visitor will let himself in."

Bowler's last act is to rip the peignoir from my body. It floats to the floor.

Before he leaves, his hand roams over my bum, but he knows better than to mar the merchandise.

I can raise my head just enough to watch him stop when he reaches the peignoir. It's too tempting. Bowler picks it up and tosses it over his shoulder.

Did he tear it at the seams? If not, he'll need a delicate darning hand to stitch the peignoir's rip.

I'd love to strangle him with it.

AN HOUR LATER, I HEAR A KNOCK ON THE DOOR.

It opens and shuts with a click.

The footsteps are slow and deliberate.

They stop at the threshold.

"Ah, there you are, waiting anxiously, just as Jerome said you'd be." Edmonton chuckles. "Oh, how I've dreamed of this moment! You, just like this!"

He loosens the ball gag and tosses it on the bed. I cough and swallow so that saliva can fill my mouth again.

"Usually, he can predict my moods, my whimsies. But today, he jumped the gun." Edmonton bends down. He then tilts my head so that I can look him in the eye. "Say you're sorry, dear Donna."

I gulp for more saliva, then whisper, "I'm sorry, Bradley."

He chuckles. "I can't hear you...." The phrase is sung softly, like a lullaby.

"I'm sorry, Bradley. *I'm truly sorry!*"

He crams his mouth onto mine. His tongue darts around. I try not to gag.

"Donna, dear Donna! What am I to do with you?"

I stay silent.

Edmonton takes my hair in his fist and jerks my head back. "Answer me!" he screams.

"I don't know," I mumble.

He snickers. "Then...you're leaving it up to me?"

"You...you want to make love to me," I whisper.

"Love?... *LOVE?*" His cackle fills the room. "Love has nothing to do with what I want to do with you! On the contrary, I want you to feel...*pain.*"

A finger roams from my neck to my spine. When it gets to my ass, I feel it slide between my butt cheeks.

I flinch.

Edmonton chortles at having instilled some fear in me.

"Not to worry. Pleasure before pain—*mine, anyway.*"

I hear the yank of a zipper and the rustle of pants dropping to the floor. He shuffles out of them and then positions himself behind me. His thighs lean into my haunches.

Holding onto my back, he thrusts—

But I feel nothing.

The thrusting continues, again and again—

Um…okay…but…

Nothing.

I should keep my mouth shut, but I can't help myself:

I giggle.

At the thought that Edmonton is flaccid.

That, despite all power he possesses—

He just can't get it up.

I'm laughing wholeheartedly now.

Hearing me, Edmonton freezes.

I know I should stop, but I can't. It's just…

Too funny.

Who'd have thunk it?

I feel him back away. He roars: "*How dare you laugh at me!*"

"I'm…I'm so sorry, Bradley!" I gasp through my giggles. "I just…I didn't know…about your…um…problem."

He rants, "My problem?… *My problem! YOU ARE MY PROBLEM!*"

From the bed, Edmonton grabs the ball gag in one hand and the mask in the other. In two strides, he is beside me. My neck snaps back as he secures the gag in place again. Then he shoves the mask over my eyes. He ties it so tightly that my lids are pressed against it.

I hear him pulling on his pants and zipping up.

Maybe I've embarrassed him enough that he'll just slink away…

But then I hear him walk over to the bed. The snap of the cat-o-nine-tails crackles through the air.

Yes, now I am afraid.

∾

THE FIRST STRIKE HITS MY RIGHT SHOULDER. I FLINCH AS I groan.

It's Edmonton's turn to laugh.

The next strike lands on my spine, lighting it on fire.

The whip crisscrosses as it cuts my left haunch and then my right one. When Edmonton adds new stripes across my back, some stray tails welp my arms.

The gag stifles my screams to gurgled yelps that echo in my own ears. With each hit, I fight off the agony with memories of Jack:

The look of adoration he gives me after we've been apart for too long;

The gentleness of his kisses;

The depth of his carnal thrusts;

And the tremble in his voice when he tells me he loves me.

This is what steels me from breaking in front of Edmonton.

I'VE LONG AGO QUIT COUNTING THE LASHES BY THE TIME I HEAR the front door open.

A voice calls out, "Sir! *Sir!* We have it! The intel!"

Mario.

The beating stops.

"What did you say?" Edmonton growls.

"Mrs. Craig—she was right. The intel was in the wallet, after all. The card was in a hidden seam."

Oh...hell...

But I saw Jamison take it!

Unless he took the wrong card.

I should have killed that son of a bitch.

143

Edmonton cackles gleefully. Uproariously.
Convulsively.

After he collects himself, his footsteps come back my way. He rips the mask from my eyes before yanking the gag from my mouth. He unbuckles the strap constraining my left hand. "Sorry I doubted you, dear Donna. Still, at the very least, letting Jamison slip through your fingers should have earned you a sound spanking, don't you agree? Not to mention a make-good task. But take Monday off, if you wish."

He has the nerve to kiss a welp on my back.

In my ear, he whispers, "Tell the truth: was it as good for you as it was for me?"

I turn to face him.

My spittle hits him right between the eyes.

For some reason, he finds it amusing.

Before he walks away, I notice the wet spot on the crotch of his pants.

It was definitely better for him.

Jolts of pain throb through my whole body. I'm too weak to move, let alone get off the bench.

I collapse and pass out.

14

Détente

Détente is the relaxation of strained tensions between two nations, akin to calling a truce to avoid further hostilities.

Think of the number of times you were ready for armed conflict but agreed to a détente.

Like the time you and your sister were smitten with the same boy, but then both agreed to back off on your advances. (Only to find out, years later, that she made out with him anyway. But that's all water under the bridge, right?)

Or when you and she bought the same dress, but then agreed never to wear it so as not to hurt each other's feelings. (She did anyway—to the prom. But then you forgave her, right?)

Now that you're both adults with daughters of your own, you'd think you'd both agree to give peace a chance, first and foremost. Right?

Wrong. The first rule of a strong nation: Never let history repeat itself! Should she co-opt your idea for your daughter's next birthday party, feel free to go for the nuclear option.

I FINALLY COME TO FROM MY FOG OF PAIN, THANKS TO THE HANDS
that are roaming over my body, applying relief in the form of
a cooling salve on my back.

I am lying face down on a bed.

I try to rise, but sharp pangs shoot through my body. I
groan as I fall back onto the mattress.

My savior moves around to face me.

I find myself staring into Jack's face. "Stay down, sweet-
heart. That way, I can keep rubbing you with this stuff."

Despite his plea, I struggle to sit up. "My God, Jack!
You're here! How…when? What day is this?"

"Edmonton left your place a few hours ago." Jack sighs. "I
was on the plane with George when he came for Jamison. I
was due to come in anyway for intelligence briefings with
Acme's counterparts at the various IC agencies on Acme's
ongoing projects, so I moved up my meetings."

"And you didn't bother to tell me when I was right there,
in Manassas?"

"It wouldn't have been wise, especially since Lee
mentioned that Jamison may have been tailed. If I'd been
spotted, the whole operation would have been burned, and
you along with it."

I know he's right. I close my eyes as if that will erase my
anger over this reality.

When I open them again, I look around to find I'm not in
my own bedroom…

Thank God! After what just happened in there.

I want to kill Edmonton.

But I know I can't because it would mean being separated
from my children for life.

And from Jack.

The thought brings tears to my eyes.

Seeing them, Jack leans down so that he can lay beside

me. But even one gentle touch in the wrong place has me yelping. So, instead, we keep still.

Finally, I ask: "Where am I?"

"Next door."

"What?... In Dirty Old Codger's apartment?"

Jack laughs. "Yes... well, sort of. Really, it belongs to Dominic."

"*Fleming?*" I exclaim in disbelief. Acme's ace raven is a British transplant who has an outsized ego and lascivious mind—and, I've discovered, a heart of gold. Guffawing, I add: "Well, now—*that* explains *a lot!* And, quite frankly, if I were him, I would be scared of what I'd see as my future."

"On the contrary, he seems to find the little old man act quite liberating. Or, as he puts it, 'I find it tedious to be the object of adoration all the time.'"

"Yep, that sounds like him," I mutter. "And I'll bet he doesn't mind being at crotch level either. He's lucky that no one dares slap a frail old man in a wheelchair."

"Not quite. According to Abu, he's come close to getting walloped a couple of times."

"Oh, my God! You mean to tell me that his caregiver is *Abu?*" The thought leaves me slack-jawed that my mission team's cleaner, wheelman, tech op, all-around fixer, and man of a thousand faces had me fooled completely.

"I've got to give it to Abu," Jack declares. "He's become a wizard at creating disguises. Arnie is jealous as hell that he gets to play with these latex masks." Jack hesitates before adding, "And by the way, Henry is an Acme asset as well. He came highly recommended by Ryan. Apparently, they go way back."

I ask, "Where are Dom and Abu now?"

Jack hesitates. "In your place, cleaning up Edmonton's mess."

I grimace. This time, it's not from pain but from the memory of Edmonton's glee as he beat me.

"Why didn't you tell me you had a surveillance team on me?"

"Because in your new position in Edmonton's administration, you'd have had to disclose it or be open to charges of treason," Jack explains. "By keeping you out of the loop, we were giving you plausible deniability."

He's right.

"There's even a false door between these master bedrooms," Jack adds. "We can access your place at any time without being seen in the hall."

"So, you've pretty much had me covered, haven't you?" I shake my head in awe. "I guess that's what Lee meant when he said you and the Three Amigos would 'document Edmonton's unlawful acts whenever possible.' Including...his latest." I blush at the sordid memory.

"We didn't have your back when you needed us most." Jack looks away. "I'm sorry, Donna, that you had to endure that sadist's game. You shouldn't have traded yourself for me. Had I even known—"

"Look at me!" I implore him. When he turns back my way, I declare: "I would have never thrown you to that wolf, Jack. Otherwise, the whole case against him would go out the window!"

Jack shakes his head. "It's my fault that Edmonton even had the chance to abuse you. After Dominic texted me in a panic that Edmonton called to tell you he knew you'd lied about Jamison, I made the decision to wait and see how it played out." Jack frowns. "I swear if he hadn't stopped when Mario interrupted him, we were ready to create a diversion." He points up to the ceiling. "This is a duplex. Its front entrance is on the floor above. Abu was about to go out and pull the fire alarm in the hallway upstairs. If that didn't work, we were going to call in a bomb scare."

"All I can say is I'm happy you're here now," I whisper.

Jack leans in for a kiss—

But I flinch when our lips touch. My jaw still aches from the ball gag. To cover up my soreness, I inch away. "On the upside, we now have three articles of evidence," I point out.

"But, sadly, we've yet to crack one of them," he reminds me.

I attempt a chuckle. "We'd better hurry up then. Or my joke about adjoining cells won't be too funny." Suddenly, another thought hits me: "Jack, the day I moved in—remember? Before you showed up with the kids? I told you and the Three Amigos that Edmonton came here to discuss how he wanted me to carry out his wet work. Abu and Dominic must have caught it on video, right? If we release it to the press, it should ruin him!"

Jack shakes his head. "Unfortunately, the rush to put up the two-way mirror in your bedroom left them little time to test the camera feeds secreted in the other mirrors throughout the apartment. All they got was static."

"But now we have the video of him torturing me! Seeing it wouldn't go over well with the American public."

Jack frowns. "As previous administrations have proven, there is no guarantee of that, Donna. Edmonton will claim you were a willing partner with a fetish of your own. I don't think you'd want the children to bear the brunt of that."

At the thought of their shame, I bow my head.

"All the more reason I wish you'd told me he'd been here when I showed up in DC."

Despite blushing at his reproach, I counter, "With the kids underfoot, we didn't exactly have time to talk shop…"

149

And the last thing I wanted to tell you was the terms I had to negotiate to free you from Edmonton's threat.

"Besides, you left me with the impression that Edmonton's Secret Service detail also planted a few bugs of their own," I insist.

"After we left for the White House with the children, Abu disposed of them, you'll be happy to know," Jack replies. "The apartment above yours is empty. All the mics planted by Edmonton are now in that unit. Whoever is listening in thinks you're as quiet as a mouse."

"Ha! I'll bet Edmonton was hoping to record his discipline session with me." I shudder at the thought.

"We, er, thought of that too. So that he wouldn't get suspicious, Abu loaded in our audio recording of it"—Jack's pause comes with a frown—"as well as any other conversations you have with him in your apartment, via phone or in person." Noting my horrified look, he adds, "I'm sorry, Donna. We wouldn't want him to suspect that his bugs had been found and removed. Otherwise, he'd have had them planted all over again, and they may have found ours."

I rise to my feet. I may not be able to sit, but at least I can stand and pace the room. "But...if Edmonton is recording my conversations with him, he can hold them against me later! Jack, we may never be off the hook!"

"Arnie is also trying to hack the secure cloud where Edmonton keeps his personal files. We're sure to find a few other goodies there too. When he does, Arnie will upload a Trojan that will scrub your file."

I shrug. There is no guarantee it will happen, or how long that will take, or with whom Edmonton may share the audio with in the meantime.

Perhaps even Putin.

The thought makes me want to throw up.

As if reading my mind, Jack pats my hand—one of the few places he knows is pain-free. "Donna, level with me. Besides the five tasks, did you also agree to have sex with him? Or were you..." Even as the words stick in Jack's throat, his eyes harden. "What I mean to ask is, did he hold you against your will?"

Tears haze my eyes. "Originally, the deal was only to complete all the tasks, which would get you off the hook. If I didn't, he said I should consider...trading sex for your life. Stupid me, I thought it would never come to that. But when I failed to assassinate Tom Jamison, I...I said yes..." Tears choke off my words.

"Otherwise, I get arrested for Elle Grisham's murder," Jack declares.

I nod.

"Well, then, we have to prepare for the inevitable."

"You are *not* going to jail for Elle's death!" I tremble as I make that vow. "He ordered you to take her out as a traitor!"

"And I won't allow you to put yourself in this position with Edmonton, ever again!" he argues.

"I will, if I have to save your life!" I retort.

"You won't have to do it! There may be a way around it!" Dominic's voice comes from the doorway.

Jack and I turn to see him peeking in. Abu is behind him.

"Old Girl, are we allowed entry?" Dominic's tone is the gentlest I've ever heard it.

"Sure. I'm decent."

When they are within reach, I take a hand from each. "Thank you for watching over me."

"I only wish we could have stopped him from what he did to you—preferably, with a bullet to the head," Abu mutters.

Dominic nods. "With what that oaf had planned for you next..."

Jack's stern frown shuts him up.

"As I was saying…I don't think you have to put up with Edmonton's sick antics." Dominic is trying hard for a stiff upper lip. "But, sadly, someone must. And I know just the woman."

"You mean…like a *substitute* Donna?" Jack asks.

"Yes, indeed!" Dominic pulls up a chair. "She is a member of one of my private clubs here in DC." He shrugs. "Not a proper club, mind you. But one in which the predilection for giving or receiving pain is indulged."

Abu snickers. "In other words, a sex club."

"But not just any sex club," Dominic insists. "We're not talking swinging singles or any of that role-playing pishposh. Satan's Playpen is a bit… Well, to be blunt, a bit hardcore."

"Is this, um, 'surrogate' a member too?" Jack asks.

"No. She is specifically hired by the club to attend to the needs of its clients."

"What's her name?" I ask.

"She goes by 'Foggy Bottom.'"

I laugh despite the pain it gives me. "I imagine that's true of half the subs in DC!"

"What Edmonton did to you is no laughing matter," Jack retorts.

"She has had worse, trust me." Dominic grimaces at the thought. "Her real name is Khrystyna Vashchenko."

"Ukrainian?" I ask.

Dominic nods. "She was formerly an acrobat who figured out fast that, despite the pain she endures as a sub, there is more money to be made at Satan's Playpen than hanging from the ceiling in a Cirque du Soleil tent."

"Why would she agree to do this for a perfect stranger?" I ask.

"Her hatred of Russia is intense. And for good reason: as

teens, she and her sister excelled in acrobatics. They answered a newspaper ad announcing auditions for a circus company. When they were accepted, they thought they'd accomplished their dream of leaving their tiny Ukrainian village and immigrating to the United States. In fact, it was a come-on used by the Russian mob to entrap nubile young girls as sex slaves."

"How sad!" The thought makes me shudder.

Dominic grimaces. "Their escape came at a high price: her sister's life. As you may imagine, it's quite a driving force in Khrystyna's life. If it puts your mind at rest, she is already an MI6 asset. CIA as well. With her help, they've turned quite a few of her Russian clients with footage of their salacious peccadillos."

I nod. "Frankly, that is a relief."

"And you can vouch for her, um, 'pain tolerance?'" Jack asks.

"No!" Dominic sniffs. "She's not my type. I'm into a little role-playing or some rousing rumpy-pumpy. But Khrystyna is too bloody *serious!*"

"Well, that's a first!... Oh! Wait, no. You've claimed that about me too." Now I'm laughing, which hurts my mouth since the gag put it in a painful stretch. "I take it, then, she does have a strong resemblance?"

"Strong enough," Dominic admits.

"She has to be," Jack points out.

"With the right hairstyle and a few prosthetics, it could work," Abu chimes in. "In fact, we'll create a latex face mask, too."

I sigh. "Good, then. But if Khrystyna is to be our Plan B, I want to be the one to make the request."

"I understand. If anyone can make the case honestly and fairly, it's you." Jack stands up. "Dominic, give her the address to Satan's Playpen. Donna, if you'd like me to take you there—"

"No, I'll let Henry take me—now that I know he's also part of our team." Despite my sore mouth, I kiss Jack goodbye.

15

Foggy Bottom

THIS WASHINGTON, DC NEIGHBORHOOD, LOCATED IN THE TOWN'S *northwest quadrant near Washington's Potomac River, came by its name, "Foggy Bottom," by virtue of having once been a marsh.*

And because it is one of the neighborhood's best-known occupants, US Department of State also bears the same irreverent metonym.

Fair warning: Do not discount the rumor that its nickname has more to do with how diplomacy is conducted than with its geographic location.

THE PRIVATE BDSM CLUB KNOWN AS SATAN'S PLAYPEN IS located in a stately mansion on one of the quieter blocks of Georgetown. I ring the bell and wait a few minutes, fully aware that I'm being watched by the discreet security cameras located in the antique sconces flanking the home's candy-apple-red door.

I'm in a short auburn wig. I wear dark glasses, a bulky coat, and heeled boots. Everyone in this place is incognito, so I should fit right in.

Finally, the door opens. Silently, a butler motions me inside. Because the handsome lad is shirtless under a tuxedo that hugs his muscular chest, arms, and *gluteus maximus*, he reminds me of the Chippendales dancers at my bachelorette party, courtesy of Aunt Phyllis.

Ah, good times.

Jeeves takes me into a parlor room, where a woman—mid-forties, lithe, full-chested, and dressed in a red vinyl sheath that is as tight as her topknot—stands at a podium desk. She is tapping away on a computer.

This hostess from hell leaves me standing for several minutes before she looks up. Smirking, she asks, "How may I help you?"

"I'm interested in talking to one of your...er, associates. Foggy Bottom. We're old friends. Sorority sisters. Please let her know I'm here."

Hostess from Hell's eye roll is accompanied by a snort. "*Talk?* Yeah, sure. In any event, you must sign up for membership. It's one hundred dollars. At that point, you can quote-unquote talk all you want in one of our private rooms —for another five hundred dollars."

I hold up twelve fifty-dollar bills. Money is the universal language. No matter the dialect, enough of it inevitably gets you to "yes." Especially here in Satan's Playpen, which prides itself on being a world-renowned palace of pain.

Hostess from Hell opens a drawer on the podium. From it, she pulls an index-card-sized "MEMBER CARD."

I fill it out with a fake name and address. I'm sure every other card in there is just as bogus.

Hostess from Hell takes it and hands me a room key embossed with the number 15. She then picks up a silver bell. Its ring summons Jeeves again, who waits in the doorway, silently and obediently. "Follow him to your assigned boudoir," she tells me. "Foggy is waiting there. You're allowed a quarter of an hour with her."

I won't need more time. But still, I can't help it. I snort. "Jeez! A half-dozen Benjamins buys me *only fifteen minutes*?"

Hostess from Hell snickers. "I've given you our off-hours rate. It's the best I can do for one of Foggy's 'sorority sisters.' Take it or leave it."

I shrug my assent.

"When you get tired of quote-unquote talking, the room is fully stocked with a wide range of accoutrements for your pleasure and her pain. By the way, do not get too boisterous. Otherwise, my butler here will be sent in, and you will be cast out of the club—*permanently*. He'd hate to have to break one of those pretty nails." Her eyes linger on my hand.

To send her a silent message, I fold all fingers except for the middle digit.

Hostess from Hell's chortle follows us all the way up the stairs.

BOUDOIR 15 MEASURES ONLY FIFTEEN FEET SQUARE, IF THAT. THE room's ceiling is mirrored, as is its walls.

My requested sub, Khrystyna, sits daintily on a chaise lounge in the center of the room. It is the only piece of furniture except for a wooden straight chair, which, like the chaise, is encircled by chains clipped to rings embedded in the wide-planked wooden floor.

Khyrstyna is dressed in a black leather bustier and a matching thong. Her dark hair is loose and flows to her shoulders. Her wrists are bound by black leather cuffs.

"Welcome, Mistress." Her murmur has a slight Slavic accent. Its tone is low and devoid of joy. "You'll find what you're looking for in there." She nods her head to the mirrored wall on her right.

Upon closer examination, the wall is also a closet. With a push of a button, its mirrored doors fold apart.

As promised, it holds a treasure trove of devices designed for ultimate pain, pleasure, and submission. Gags, muzzles, collars, harnesses, cock rings, hoods, shackles, and cuffs hang from hooks at the top of the closet. One shelf holds dildos of all sizes. Another below it holds paddles of varying shapes.

Some of these goodies have signs of wear and tear. One is specked with blood.

Points off for lackluster sanitary procedures.

Spreader bars line the inside of one door. Ticklers, whips, crops, slappers, and floggers run the gamut from feather to leather.

It is duly noted that the ticklers look untouched.

I move the straight chair so close that we are face to face. Having been duly warned that there are eyes and ears on us, I tap my phone to a music app and turn it up all the way: It is playing Donna Summer's *I Feel the Love*.

"Dance for me," I command her.

Her moves are languid and broad as if she has all the time in the world. I've seen enough videos of the songstress to know the dancer is channeling her every move.

Whereas Khrystyna starts out at the wall farthest from the settee, each step, timed to the song's Euro-pop vibe, brings her nearer to me until we are close enough to touch.

But she doesn't. A good sub knows the rules of engagement.

So that Khrystyna knows the purpose of our time together, when she leans down, taunting me with lips close to mine, I murmur the password code: "Life is but a dream."

Khrystyna's sensual gyrations stop for a mere second. Then, like me, she speaks through a smile without moving her lips: "If only that were true."

This is her way of telling me *I'm at your service.*

Through my grin, I ask, "I take it we're being watched?"

Her nod is accompanied by a sensual shimmy. "Wall to your right."

"Cover me so that I can talk without them watching me."

Is it Jeeves? More than likely, it is Hostess from Hell. She was too curious for her own good.

When I know I'm covered, I tell Khrystyna the plan:

That she'll be paid well to leave this job and be at the beck and call of a particular gentleman caller.

So that she is available at all times, she is to move into an apartment in the Watergate. It has a secret door that opens up into mine—specifically, through our back-to-back bedroom closets.

After a makeover that will include a few prostheses, she will pass as my double.

All assignations with the adversary will then take place in my bedroom.

I don't tell her that I hope she never has to meet my tormentor.

Khrystyna's chuckle bounces off the walls along with Ms. Summer's thrumming technobeat.

"Is that your way of saying it can't be done?" I ask.

"Not at all." As she turns to face me, she drops low to her knees into a sexy groove. Even as she bops her head, she scrutinizes me. "We are the same height and build. And I saw how you moved when you came in. Like me, you do not hide your sensuality. Instead, you revel in it. Still..." Her shrug is hidden from the camera's eye. "Does this man know your body well enough to tell us apart?"

"As in any birthmarks? Nah. He's into his own pleasure."

This allows me to segue to the clincher: that her gentleman caller's tastes won't be easy to stomach.

She actually guffaws at this. "I'm sure it won't be anything I haven't already done. Or felt." As Khrystyna turns to face the camera again, she lifts her backside, twerking it as she whips around so that she may hide her face as she mutters, "What if he wishes to engage in pillow talk? From my accent alone, he will know I'm not you."

"He prefers his conquests to remain silent. In fact, he insists on it." I try not to shudder at the thought of my recent experience with the ball gag. "By the way, he's a very public figure." I hesitate before adding, "The President of the United States: Bradley Edmonton."

Hearing this, she stops, shocked. Then, in time with the music, she starts a shimmy that brings her around to face me again. Through clenched teeth, she hisses: "But...*you are an intelligence agent.* He is your Commander in Chief! Why would you do this?"

I close my eyes. If a voyeur can indeed catch a glimpse of my face, I doubt he would think my demeanor is anything but ecstatically enthralled, when in fact, I'm just bone-weary. "Khrystyna...*Edmonton is a Russian spy.*"

I have to give her credit. Her pause could be interpreted as a part of her erotic dance.

Her silence worries me.

Finally, I ask, "So, are you in?"

Her raucous laughter is covered by Donna Summer's

soaring finale. This time, when Khrystyna faces me, her eyes are flaming with resolve. "I'm an American! What do you think?" Then she leans in, so close that we are nose to nose. "Slap me," she hisses. "Chain me down. Then do your worst to me. Or else...*they* may suspect."

My stomach lurches at the thought that not playing this game may put us both in danger.

My quick backhand sends her tumbling onto the floor. Before she has a chance to get up, I drag her by her hair to her feet. I point to the rolled arm of the chaise. "Bend over it."

She does as she's told.

I walk over to the closet, knowing that Hostess from Hell's eyes are watching me, and that I will be judged by the accoutrements I choose. I take what I think Edmonton would use: a thick wooden paddle riddled with holes, a leather flogger, and a cat-o-nine-tails.

I kick Khrystyna's legs apart before hooking her ankle cuffs to the floor rings that leave her spread-eagled. I then grab the chains directly next to the front of the chaise. "Hold out your arms," I growl.

Hesitantly, she does as she is told.

I hook her cuffs to the chain and then yank it across the chaise, pinning it to the floor rings so tightly that she strains to keep her toes on the floor.

Her ass cheeks sit high on the rolled arm of the chair.

I start with the paddle: slow, firm slaps at first.

Khrystyna doesn't make a sound.

The hits come faster and harder, eliciting an occasional grunt.

I pause for more than a minute. Then—

WHACK!

Khrystyna cries out.

I follow with another whack but wait one long moment before hitting her with a third one just as hard.

Her cheeks are so red that I can't help but feel for her.

"I am not worthy, mistress!" she mutters.

She's asking for more?

So be it.

I toss down the paddle. Skipping the flogger, I pick up the cat-o-nine-tails instead. Remembering how its lashes felt, I take aim.

The tails slash left, breaking the skin on the right side of her back.

Khrystyna gasps from the strike.

With the next hit, they cut right through her skin.

She screams out. The sores are deep. Blood runs down her back.

But still, no tears are shed.

I can't take it anymore. Sorry, I am not a natural sadist.

I throw away the whip. Quickly, I unhook the chains from Khrystyna's wrist cuffs and then do the same for the ones pinning her legs apart.

Still, she doesn't move. Is she afraid of what I may do next?

I roll her off the arm of the chaise and onto its seat.

Then I hold her in my arms and whisper, "I'm so sorry!"

I don't hear the door open. Slinging me away from Khrystyna, Jeeves snarls, "You broke the cardinal rule—'*no show of affection to a bottom!*'"

He shoves me out the door, locking it behind him.

Shaking, I stumble down the steps. Somehow, I find my way onto the street.

I have to say, I admire the way the club looks after its people. If Jack's plan must be implemented and Khrystyna must bow to our Fetishist-in-Chief, I'll have to be just as vigilant for her.

Otherwise, appeasing Edmonton on my behalf will be a sacrifice she may come to regret.

In an hour, Dominic will call her. He and Abu will arrange to pick her up and bring her to their apartment. She will live there as long as the operation is in play.

If her luck runs out, so does mine.

16

Central Security Service

Under the auspices of the National Security Agency, the Central Security Service supervises the coordinated efforts of our country's military cryptologic community, which decodes our enemies' covert communications—a.k.a. "Signal Intelligence."

Sorry, but no: you cannot ask the CSS to hack your children's cell phones and report on their most shocking texts, cryptic emojis, or incomprehensible slang.

However, by putting every great mind in your million-mommy network on cracking these confounding codes, your makeshift CSS will prove just as powerful as the real one!

It is Sunday. After Jack's last scheduled meeting, he will fly home.

I wish I could go with him.

Heck, I wish he could touch me without making me flinch or shout in pain, so maybe it's for the best.

As much as I would like to take Edmonton up on his offer

165

to take Monday off and recuperate, I can't. It would delay the mission of taking him down by twenty-four hours—something neither Jack nor I can afford.

Let alone the rest of the world.

Dominic informs me that Abu has been sent to pick up Khrystyna, and that in her honor, he's throwing a dinner party.

"I'll bake an orange chiffon cake, if you'd like," I offer.

Sure, why not? It's not even six in the morning on the West Coast, so I've got a few hours to kill before I can call the children. Besides, I need to do something to keep my mind off my still-tender skin and the week ahead.

"A welcomed gesture indeed, Mrs. Craig!" Dominic exclaims. "And the perfect compliment to the meal. I'm making a hearty lentil soup to start, followed by beef bourguignon, mashed potatoes, and crispy green beans."

"I'm impressed, Dominic! I never knew you are such an accomplished gourmand."

"I've learned that the quickest way into a woman's bed is through her stomach."

I guffaw. "That's only because the supermodels you date are half-starved!"

"It hasn't failed me yet," he assures me. "But you may have a point. It wouldn't work as well if I were attracted to more well-fed lasses"—Dominic tilts his head as he assesses my backside—"like yourself."

The pot I throw at him bonks him soundly on the head and sends him scurrying back to his apartment.

HENRY, WHO KINDLY FULFILLED MY GROCERY SHOPPING LIST THIS morning, is hanging out with us through dinner. Right now, he sits at the dining room table, nursing a cup of coffee. Between curses over today's very vexing *New York Times* crossword puzzle, he regales me with tales of Ryan's derring-do as a young CIA operative.

As I pull my cake from the oven, Henry asks, "Did Ryan ever tell you about the time we broke into the Chinese Consulate in São Paulo? Not only did we walk out with the intel we came for, but we also exfiltrated a political dissident being held captive there."

I shake my head. "In Brazil? That must have been quite a feat!"

"You're telling me! We pretended we worked for the consulate's linen service. We entered through the basement door with a large laundry basket. I had the joy of climbing through the heat vent and crawling my way to the office. Its safe contained microfilm with a detailed map of the United States Naval Support Detachment Base. While Ryan covered for me, he heard some poor guy moaning in the basement. Ryan broke him out and hid him in the dirty laundry."

I shake my head in awe. "That took guts!"

"You said it! We only knew a couple of Portuguese phrases. If anyone in the embassy had asked us a question, we'd have been toast." He shrugs. "Good times indeed. But after Ryan met Natalie, he transferred to a desk job." Henry sighs. "I never thought I'd see the day Kamikaze Clancy would give up that adrenaline rush. In hindsight, it may have kept him alive—and sane."

Ryan's devotion to Natalie sidelined him to a desk: first as one of the CIA's best handlers, then as Acme Industries' founder and Chief Executive Officer.

"God rest her soul," I murmur.

"Yeah, when she died… Well, those were sad times." Henry frowns. "It was an accident, wasn't it?"

I nod.

But I know the truth. Ryan had never leveled with her as to the real duties of his government job. Not the killing part, anyway. When Natalie found out, it gutted her. She confronted Ryan, asking him to deny it.

He couldn't lie to her.

Upset, she ran out into their backyard. Ryan never knew if she jumped or slipped off the ridge at the edge of their ocean view property. Either way, he's always blamed himself.

I feel Henry's eyes on me. When I turn, I wonder: Did Ryan confide his guilt to him?

Maybe, but I doubt it. Ryan is the stoic type. It's a trait that allows him to shoulder the cause and effect of Acme's crimes and misdemeanors.

"When you left the service, he recruited you for Acme, didn't he?" I ask.

Henry nods. "Kamikaze Clancy is gone. But he's the best boss in the biz."

"Can't argue there."

Ryan is back in the field now, hiding in plain sight of Acme's most dangerous adversary. Should he give Edmonton reason to doubt him, this mission will be blown sky-high, and we will all pay the price.

Henry knows it too.

I lay my palm on the cake to see if it's cool enough to ice. It isn't. That's okay. The kids should be up by now. And by the time I get back, the cake will be ready for its orange glaze.

Henry looks admiringly at my masterpiece. "That would sure taste great with this coffee."

I wag a finger at him. "Sorry. As tempting as it is, we have to bide our time."

Henry laughs. "That's an apt analogy for so much of life."

~

I DEBATE WHO TO CALL FIRST. HAD MARY ALREADY HEARD FROM Berkeley, I'd have been flooded with texts filled with happy faces. No doubt she's still bemoaning that there's been no word, so the call will be all moans-and-groans.

Ah, well. I might as well get it over with.

I punch in her cell phone number. "Mom! Wow, I'm so happy you called!"

Ha...*What?*

Just go with the flow...

"Thank you, Mary, darling! I've been missing you too." I sigh, relieved. "So, I take it you've had some good news?"

"News?...Oh! You mean about Berkeley. *No.* But it's all right. If it's meant to happen, it will."

"Wow... That's a—a very *mature* attitude."

"It's idiotic to put all of one's eggs in one basket, don't you think?"

"Totally. Completely." *Yes! Yes!* "And UCLA also has an excellent Business program."

"Yeah, well...wherever I get in, I'm going to apply for a year postponement."

"You mean take a gap year?... Sure, I'd support that. Travel is a maturing experience—"

"I may take an internship instead."

"Oh! Well, that's a good idea too..."

"You mean, you wouldn't mind? Wow, Mom! Thanks! Then I'll write back and accept it immediately!"

"Wait... Where?"

"There, in DC! ...You know, with you!"

"I...Honey, I can't have you interning for me!" *Hell no! No way!*

"Mom, it wouldn't be for *you*. It would be for President Edmonton. When he wrote to me and offered it to me—"

"He wrote to you?"

"Yes! I was shocked, too, believe me. And it wasn't one of those form letters everyone gets. He remembered how interested I was in the portrait of George Washington and was impressed that I'd already studied its origins. He even offered to give me a personal tour of all the art in the White House after I started! As if it was already a done deal! But, of course, it is, since he's the president." Mary giggles. "And just think, Mom—we'll be roomies!"

"Mary, I don't think that's a good idea!"

"Well, that's a relief! I thought you'd insist on it. But since you aren't, I'd much rather get an apartment with a couple of the other interns. We'll still see each other all the time in the West Wing. And in the evenings we can meet up for runs or for dinner—"

"No! What I mean is that interning at the White House isn't—"

"Mom, I'm sorry! Jeff is dying to get on the phone! Maybe we can talk tomorrow about it? The president's letter was so kind. And *so inspiring*! Love you!…"

No! Never ever, ever, ever—

"Hi, Mom!" Jeff also sounds upbeat, thank goodness. "Hey, so Dad told you about my game, right?"

Here it comes.

I brace myself for recriminations about missing his game. "Yes, sweetie! I'm *so, so* proud of you! And I am so sorry that I couldn't be there to support you—"

"No, Mom, I don't want you to feel guilty at all."

Wow! In my absence, my son is maturing too—

"—In fact, even when you come home over weekends, I think you should sit out the rest of the season."

"I... *BEG YOUR PARDON?*"

"Believe me, it's nothing personal!" Jeff insists. "It's just that Cheever brought up something I'd never noticed, and frankly, he's right."

"*Cheever Bing*? Hasn't experience taught you that he's the last person in the world who should give you advice?"

"Statistics don't lie," Jeff argues. "And statistically, I score better when you're not in the stands. Like *phenomenally* better! And with the county tournament starting next weekend... All I'm trying to say is don't feel as if you need to rush home."

"Look, Jeff, don't buy into some old wives' tale that Cheever is peddling—"

"That's what Cheever called it too! But like he pointed out, it makes sense, since you're an old wife."

I'm so shocked that I'm sputtering.

"Mom, please don't take it personally. Cheever noticed it about his mom too."

I mutter, "Well, I can believe it about *Penelope*—"

"Got to run! Hey, Trisha wants to say hi!"

"No...I don't!" His younger sister's exclamation is loud enough for me to hear even without her holding the phone.

I hear a muffled struggle. I guess Jeff finally shoved the phone in her hand because the next thing I know, Trisha is crying in my ear.

My poor baby.

"Trisha, your father told me about your hair...and about your suspension."

"I know." Her voice is barely a whisper.

"It was a cruel thing for Janie to do to you. But what you did to her was just as mean."

"I know, Mom, okay?" Trisha mutters.

"Have you heard from Janie?" Do I sound too hopeful? That's because I am.

"As a matter of fact, yes. She sent me a video."

The next thing I know, my phone is pinging with a text from Trisha. "Go ahead, watch it."

I click it to see Janie on the screen. "Trisha Craig, what you did to me was totally sick! It makes me puke to think I spent almost my whole life being friends with someone so gross. But now I have a real friend who is smarter and prettier than you and would never hurt me, ever, in a million years. So, whenever you pass Riley and me, just look the other way, bee-hatch! Or better yet, turn and run! Oh, and good luck finding someone else who is stupid enough to be your friend."

Janie doesn't smile the whole time. Not even when Riley puts one arm around her waist and raises the other to her forehead, making an "L" with her thumb and index finger.

Janie winces, but she copies her.

"So, this is Riley's way of telling you she chose Janie as her bestie, right?"

"Yes," Trisha mumbles. "Mom, please—*I never want to go back to that school!*"

"Trisha, if you don't, *they win.*"

"And if I go back, what exactly do *I* win?"

"Your pride. Their respect. And everyone else's too."

"You mean, *you* won't respect me if I change schools. Isn't that what you're saying?"

"No! I'm saying you won't respect yourself."

"I'll hate it!" she warns me.

"At first. But staying there will be Janie's big shame, not yours."

"But *she* won!"

"What did she win, exactly? I've seen Janie when she's happy, and you have too. Did she look happy to you? Did she look triumphant?" I sigh. "Trisha, let me ask you a question:

how would you have felt if that were you in the video? Would you have been proud of yourself, doing that to your oldest and dearest friend?"

"No. I...I would have hated it..." Trisha pauses. "But I'd do it to her now."

"You mean, out of revenge?"

"Yes," she exclaims.

She clicks off.

Oh, no...

My daughter is me.

WHEN THE PHONE RINGS AGAIN, I PRAY IT'S JACK—

But it's not. It is Edmonton calling.

"What do you want?" I mutter.

He chuckles jovially. "Top of the morning to you too! I hope you're not feeling too tender."

"What do you need, Bradley?" I steel myself at the thought.

"One simple request, really. A retrieval."

"No extermination?"

"Not unless it takes that to get what I want. But I doubt it. Does that disappoint you?"

"Not if it were a mercy killing. Like, say, yours. Where and when is the retrieval to take place?"

"Bethesda. The soirée begins in a few hours, in fact. Three o'clock. It's by invitation only, so you'll have to figure out a way to crash it."

"What's the event?"

"A wedding. Ethan Mankoff's daughter is getting married."

"Thanks for the heads up," I mutter. "Isn't General Mankoff the Chief of the Central Security Service?"

"Yes, one and the same," Edmonton declares. "That four-star pompous ass married old money—old enough to buy a historic four-story Georgian mansion on a grand estate. Everyone will be upstairs in the grand ballroom except for the catering staff."

"What is the intel?"

"A file on"—he pauses—"the latest US SigInt codebook. Mankoff is old-school. His aide prints out everything for him, so it should be a paper file."

"Is he dumb enough to leave it on his desk?"

"I find him insipid, so perhaps."

I've met Mankoff. Edmonton isn't giving him much credit.

"In any case, get it for me. Deliver it to me afterward." He clicks off.

17

Dezinformatsiya

THE RUSSIAN TERM FOR OPERATIONS THAT ARE DESIGNED TO PASS *false information to the enemy is "dezinformatsiya."*

You may call it something similar: "a little white lie." You use it to deflect anger, anxiety, or rudeness. So all good, right?

Gain proficiency and you may be recruited by the US Diplomatic Corps. Little white lies have started wars. Perhaps they can stop them too.

MY COVER IS COMES DOWN TO ONE OF TWO THINGS: A GUEST, OR a cater-waiter.

To get in without an invitation, I opt for the latter, which usually means black pants and a white button-down shirt.

But just in case, I take a cocktail dress too—a beige form-fitting Body-Con that I wear under my blouse but roll down to my waist.

After icing it with an orange glaze, I take the cake too.

Henry frowns when he sees me boxing it up. "Hey, where are you going with that?"

"To a wedding. Hopefully, it'll come back in one piece." I reach for his key fob. "I'll make the same promise about your car."

"Wait!... *You're taking my car?*"

"It's an emergency. I'll be back as soon as I can. Promise."

I go out through the bedroom closet's hidden door, into Dominic's closet—

And grab one of his many formal black tuxedo ties. My God, there are enough for him to wear two weeks straight without re-using one! And from the laundry receipts tagged on them, he has them dry-cleaned.

For that matter, he's got a baker's dozen tuxedos too. Between his love for cooking and his wardrobe, he could open a restaurant.

If I told him it would make it easy to pick up babes, would he do it?

Probably not. Having a license to kill from the Department of Intelligence is a more significant ego-booster than having a license to serve food from the Department of Public Health.

I ARRIVE NINETY MINUTES EARLY, ON PURPOSE. IT'S A GOOD thing, too. Cars snake all the way down the Mankoffs' tree-lined driveway, almost to where it meets the street.

The mansion, five miles into the thirty-acre-square estate, is so humongous that it makes Downton Abbey look like a cabana house.

Okay, maybe I'm exaggerating. But you get the picture.

There are four security guards at the entrance to the drive-way, hopscotching the cars as they check invitations.

When one reaches me, I point to the cake box on the floor of my car's passenger seat: "I'm with the caterer! I've got the groom's cake, which they've been waiting for."

"Step out of the car with the box and open it."

I do as instructed.

He grins at the cake. "The groom has good taste! Go ahead and follow the lane beyond the guest parking area, all the way to the back door. It's the pantry entrance."

I smile and wave as I sail through the gate.

I CARRY THE CAKE INTO THE HOUSE BY WAY OF THE WALK-through pantry, which is the size of my kitchen.

Yes, I'm insanely jealous.

I'm just about to hide the cake on a shelf when a woman blows a whistle at me. I freeze, which, I guess, is what a dog would do in the same predicament.

She motions me forward, into a kitchen that is the size of my whole house. Chefs and waiters anxiously scurry about.

"What is that?" Whistler asks.

"It's the …um…the groom's cake." I open the box to show her.

"Ack! So *plain!* Ah, well, that's the trend these days. Something sentimental"—she rolled her eyes—"even if it's homely and pathetic."

I stifle the urge to smash her face into it.

Whistler frowns. "Well, set it down and pick up a champagne tray." She points to one of several sitting on a sideboard. "Take it up to the ballroom on the fourth floor via the servants' elevator, right over there. I can't believe how many guests are already here!" She shakes her head in frustration as she shoos me out with her hands.

Before getting out on the second floor, I slip on thin latex gloves.

There are four rooms on either side of the hall and one at the very end, facing the front of the estate.

Only two doors have been left open. I hold off on peeking through the closed doors, assuming they may be the bedrooms of out-of-town guests. Instead, I glance into an open doorway across from the guest elevator. It is a powder room. The other open door leads to a sumptuous bedroom. I leave the champagne tray there. If some horny guests decide to take a tumble in the empty room, they are sure to appreciate the gesture.

Since I now have to guess which room is Mankoff's study, I go for the only door facing the front.

Bingo.

The room, walled in knotty pine, has expansive windows in the front. Its other walls are lined in floor-to-ceiling bookcases.

Two burgundy leather-tufted Chippendale couches face each other in front of the desk. There are two paintings on the wall. I check to see if they hide a safe.

They don't.

The desk, an authentic William and Mary, has only five drawers. They are locked, but easy enough to pick. Again, I come up empty for any files that may have been stashed in there.

I tap its sides, top, and bottom for a hidden panel.

I am doing the same to the bookshelves—searching for any hidden releases—when I hear voices coming down the hall: two men.

I look for a place to hide. The desk doesn't have a privacy

panel, so that doesn't work. My only option is to slip under one of the couches, but it'll be a tight squeeze.

I do it just in time. Two sets of feet enter. Both belong to men.

One—General Mankoff, I assume—takes the chair behind the desk as he says, "—long overdue for an overhaul to our SigInt codebook. For the life of me, it's dismaying how easily Russia breaks it, time and time again. One would think we have a spy in our midst—*at the highest level.*"

"I would assume nothing less." The other man is Ryan.

When he sits on the couch, it sags so far down toward my face that I couldn't turn my head if I wanted. I guess Ryan is eating well in his new fancy position. Thank goodness I'm looking out into the room.

He places his briefcase beside his feet.

Mankoff discharges a heavy sigh. "And your presumption is that it's..." His voice trails off.

"Sadly, yes, Ethan. But even as we speak, the incontrovertible proof is being readied. Congress' Intelligence committees will have what they need for the one solution our country's forefathers gave them to deal with such treason."

"And you feel the SigInt Codebook is safer here than in the Pentagon?"

"Your lament is proof of that! The fact that you'll be safekeeping the only copy means neither he nor any operatives he has will be able to get his hands on it." Ryan picks up his briefcase. I hear its locks click open. I assume he's pulling out the file containing the codebook.

Mankoff rises from behind the desk. He comes toward Ryan. When his feet move away, I assume he has taken it.

He walks over to the bookcase on the opposite wall. The next thing I hear is a slight creak.

Ryan laughs. *"War and Peace?* Isn't that somewhat obvious?"

Mankoff chuckles too. "It's the right thickness, and no one ever reads it. So sure, why not?"

I hear a few clicks. I try to count them, but they are too faint.

Ryan adds, "That's one beauty of a safe! Another antique?"

"It came with the house, but I had the tumblers reset."

"Hopefully, nothing sentimental! You of all people know the folly in that."

"Because this is my personal safe, the combination is something easy enough for my wife to remember too."

"Let me guess: your beautiful daughter, Lydia's birthday?"

"Nope, nothing *that* easy. Do you remember I told you that Lydia chose our wedding day to have as her own?"

"Ah, yes! And today, twenty-eight years later, it's the sweetest gift she could have given you and Patrice," Ryan says softly.

Mankoff snorts. "I'll remember you said that as I pay the bills for this hootenanny."

The safe door clicks shut.

The tumblers roll.

With a gentle creak, the book goes back on the shelf.

And once again, I must decide if being a traitor to my country will save my husband from the same fate.

Ryan gets up. When he reaches down to pick up his briefcase, a tiny slip of paper drops to the floor.

I freeze. Will he reach down for it and see me?

Or, worse yet, will Mankoff?

To my relief, their footsteps move to the door. A draft

enters as it opens. The paper floats toward me but stops when the door closes again.

I reach for it. In Ryan's almost illegible scroll, it says:

Yes! Take it!

I roll out from under the couch. *War & Peace* is found on the bookcase all the way to the right, on an upper shelf. I pull it out.

There's the tiny button. I tap it.

A wood slat slides to one side. The safe is revealed.

I put in today's date minus twenty-eight years. The safe door swings open with a slight creak.

The codebook feels like a slim binder in a sealed envelope, one that is explicitly used for top-secret Pentagon interoffice correspondence.

As instructed I don't open it. After what Ryan wrote, I realize it's chickenfeed anyway.

I peek out the door before heading to the service elevator.

The kitchen staff is too frantic to notice me slip away.

To my dismay, my cake isn't where I left it. I hope the happy couple enjoys it.

I wave at the guards as I drive out.

I TOSS THE ENVELOPE ON EDMONTON'S DESK. HE NODS WHEN HE sees the seal hasn't been broken.

"Good girl! I take it you've learned your lesson?" He looks sideways at me as if seeking confirmation.

I will not give Edmonton the satisfaction of an answer. And I certainly won't let him know how furious I am about his offer to Mary.

Not yet, anyway. I'll save that for the appropriate time. Say, when I'm torturing him, not the other way around.

~

ON THE WAY HOME, I STOP AT A BAKERY.

No orange chiffon cake. Even if I'd found one, it wouldn't be as great as mine.

Still, I can't return empty-handed. The only thing that looks halfway decent is a chocolate cake with coconut icing.

Sold.

~

BY THE TIME I GET BACK, ABU AND KHRYSTYNA ARE ALREADY AT the Acme bachelor pad. Dominic sends me upstairs to tell them dinner is ready. As I head up, Henry peeks into the bakery box. He frowns when he sees what's inside.

"It was a casualty of war. I'll make it up to you," I promise him.

Abu has situated Khrystyna in one of the duplex's spare bedrooms. I welcome her with a smile and a nod. She has brought just two small bags with her. Hanging in the open closet are several pairs of loose flowing pants, a few long-sleeve cotton sweaters, a heavy jacket, and a couple of pairs of jeans like the pair she wears now.

Khrystyna looks totally different now that her long dark brown hair is tied into a ponytail. Devoid of any of her BDSM garb and elaborate makeup that went with it, she looks like an innocent, freckled-face thirty-something.

Before turning their attention on me, they finish their intense discussion. I catch just the tail end of it. They are comparing the meditation methods they try when under duress.

"We're trading mantras," Abu explains with a shy grin.

He's sweet on Khrystyna.

From her smile, his interest is reciprocated.

Sadness chills me. How is Abu going to react if Khrystyna is called into duty?

THE MEAL IS AS GOOD AS DOMINIC HAS PROMISED.

I might have lingered longer after dessert and coffee if the cake had been half as good as mine. Or perhaps if I hadn't had a lousy weekend, starting with an exfiltration that went to hell, a beating that hurt like hell, and the recruitment of a double who is too sweet for the assignment from hell.

The only upside was handing off disinformation to Edmonton to pass forward to his Russian handlers. Score one for the good guys.

I beg off for the rest of the night. Henry follows suit. Dominic is disappointed, but only because he sees he's now the third wheel in the blossoming relationship between Khrystyna and Abu. Too bad. He can console himself that if it hadn't been for him, these two crazy kids would have never met up. Maybe it'll be the gist of his toast at their wedding.

Am I jumping the gun? I hope not. Everyone deserves a love story. Abu is long overdue.

And from what Dominic said about Khrystyna, she is too.

As I disappear through Dominic's closet, I wonder if he'll ever settle down.

He'd sure make some lucky lady a wonderful beef bourguignon.

~

I'VE JUST SETTLED INTO MY JAMMIES WHEN THE PHONE RINGS. I brace myself before looking at the Caller ID, but breathe a sigh of relief when I see it's Jack.

"You made it home okay?" I ask.

"I did indeed," he replies. "Hey, listen, I've got Emma on the line too. She's got some great news. I told her she should tell us together."

"Spill it, girlfriend," I declare. Because, heck yeah, I need it right now.

"The cipher on the intel Milo passed to Volkov has been broken! It's a numbered bank account. Swiss."

"Well, what do you know!" Jack exclaimed, awed.

"Who is the account registered to?" I ask.

"Scorpio Industries," Emma replies.

In other words, Edmonton.

"Congratulations, Team Emma!" I reply.

"I wish I deserved your praise." Emma's long sigh is weighted with frustration. "I'm ashamed I didn't think of the cipher previously since it is literally child's play."

"How so?" I ask.

"While on my break, I went into the Acme nursery to check on Nicky. His teacher had numbered the whiteboard from one to twenty-six. Each number had the sequential alphabetical letter beside it. With where the dashes are placed, it dawned on me that it may be a quick, simple code for an international bank account number, or 'IBAN.'"

She texts us the unbroken code:

CODED:
38HA - POOR- LULU - WILL - HATE - U
KEY:

1: A / K / U
2: B / L / V
3: C / M / W
4: D / N / X
5: E / O / Y
6: F / P / Z
7: G / Q
8: H / R
9: I / S
0: J / T

DECODED:
CH81-6558-2121-3922-8105-1

"The Swiss IBAN uses twenty-one digits, broken into four parts. The cipher's first two digits, which are really letters, indicate the bank's location—in this case, Switzerland," Emma explains. "The two letters beside them are the check control digits, which is determined by an algorithm. The next five letters coincide with its bank identifier number, whereas the last twelve numbers are actually the account number."

"How do you know that the zero is the tenth digit as opposed to the first?"

"Because if zero were keyed as an A, K, or U, it wouldn't have fit any of the IBAN country codes."

"Well done!" I exclaim.

"So, the account is Edmonton's slush fund," Jack reasons. "How much is in there?"

"We won't know until we can hack into it."

"Great, then that's our next task. Thanks, Emma. Get Arnie on the line, please."

The next voice we hear is her husband's. "What's up, boss?"

"I need you to hack an offshore bank account."

Arnie's snort reverberates through the phone. "Is that all?"

"So, it's doable?"

"Yeah. I mean, it has been done." He sighs. "But…it's not easy. It may take me a week—"

"We don't have that sort of time," I remind him.

"Well…there is someone who can do it quicker."

"Who is that?"

"Mad Hacker."

"Now, there's a trip down memory lane!" I murmur.

"There's no guarantee she'll go for it," Arnie warns me. "She's not exactly a fan of the US intelligence community."

She had reasons to be wary of it. In the past she was viewed as an enemy attacker because she had hacked the DNI's secure server. But her doing so allowed Acme to prove to then-President Lee Chiffray that my ex, Carl—his Director of National Intelligence—was in fact the traitor we claimed he was all along.

At the time, Acme didn't know if Mad Hacker was male or female, let alone ally or adversary. By saving Jack's life and mine—almost at the expense of her own—she proved to be someone we could count on.

"Call her. Tell her I'm asking."

"On it," Arnie assures me.

Here's hoping she'll take on this assignment despite her past experience with us.

18

Decoy

In IC parlance, a "decoy" is an imitation in any sense of the word, be it a person, object, or an event that is intended to deceive enemy surveillance, or to mislead the enemy's assessment of the situation.

Decoy deployment is a staple in the art of housewifery. A good mother knows how to make nutrient-rich food look "fun," even if its taste is less than yummy. At her husband's Christmas party, she will pretend to be deaf when his boss says something inappropriately lascivious. When her mother-in-law comes for dinner, she will be fêted with a coq au vin worthy of the best French restaurant in town (thanks to said restaurant's delivery service).

No matter the reason for subterfuge, a decoy is a necessary evil. A housewife must keep up appearances at all times if only to avoid being called a slob without a job.

My first meeting on Monday takes place at DARPA—the Defense Advanced Research Projects Agency—which invests in technology breakthroughs that advance our nation's security.

Today, a few of its project leaders are walking the IC through its PIPES program, which will innovate the connectivity of microelectronics for covert communications in the field.

When a break is called, Ryan, with a folder in hand, follows a few others into the hallway.

I wait a few minutes before doing the same, taking a glass of water with me.

I find Ryan near a scrum of like-minded leg-stretchers, but far enough away from them that we can stand close and murmur to each other without appearing to stand together.

"Good news. Jamison's intel is a game-changer." Ryan's mumble, made through a frozen grimace, is so low that I think I misheard.

I drop my head before whispering, "Made it worthwhile, then."

Ryan knows I'm talking about the beating because, as he turns a page, he shakes his head slightly. "You went well beyond the call of duty."

I nod slightly, acknowledging his kind words.

"Did he get it?" Of course, Ryan is referring to Edmonton and the codebook.

"Yes," I murmur. "How did you know I was there?"

Ryan snickers. "Your signature cake made its appearance. By the way, it went over big with the groom."

He meanders back into the meeting room.

Two compliments in one day, and it's not even noon yet! My head is spinning.

It doesn't get better than this.

~

Sadly, I'm right. The minute I get back from DARPA, Edmonton summons me into the Oval.

As usual, he keeps me standing, electing to stare out the window until he's ready to speak. I glance down at his almost empty desk. One thing that stands out is a beautiful antique desk clock. The background beneath the clock's face has a pen and ink rendering of Edmonton's alma mater, Stanford University.

When Edmonton turns around, he finds me looking at it. "A gift from an old friend," he mutters.

"Is it anyone I know? You had at least eleven of them while at the university," I remind him. "Twelve, if you include your illustrious professor, Arthur Yates."

"In this case, none of the above. In fact, the gift is from no one who attended Stanford, just someone who wanted to commemorate my accomplishments while I was there."

"Do tell." My yawn demonstrates my degree of interest.

"As it turns out, you know her too." He nods toward the door leading to his secretary's office.

"Mildred?" I coo. "Such gracious condescension!"

"I thought so too until I found out it was also a recording device." Edmonton shrugged. "It's been back-channeled to me that she's a double agent for the Chinese." The thought makes him shudder.

My eyes open wide. I can't help myself as I guffaw. "Well, well, well! What a disappointment it must be for you to find out your most loyal aide and confidante has been anything but, for all these years!"

"It proves my point that no one can be trusted"—he stares point-blank at me—"unless the stakes are too high to betray me."

I shrug. Edmonton has made his point.

"Considering the extent of her betrayal, I would prefer

you make it a painful death. However, do try to make it look like an accident. Otherwise, local law enforcement will feel the need to go above and beyond the call of duty in finding her murderer. And what would I do without you?"

It's almost on the tip of my tongue to say, *let's try it and see.*

Does it bother me that I'm to dispose of his enemy? Not at all. Her treason has nothing to do with how it affects Edmonton and everything to do with how it has hurt our country.

For once, he and I have a common goal.

THREE DAYS SPENT SHADOWING MILDRED REVEAL SOME SLOPPY spycraft on her part. She never alters her routine. For example, every day she takes lunch at her desk. She leaves her apartment on the top floor of a ten-story mid-last-century apartment building in Foggy Bottom every morning at five-thirty. She walks to the GWU Metro Station and takes the Blue Line to the McPherson Square Station, which is the one closest to the White House. At six-fifteen in the evening, she reverses the pattern.

If Mildred stops on the way home, it's at her local corner market, where she stocks up on canned tuna, oatmeal, rice, spaghetti noodles for her, and at least twenty tins of Fancy Feast for her cat.

Make that *cats.*

As in five of them: three Persians (black, white, and chocolate) and two tabbies: a full-grown tiger stripe, and a calico kitten.

A cat door allows them to hang out on her balcony. But when they hear Mildred enter the apartment, they run through it to greet her.

Just like they come to me, as I break in.

I shoo them away, except for the one that whines the most —the calico kitten. I scoop him up and take him with me out onto the balcony. From there, I climb up the fire ladder onto the roof with Calico Cat.

A half-hour later, when Mildred gets home, she realizes Calico Cat is missing.

She goes out on the balcony to search for her.

Hearing Calico Cat's plaintive cries above her head, Mildred looks up and sees his sweet little face staring down at her. Mildred's fretful fussing assures me she has deduced he may be stuck, or is afraid to climb back down the ladder's narrow vertical steps on what has become a dark and stormy night.

As I imagined it would, it breaks her heart to think of the tiny kitten shivering by itself in the cold. She climbs the ladder to rescue her baby.

The building is almost one hundred years old, and the ladder is the original one. It would not surprise a fire safety inspector that the rungs were too narrow and too slippery for Mildred. Nor would he question that the bolts holding the ladder over the lip of the roof's balcony were weak enough to tear away from the building as she struggled to hang on when it fell with her to the pavement.

Throughout the ordeal, Mildred is looking up at me.

When one is merely watching, such a fall seems to take place in a blink of an eye.

But now, seeing the many varied emotions play out on Mildred's face during these few fleeting seconds, I realize it may seem different to the victim.

Perhaps, the inevitable becomes interminable as well—

Especially for one who realizes that her sad, quick death is the right price to pay for a lifetime of dubious deeds.

I drop the cats at an animal shelter renowned for making great matches between pets and owners.

Huzzah! I now owe Edmonton one last task.

I AM RUNNING A HOT BATH WHEN MY PHONE RINGS. MY CELL IS on the vanity. I glance over at it:

Jack is calling.

I turn off the spigots before answering.

"Our old friend, Mad Hacker, has finally responded to Arnie's entreaties," he exclaims. "Actually, it was to Emma's call to arms."

I sigh, relieved. "I'm glad Arnie thought to have Emma reach out, even if it meant putting his ego in his pocket."

"More like his idol worship," Jack counters. "Something Mad Hacker abhors."

I chuckle. "Well, too bad. With her rep, she'll always have her fanboys."

"The good news is that Emma's request for a meeting of the minds with you was accepted. In fact, Mad Hacker is in DC. She will meet, but only if you come alone."

"I'm on it," I reply.

"I'll tell Emma. Mad Hacker will reach out to you with the details of where and when."

Mad Hacker's timing couldn't be better. The sooner we learn what's in that bank account—and how to steal it—the better.

19

Foreign Affairs

THE TERM "FOREIGN AFFAIRS" DESCRIBES A COUNTRY'S POLICIES *regarding furthering its national interests, first and foremost, through diplomacy.*

When it comes to developing relationships that align with her family's interests, a savvy housewife is also its ambassadress!

For example: If Hubby calls a half-hour before he's due to come home for dinner with the grand news that his regional manager will be joining the family for "the feast I'm sure you've prepared—along with your world-famous chocolate mousse," she will hustle back to the grocery store (or the local Whole Foods prepared meals counter) to secure a dinner befitting her victorious road warrior and his superior.

And, should his superior make a pass at her while her husband is out of the room, she will keep this tidbit to herself.

Retaliation for the regional manager's vulgar indiscretion will come later, delivered by the dark chocolate Ex-Lax glaze atop his slice of chocolate mousse.

∼

I'VE BARELY SITUATED MYSELF IN MY OFFICE WHEN MILDRED'S replacement—a young, pretty administrative assistant named Julia—calls to tell me that Edmonton would like to see me.

So, here it is: my final task.

When I knock on his door, he barks, "Come in."

Edmonton stands with his back to me, looking out his window. He is obviously in a pissy mood.

Great.

When, finally, he turns around, he slides a card across the desk.

I pick it up. It's one of Ryan's official business cards.

"You've got to be kidding!" I declare.

"Do you really want to test that theory?" Edmonton asks. "It's a conundrum, no doubt. Should you sacrifice your father figure for the man you married?" He rolls his thumb and forefinger together as if playing a tiny violin.

I answer his jibe with a middle-finger salute.

Edmonton chuckles at my audacity. "A Biblical dilemma deserves the proper setting. Why not invite him over for, say, a last supper? He can conveniently have a heart attack—a simple yet effective solution."

"You hired him," I retort. "Why don't you just... oh, I don't know, say, fire him?"

"What would be the fun in that?"

"Bradley, hon—*this is my fifth and final task.* Why waste it on tickles and farts?"

He grabs my mouth and purses it until it hurts. "Because I know what he means to you. Besides, it's the best way to test your loyalty."

"Here's a news bulletin: *don't bother, because I'm not.*"

My insolence earns me a hard slap.

My face burns from it, but I don't give him the pleasure of covering it with my hand, let alone shedding a tear.

"Get out of my sight," Edmonton growls. "Call me at midnight with the news I want to hear. Or else."

I don't have to ask, "Or else what?" I leave, knowing this was his end game all along.

"DINNER, AT YOUR PLACE?" RYAN EXCLAIMS. "WHAT'S THE occasion?"

"Does there need to be one?" I counter. "We're old friends, and I'm homesick. And since when does Ryan Clancy turn down a home-cooked meal?"

"You're right. How foolish of me! Go ahead, tell me what's on the menu. Make my mouth water."

"I'm thinking pot roast, mashed potatoes, Brussels sprouts, and lemon meringue pie for dessert."

"All are my favorites!"

"I know."

"Are you trying to tell me something?" Ryan's tone is wary. "In fact, if this were my last meal, it would be perfect."

I'm laughing so hard that all I can do is sputter. When I get ahold of myself, I gasp, "See you at seven, promptly."

"Yes, ma'am." He hangs up with a chuckle.

THE POT ROAST IS SO SUCCULENT THAT IT FALLS OFF THE BONE. The potatoes, Yukon Gold, melt in one's mouth. The sprouts are just soft enough and spiced perfectly.

By the time Ryan is on the last bite of his second piece of pie, I break the news to him:

"You know, Edmonton asked me to invite you here so that I could kill you."

JOSIE BROWN

Ryan shrugs. "Your cooking isn't *that* bad." A second later, it dawns on him that I'm not kidding. Slowly, he puts down his fork. "Give it to me straight: was anything on my plate poisoned?"

"Jesus, Ryan! You sure know how to hurt a girl!" I throw down my napkin. "Besides the irreparable damage it would do to my reputation as a hostess, do you really think I'd follow through on Edmonton's bullshit task?"

"Let's not forget the last time I was your target," he counters. "Granted, it was also to save Jack's life."

I flinch. "I'm sorry about that… Especially when I thought you were a goner."

"Nope, just a good actor. I missed my calling." Ryan smiles. "And besides, I know there have been other times you've wanted to kill me—"

"Only metaphorically speaking," I point out. "Ryan, this is no laughing matter! You're like a father to me. If you had any hair left, I could assure you, I wouldn't hurt one of them!" I sigh. "Edmonton is a sick puppy. But I still can't believe he'd do this out of spite."

"I would." Ryan pats his mouth with his napkin. "In fact, he asked me to exterminate *you.*"

I'm laughing so hard that I choke on my coffee. "Well, I'm glad we're forgoing our deathmatch—this time, anyway. But fair warning: *don't ever knock my cooking again.*"

We're both laughing so hard that we tear up.

When I can talk again without gasping through my giggles, I retort, "Talk about paranoia!"

"I respectfully disagree. It was Edmonton's test of loyalty for both of us." Now assured of his longevity, Ryan cuts himself a third slice of the lemon meringue. "As I understand your deal with our Fetishist-in-Chief, this puts you in a quandary, correct?"

"Absolutely." I shudder at the thought. "But I can tell he *wanted* me to turn it down. You're right, he's doing it out of spite. But whether it's for you or for me, I really don't know."

"Possibly neither of us." Ryan leans in. "Milo is getting to him."

I'm all ears. "Meaning?"

"Edmonton has had all the intelligence agencies on a full-on manhunt. He's cracking, Donna. And the Congressional Intelligence Committee chairs are getting suspicious. The sooner Acme comes up with the goods, the better."

I suppress the urge to do a happy dance. "Edmonton is not just a lame duck, he's a dead one too," I say. "So, why don't you take a flyer?"

"We've always been on the same wavelength, you and me. In fact, my resignation is being delivered to the House and Senate Intelligence Committees first thing tomorrow." Ryan looks at his watch. "I'm wheels up at dawn, in fact." Ryan stands up. Looking me in the eye, he adds, "I wish you could ride along with me."

I frown. "We both know I've got to see this through to the bitter end."

Ryan nods sadly. "As soon as we have our hands on Edmonton's ill-gotten gains, Khrystyna will be well-paid for her efforts—enough to retire from the business for good." He stands up and pecks me on the cheek. "I'll see you back in Los Angeles—real soon."

I hope he's right.

∾

RYAN HAS JUST LEFT WHEN I RECEIVE A TEXT TO ONE OF MY burner phones.

I don't recognize the number as any belonging to my mission team members. It reads:

Don't be late for this very important date!

"The **Caterpillar** and **Alice** looked at each other for some **time** in silence: at **last** the Caterpillar took the **hookah** out of its mouth, and **addressed** her in a languid, sleepy voice."

The Mad Hacker—*finally!*

The quote from *Alice in Wonderland* is the tipoff, as is the fact that it is coded in such a way that I can't make heads or tails of it.

I call Emma. "Okay, so I heard from the Mad Hacker. What do you make of this gibberish?"

I forward the text to her.

Seeing it, Emma laughs. "Since we can't shine a searchlight with the Mad Hacker insignia over the lens, she and I worked out a really simple code." She takes a moment to scrutinize it. "In this case, the highlighted words indicated the who, where, and when."

"Let me guess. Mad Hacker is referenced by the book's crazy characters, and I'm Alice."

"Yep, just like in the old days," Emma assures me.

"A trip down memory lane, for sure," I mutter.

A bittersweet one, in that it ended with Carl's death. Despite tossing me, hogtied, overboard into Washington state's Salish Bay, he was the father of my children, so I owe him that.

"The next two words that are bolded—'time' and 'last'—indicate the best time to meet with her. In this case, it's tonight," Emma explains. "And you've only got a half-hour to get there."

"Just where is 'there?'"

"You'll notice that the word 'hookah' is also in bold, followed by the word 'address.' This is her way of saying that the location she's chosen is a lounge that caters to that type of smoking. In DC, there are a bunch of them, but there is only one on her drop-point list: Betty's Gojo Hookah Lounge."

"Use the code to confirm I'm leaving now," I reply.

"Already done," Emma responds.

THE LOUNGE IS NORTH OF THE CITY, ON GEORGIA AVENUE, JUST before you enter Silver Springs. It is housed in a square brick storefront.

The lounge is small enough that Mad Hacker is not hard to find. She sits in an alcove. Her hookah is topped by a pineapple. Its vapor creates a sweet-smelling cumulus cloud.

Mad Hacker is twenty-four, maybe twenty-five years old. She wears large-framed black glasses, and she has several nose rings. She's also wearing ripped jeans and an oversized boat-neck sweatshirt.

Not much about her has changed except for her hair color. Once a neon fuchsia, it's now lime green. Its gamine pixie is spiked with fluorescent yellow tips.

In other words, she's still the same disaffected twenty-something rebel with a very serious cause: using her hacking skills to stop injustice, be it that of terrorists or a government that abuses its power over its citizenry.

Okay, yeah, I'm a duly awed fangirl.

Mad Hacker holds out the hose. "Care for a puff?"

"Nah, not really. I don't smoke."

"Neither do I, but it makes it harder for us to be seen."

I get her point. "Does the pineapple mask the taste of the tobacco?"

"It would," she acknowledges, "if I were smoking *tobacco*."

I sniff the air. "I don't smell pot—not from this hose, anyway." Although its odor wafts throughout the lounge.

Mad Hacker chuckles. "I haven't touched the stuff in years. Considering the target on my back, I don't need to numb my senses. I assume that's the reason you lay off of it too."

"Well, yeah. That, and I've got kids. Bad example, and all that."

"Sure, I get it—not part of your 'perfect wife and mother' vibe." Mad Hacker eyes me through the sweet-smelling cloud surrounding us. "I get that you are all about setting the right example for your kids—although I can't for the life of me know how you explain your kill rate."

I shrug. "When the time comes, I'll figure it out."

Mad Hacker snorts. "I'd love to be around for *that* conversation!"

"I'm doing it in a one-hundred percent unhackable cone of silence," I warn her.

Between laughing and smoking, she's now coughing too. When she catches her breath again, she retorts, "Way to throw down the gauntlet, Mrs. Craig!" Mad Hacker holds out her hand. "Game on!"

I take it, and we shake.

"Now, what exactly can I do for you and your merry band of covert misfits?" she asks.

"We need to hack an offshore bank account."

"Why?"

"To prove that a mole has infiltrated the White House and is benefiting from it," I explain.

Mad Hacker arches her neck before exhaling. "Interesting. Who's paying this supposed mole?"

"Russia."

"An oligarch?"

"Our guess is that the contracting party is even higher up on Russia's totem pole. But we won't know until you break into the account and verify the balance as well as where the funds came from."

She nods. "What can you tell me about your target?"

I frown. "I can't disclose anything. You know that."

She smirks. "Fair enough. Once I get in, what do you want me to do with it?"

"You'll be given another account in which to transfer the funds."

"Groovy." Mad Hacker takes a long drag on the hose. "My commission is five percent, not to exceed five million dollars, which I'll take from the account before transferring the rest to you."

"Um... Sure, okay." Jack will bust a gut, but he'll just have to live with that. Ryan would have done so too, but I could have sweet-talked him around it with a cherry pie.

Jack will expect a different sort of assuagement. But, yeah, I'm up for that too.

"Thanks." I shake her hand. "Emma will give you what you need."

"As long as it's her and not Arnie." Mad Hacker rolls her eyes. "Seriously, when that dude goes all puppy love on me, I can't keep from laughing." Her smile fades. "By the way, you were followed over here. Tell your driver, Henry, he needs a different pick-up corner and a new set of wheels, too."

A chill of dread rolls through me. "Thanks for the heads up."

"Give me a moment to leave first," she requests. "Then use the side exit on the right. It'll take you into the pawnshop next door. Go out the back."

I nod.

Mad Hacker is gone in a flash.

I look out a moment later. The beaded curtain on the side door is still tinkling softly from her exit.

THE DREADED CALL FROM THE WHITE HOUSE COMES THROUGH at five o'clock in the morning.

It is not made through Julia but by Edmonton himself.

His screams of obscenities are so loud that I have to hold the phone far from my ear.

When I hear silence again, I say, "I take it you know that I was unsuccessful in completing my task. Does this mean you're firing me?"

"That would make your life too easy," Edmonton snarls. "Don't bother coming into work."

"Bradley…wait!"

Here it is: the moment he's been waiting for: will I once again sacrifice myself for Jack?

Yes—even if Khrystyna hadn't agreed to take on Edmonton's punishment.

He hasn't hung up, but his silence indicates his contemplation to do so.

Finally: "What is it, Mrs. Craig?"

"I'm… I'm asking for your forgiveness."

He snickers. "*Asking*?"

"No, Bradley… *I'm begging you.*"

More silence.

Then he hisses: "My forgiveness comes at a price."

"And I'm… I'm willing to pay it."

His breathing is long and labored. I envision the pleasure

he takes from this exchange—emotionally, but also physically, which reveals itself in his sharp gasp.

Revolting.

When he has recovered from his self-gratification, he mutters, "You'll need to prepare for my visit. Jerome will deliver the necessary items."

I've been duly warned.

By the time I'm able to stumble to my feet, I'm bathed in sweat.

I head to the shower. No matter how hard I scrub it, my skin still crawls at the thought of Khrystyna's predicament.

Will she ever forgive me?

Abu won't.

I know that.

20

Assault

IN MILITARY TERMS, AN ASSAULT IS A SHORT, VIOLENT, WELL-*ordered attack against a local objective.*

Various forces, tactics, and weapons may be used in the assault to assure its success.

Should you find yourself being assaulted, standing your ground may make you a hero—perhaps, unfortunately, a dead one.

By taking cover or falling back while comrades are felled, will you be branded a coward? It depends on the circumstances.

Whatever your reasons, the outcome is the same: you'll live to fight another day.

AS PROMISED, APPROXIMATELY AT NOON, THERE IS A KNOCK ON my door.

Same courier: Jerome.

Again, with the bowler? Jeez! The dude needs a new look.

This time, I open the door only as wide as the metal safety lock allows.

He sneers as he drops a red suitcase to the floor. "Your gentleman caller will be here in an hour," he murmurs. "Enjoy your date!"

Because he doesn't expect me to open the door any wider, my kick to the balls does its job and wipes the smirk off his face.

He's still cursing between giggles as he stumbles toward the elevator.

It's a Pyrrhic victory. We both know it. When he tells Edmonton, there will be hell to pay.

Could it be any worse than what is in his latest goodie bag?

I doubt it.

I open it anyway to see what's inside. It holds a different gag: one that works like braces, but leaves your mouth open. It also contains a full-body harness and a spread bar. Four cuffs-and-chains. Three dildos of varying lengths and girths. Two paddles.

A bamboo switch.

A wooden cane.

There is also a typed note that reads:

YOU SHALL LAY OUT EACH INSTRUMENT ON THE BED,
EXACTLY FOUR INCHES APART.

YOU SHALL WAIT FOR ME, KNEELING AT THE FOOT OF THE BED,
WITH YOUR HANDS BEHIND YOUR BACK.

YOU SHALL BE WEARING THE HARNESS.
YOU SHALL BE GAGGED AND BLINDFOLDED.
ONE HOUR.

We have no time to waste.

As we agreed, I text Khrystyna from my Acme burner cell to hers. The message says:

The movie starts at 1:45! Bernard is saving you a seat.

The coded message:

I'll be coming over via the secret panel through both apartments. We've got one hour to prep for Edmonton's visit.

A moment later, Khrystyna texts back:

Can't wait to see it with you!

I head for the bedroom. From there, I slip into my closet and tap out the code.

Dominic opens the secret panel. I've never seen such sadness in his eyes. "Abu will be gutted," he murmurs.

And it's all my fault.

Abu and Khrystyna are sitting together on the large circular couch in front of a sterling silver tea service and two tiered tea stands. One holds sandwiches. The other has petit fours and other sweet goodies.

They are holding hands. Their conversation is intense enough that at first they don't notice Dominic and me.

Khrystyna must be filling him in on my text.

Dominic whispers into my ear, "She's worried."

I grimace. "Cold feet?"

Dominic shakes his head. "She knows it's why she's here. She's just ashamed that Abu will have to see her that way."

I know how she feels. It's precisely what I went through when Jack walked in after Edmonton's last visit.

"Frankly, I'm glad she and Abu are close if only to pick up the pieces after our Fetishist in Chief is done with her," I reply. "We'll have to get going. We have less than an hour."

They hear me. Reluctantly, they stand up. Khrystyna wears a sheer robe with nothing underneath it. If she and the rest of the mission team watched as I laid out the harness and gag on the bed, she knows it's all she'll be wearing during Edmonton's torture session.

We head for the dining room table. There, Abu has set up a lighted three-panel mirror next to the box holding a latex mask molded into my face. There is also a tackle box filled with the same tubes and tins found on the styling tables lining every Fashion Week runway.

In other words, Abu has everything he needs to turn Khrystyna into me for the performance of a lifetime.

She sits down on the chair in front of the mirror and the transformation begins.

"Remarkable!" I whisper.

Khrystyna and I stand, facing each other. It's as if I'm looking in a mirror, down to the fake scars on her back, which mirror my own.

"Abu..." I turn to look at my dear friend with awe.

He tries to smile. "I've seen enough makeup tutorials online to get certified as a Sephora collection ambassador.

Hey, I wonder if I can get my union card and work on a movie set or something? I hear the pay is great."

Abu is always on the lookout for a gig that doesn't include dumping bodies. Maybe he can combine the two skill sets.

I shake my head. "I'm sure it is, but it's a competitive field. Hey, I'll bet funeral directors would hire you in a minute. If you want, practice on a few of our exterminations. You can take pictures for your portfolio."

"Not exactly what I was looking for," he mutters.

Can't say I blame him.

Dominic, who is still scrutinizing Khrystyna, declares, "She isn't an exact match, Old Girl. She's *a bit* slimmer. And her breasts are *definitely* larger—not to mention *much* firmer." He sighs. "But of course, that would have something to do with her age, I suppose. And her workout regime doesn't include as much baking as yours—"

"Alright, enough! I catch your drift." To make the point, I slap his shoulder. "The big question is, will it be noticeable to Edmonton?"

Khrystyna shrugs. "Doubtful. He'll be too busy trying to break me."

Abu winces at the implication.

"Wow! With the voice alteration app on, she even sounds like me," I murmur.

"We need to test Khrystyna's earbud to make sure she can hear us." Abu's reply is curt.

Yes, he is worried.

Khrystyna takes his hand. "Whisper sweet nothings in my ear, my darling, and all the pain will go away."

"I will," Abu promises.

Khrystyna's languid kiss holds Abu in a trance. Reluctantly breaking away, she steels her shoulders before sauntering into the closet and through the hidden door.

Through the two-way mirror, we watch as Khrystyna drops the robe, replacing it with the harness. Next, she puts on the gag. Finally, she puts on the blindfold.

She then positions herself on the floor, per Edmonton's written instructions: kneeling, facing the bed, with her hands behind her back.

Abu says, "Khrystyna, nod if you can hear me."

She does so, slightly.

Not a moment too soon.

The faint creak of the front door alerts us that Edmonton has arrived. He has kept his promise to me: his Secret Service detail stays outside.

I now know his tread by heart, and I dread it: the light, quick steps as if he hasn't a care in the world.

Today, he adds an off-key whistle. From what I can make out, it's some old Broadway tune—Richard Rodgers, I think. The thought that he finds levity in what he assumes is my pain makes my blood boil.

He slows down when he reaches the open bedroom door. He sees Khrystyna's prone figure and chuckles. "Very nicely played, Mrs. Craig. If you can stay completely subservient, we will both be the happier for it."

Slowly, he starts toward her. It takes him fourteen steps to reach her. Bending down, he grabs her by the hair, jerking her head straight back.

"I see the gag is a perfect fit! I had to guess at the size of your pretty little mouth. Hopefully, it won't stretch it out too badly." He lets Khrystyna's head drop.

"Kiss my feet," Edmonton commands her.

She raises her head so that her mouth skims the tops of his brogues.

"That's a good girl. Now please stand up."

Khrystyna does as commanded.

Edmonton circles her. His hand roams lightly over her supple skin. When he stops, I hold my breath, but let it go again when he kneels behind her—

To lick her waist.

When she shivers, he punches her in the kidney.

She bends over, gasping.

He yanks her head up and hisses, "I was disappointed that you weren't more gracious to Jerome, my dear Donna. Although I don't know why it surprises me. Disrespect is all I've gotten from you since you arrived in Washington! You act as if I were...*beneath you.*" He laughs when he realizes his double entendre. "I guess we now know who is really on top here. There are no excuses. You were duly warned what would happen if you didn't follow my orders to a tee! But you let your sentiment get the better of you! Because of it, I now have two traitors taunting me, not just one! Someone has to pay for it! And, unfortunately, it's you."

He reaches down for the bamboo whip. Taking it in hand, he flexes it. Then, gently, he runs it down Khrystyna's back.

This time, she doesn't move a muscle.

Frowning, Edmonton throws back his arm. The whip sings through the air before slashing her shoulders.

The beating begins.

FOR THE LONGEST TIME, KHRYSTYNA STAYS STILL AND SILENT.

Lash after lash raises ruby welts on her backside, shoulders, arms, and legs. Soon, streams of blood run down her legs.

All the while, Abu's murmurs continue. It is almost as if he has willed Khrystyna into a trance.

One that Edmonton can't break.

This only made makes him angrier.

Finally, he throws down the whip and picks up a paddle. With the first wallop, Khrystyna loses her footing, and Edmonton cackles triumphantly. The next, even harder, has her standing on her toes. The smacks come now, faster. The sound of board slapping skin has even Dominic groaning.

I bite my fist to keep from crying, but I can't stop the tears from rolling down my face. I've put her in that position. It's all I can do not to grab a gun and walk back in there to blow Edmonton's head off.

Now I must watch as her skin goes purple before bruising to black.

Unlike me, Khrystyna doesn't shed tears. Edmonton has also realized this. He taunts her with foul names and cruel slurs that are meant to shame her.

Still, no tears.

Angrily he heaves the paddle at the two-way mirror—

Instinctively, Dominic and I duck.

Thankfully, the mirror doesn't break.

Somehow Abu keeps up the mantra that is entrancing Khrystyna.

Incensed, Edmonton stalks back to Khrystyna and slaps her so hard that she falls, face down onto the bed.

Seeing this, Abu jumps up and rushes toward the closet.

I run after him, grab him, and hold him tight. "Abu, you can't! It'll blow the whole mission—everything we need to put an end to this monster!"

Abu's anger comes out in a muffled groan, but he stops fighting me. Shaking, he nods.

I walk him back to the monitor.

By now, Edmonton has picked up the cane. He strikes her back, again and again. Her grunts can barely be heard over her cracking bones.

I can't take it anymore. I shake Dominic. "Do something! *Now!*... The fire alarm—the one upstairs! *Pull it!*"

He nods frantically and runs out of the room.

I hear him taking the stairs two at a time to the second floor. A moment later, the fire alarm blares through the building.

But it's too late.

Edmonton has beaten her to death.

Even he can see this.

He tries to raise her, but she is limp, like a rag doll.

He turns her over to check for a heartbeat but finds none.

He takes off the gag, and tries to resuscitate her, only to choke on the blood trickling out of her mouth.

The realization leaves him bent over, heaving onto the floor.

Edmonton takes a moment to catch his breath. When he can stand upright again, he stares down at the dead body—at the woman he thinks is me—and cackles hysterically.

In time, he picks up his jacket from the chair. As he shirks it on, he strolls over to the mirror. He stares into it for so long that I wonder, can he hear Abu crying?

Does he see us?

No. He only sees the specs of Khrystyna's blood that fleck his face.

He rubs them off with his kerchief. Then he pats down a wayward cowlick.

He whistles as he walks out of the room. I only know this because I see his lips puckering. But I can't hear him because Abu is sobbing incoherently.

213

SUITED UP WITH LATEX GLOVES AND HAZMAT SUITS, DOMINIC and I take pictures of the crime scene. We also search for latent prints on the fabrics and surfaces touched by Edmonton, bagging all evidence samples from surfaces where Edmonton may have left his fingerprints or DNA.

Afterward, we strip off what is left of Khrystyna's harness and wash off her blood.

We lay her out on my shower curtain. I know it doesn't matter now. Still, I put her in one of my dresses, brush her hair, and apply makeup.

By now, Abu is enough in control of his emotions to come into my apartment and pay his respects. He holds her face in his hands and kisses her gently. Then, sighing deeply, he mutters, "Goodbye, my dear, brave love."

I bend beside Abu. When I lay my arm on his shoulder, he doesn't shrug it off. Instead, he looks up at me.

I don't expect him to forgive me for putting her life in danger.

It's all the more reason I'm shocked when he whispers, "Donna, I know you mourn her too. And that you are upset to have caused me this grief. Khrystyna was a hero. She gave her life for our country. She chose to do it. In fact, she knew his bloodlust might bring about her demise."

"How is that even possible?"

"As part of Khrystyna's preparation, she had asked me to play the video of Edmonton's sadistic session with you. She made this prediction after seeing it. And yet, she never turned down the role." Abu looks away. "Not even when I begged her to do so." When he's able to face me again, he adds: "Donna, you are one of my dearest friends. But beyond that, I don't know how Acme—or Jack, or your family—would survive if we'd lost you instead." He rises. Taking my hand, he murmurs, "Let's not waste her sacrifice."

With Dominic's help, Abu lifts Khrystyna gently into a laundry cart. In case he passes someone with prying eyes, he lays a quilt on top of the cart before rolling it into the service elevator that will take him down into the garage.

He will then whisk her away in his van. Henry knows of an abandoned industrial ceramics factory with a furnace large enough to cremate Khrystyna's body.

"I'M SORRY, DONNA." JACK'S VOICE ON THE PHONE IS DEEPENED by his emotions.

"You know about Khrystyna, then?" I ask.

"Yes." His silence speaks volumes. He realizes it could have been me.

Finally, he adds, "I've just landed in DC. I came in for a meeting scheduled for tomorrow...but I've called it off. Your currently unreported 'death' is more important."

"Ya think?"

I may have tried for levity, but my voice trembles enough that Jack replies, "I'll be there as fast as traffic permits, honey."

"The sooner, the better."

This time, I can't keep the sobs out of my voice.

I need to feel Jack's arms around me.

THE DOORBELL RINGS. THANK GOODNESS! THE TRAFFIC GODS smiled down on Jack—

But no, it's Mario Martinez.

Oh.... *shite.*

I recognize him despite the hat, sunglasses, and gloves he

wears. Apparently, he doesn't want to be caught on any security camera.

Mario pauses in front of my door, but he doesn't knock.

Instead, he unlocks it.

He has Edmonton's key.

Double shite!

I run to my bedroom and into the closet. As quickly as I can, I dive through my hanging dresses, then slam my fist against the sliding door's tiny button.

Why does it open so slowly?

I hear his soft, cautious footsteps coming my way—

Just as the panel slides open.

I leap through it and hit it again.

It shuts just as Mario walks into my bedroom.

How did he duck our surveillance?

Dominic's tea service is set up on the far side of the surveillance room. He stands there doctoring his cup. Noting my alarm, he exclaims, "What? … *Oh*! But of course! You'd like a cuppa too. Darjeeling or Jasmine Flower Bell? And the cakes are flown in specially from the Lanesborough. Scrumptious!"

I point at the rows of monitors, where he should have been sitting. "Sorry, Dom, but the cucumber sandwiches and scones will have to wait. Looks like I have another visitor!"

"Blimey!" he mutters, as the intruder steps into my bedroom.

MARIO'S EYES SHIFT SLOWLY AS IF TAKING IN EVERY SQUARE INCH of the room.

His eyes stop when they reach the closet.

He starts toward it.

Shit…

Why?

I watch as walks over to it—

Into it.

Dominic instructs the camera to zoom in. We look on as Mario stares at the hanging clothes in front of him. He sees a woman's life as detailed by her fashion taste: an array of monochromatic dresses, black slacks, fitted jackets, a few party frocks. Lots of expensive handbags.

Too many designer shoes.

Suddenly, Mario shoves some of the hangars to one side—

But no Dead Donna.

Slowly, he walks over to the bed. He stares down at its stark white comforter, so smooth and pristine. Next, he walks around the room—looking under the bed, pulling out drawers, checking the lamps and their shades.

He searches the other rooms too but doesn't find me.

Finally, he walks out.

I wonder what he will tell Edmonton, that I'm a ghost who has disappeared into thin air?

He should only wish that were the case.

Unshackled to Edmonton's false promises, I am his worst nightmare.

"DONNA—JACK IS HERE!" DOMINIC MOTIONS AT THE MONITOR trained on the Watergate's lobby.

He's right. Jack stands at the elevator bank. He is surrounded by the animated crowd waiting for one to take them to the upper floors.

Mario is in the only elevator going down.

I can't let them run into each other.

Fourteenth floor… Thirteenth floor…

I scramble for my burner phone. I punch Jack's number.

Twelfth floor… Eleventh floor…

We watch as Jack checks his coat pocket. He then realizes it's in his pants pocket instead.

Tenth floor… Ninth floor…

Jack stares down at the number. Surely, he recognizes it! Pick up, damn it!

Eighth floor… Seventh floor…

Finally, he taps open the line.

Sixth floor…

"Don't ask any questions. Just do as I say!"

Jack covers his other ear so he can hear more clearly. "Donna? I can barely hear you…"

Fifth floor… Fourth floor…

"Turn around! Don't face the elevator! Instead, walk toward the fire exit!"

Third floor… Second floor…

My words sink in just as the elevator's bell chimes. Its door opens—

And Mario steps out.

The crowd streams in around him. As he walks toward the front door, he hears the beep as the fire exit opens—

At least he thought it did. But no, the door is shut.

Mario walks out of the Watergate.

I FLING OPEN THE DOOR TO TAKE JACK'S ARM AND PULL HIM IN close to me.

We hug as if we never want to let go.

21

Ultimatum

IN WARFARE, AN "ULTIMATUM" IS THE STATEMENT INDICATING ONE *warring state's final position with its enemy state. Take heed! This could be the final demand prior to military action.*

In essence: WAR.

In a marriage, periodically, the need for ultimatums arise. A sample scenario:

Your spouse is adamant about betting the bulk of the family's nest egg on some sort of cryptocurrency. Despite your calm protests against this cockamamie scheme, your warning goes unheeded.

Before his stubbornness tips the balance on your already precarious financial reality, pull out the heavy artillery—say, cramming his computer into the trash compactor.

He will shout. He will cry. He will sulk—

And that's okay. Threatening to take the nuclear option will save him from himself.

Eventually (when you are proven right), he will call for a truce, and you will agree.

As you should. Or, as your hippie parents could tell you, it's so much more fun making love than war.

I state the obvious: "As far as Edmonton knows, I'm dead."

Jack nods. "And now that he's through playing cat and mouse with you, I'm a dead man, too."

"All the more reason we should just get out—*now!*" I declare. "We have to disappear! Emma and Arnie can put the kids in the Acme jet so that they can meet us somewhere he can't find us—"

"You're panicking, Donna," he replies. "Stay calm! *We have what we need to get Edmonton. He's killed someone!*"

"He thought he killed *me!*" No matter how hard I try to stop it, Khrystyna's brutal murder plays in my head like a video loop. "Jack, if I waltz back in as if nothing happened—"

"But something *did* happen," Jack counters. "We have proof of that. You—*we*—now have the leverage to get out of this sick pact with him. Show it to him."

He's right. Otherwise, our work throughout our lives—the lives we've built for us and our children—is for naught.

Life on the run is not what I want for either myself, Jack, or them.

Then it dawns on me: "Jack, even if Edmonton agrees to let us off the hook, we still have a Russian asset sitting in the Oval Office."

"Until Mad Hacker breaks into Edmonton's account," he reminds me. "Which she thinks will happen soon."

"Like how soon?"

"She says at the most, another twenty-four hours."

Then we can take Edmonton down.

"Donna, you never asked why I'm here in DC."

I guffaw. "And all this time, I thought it was to see me!"

"I wish it was a well-timed pleasure trip—but no." Jack

grimaces. "What we'd hoped for has happened. Edmonton requested a face-to-face meeting with Milo."

"Oh." He's right. It's what we'd wanted. After seeing what Edmonton was capable of doing to Khrystyna, I can only wonder what he has in store for Milo.

Or, in this case, Jack.

"You can't do it," I plead.

"I have to. But don't worry. The meeting is happening on Milo's terms."

"If you say so," I mutter.

He knows I'm far from convinced.

"At the very least, we've got to get out of the Watergate," I point out. "Does Acme have a safe house in DC?"

"Yes."

"We should move our operations there."

"Agreed. Henry brought me over. He'll take us there." Jack heads for the secret door. "I'll let Arnie know to block any cameras that may see us leave. Still, in case Edmonton has Mario watching this place, we should take a circuitous route. I'll get Dom and Abu to do the same. We should all go out through their door on the floor above."

Together, we pack up my stuff.

HENRY TAKES US TO A SHABBY THREE-STORY VICTORIAN ON A quiet dead-end street in the Berkley neighborhood. It sits deep on the lot. Thickets of trees in both the front and back yards shield it from its neighbors.

While touring the home's basement, Henry divulges one more thing that makes it an ideal hiding place. "Its history as a safe house goes back to the time of the Civil War. In fact, it was owned by an abolitionist and was part of the Underground Railroad. Proof of this is the tunnel built under the backyard and Canal Road, which parallels the Potomac River. It was used to ferry escaped slaves on their journeys farther north."

We park our vehicles in the garage, which is located toward a far corner of the backyard. Henry shows us its false back wall that opens onto Canal Road. Both are adequate escape routes—the former by foot, the latter by car—should we find ourselves cornered.

Hopefully, we won't.

Abu hasn't said a word since he got back from cremating Khrystyna. He excuses himself from our quick dinner of burgers and fries to go to bed.

"He'll never get over her," Jack murmurs.

This saddens me.

Abu has always been able to keep our missions from darkening his soul. Should his mourning for Khrystyna cause him to leave Acme, I will certainly understand.

Still, Abu's loss would be significantly felt. His quick, innovative responses, especially while under pressure, have saved our missions on innumerable occasions.

Most of all, I would miss having my dear friend as a regular part of my life. His wry sense of humor has buoyed me in dark times. His ongoing quest for some less treacherous job that gave him the same financial rewards and a better chance of survival was usually cockeyed and the prospective gigs were undoubtedly dull. Otherwise, Acme would have lost him long ago.

Jack leans in for a kiss. "I would never get over you. But I would make sure to avenge your death."

I realize Abu may feel the same.

And we will help him do it.

Knowing that the removal of "Donna Craig's" body may

put Edmonton on the warpath, everyone is still on edge over his next move. In case our getaway wasn't as clean as we hoped, we decide that one of us must be on guard at all times.

I will take the first three-hour shift, followed by Jack, Henry, and Dominic. Tapping into Acme's satellite and radio feeds of the DC metro area gives us eyes and ears on any SWAT operation coming our way.

Even after Jack takes my place, I spend a sleepless night.

I'm wide awake before dawn. I dress to go back to the White House and give Edmonton the scare of his life.

AT FIVE O'CLOCK, HENRY DROPS ME OFF A FEW BLOCKS FROM THE US Treasury Building. My White House credentials get me inside, at which point I head to the tunnel that connects it to the East Wing.

Since no one yet knows I'm 'dead,' my White House pass easily gets me through the various security check-points. I smile at those who know me and say hi, and I wave at others who glance over but don't really recognize me.

That's okay. Hopefully, they never will.

I slip into the president's private dining room. From there, I take the private hallway to my office. It is locked, but I still have my key. After entering, I lock it again behind me.

Since Arnie has hacked into the Oval Office security cameras, I can watch as Edmonton's new secretary, Julia, goes into her boss's office from the door her office shares with his, something he demands a half-hour before he arrives. She places his daily agenda on his desk and then closes the door behind her.

He will enter through the door from the main hall.

Edmonton won't like that his tall leather chair is facing the credenza and window as opposed to the desk.

Well, too bad.

I know when he's coming because of the show-tune whistle preceding him. This time, it's from *The Sound of Music.* The song is *Maria.*

The door opens. Edmonton closes it after he steps in.

Annoyed at the angle of his chair, he clicks his tongue.

This is my cue to turn around and say, "Missing me yet, Bradley?"

EDMONTON'S FACE, PAPER WHITE, SEEMS TO BE PURGED OF ALL blood.

He grips the back of the nearest Queen Anne wingback to break his stumble.

His eyes blink several times before remaining open. At that point, they widen. His mouth falls open, but he is speechless.

I wave. "Hey, come on over here! I think there's something you're going to want to see!"

Warily, Edmonton staggers to the edge of his desk. His frown twitches with anxiety.

Perfect.

I slip a thumb drive into his computer and tap on the monitor. Khrystyna's beating plays on the screen. Because of her silence, only his curses and the crack of the whip are heard. When Edmonton watches as he picks up the cane, he flinches.

"Where did you get this? I was assured by my people that the cameras were turned off!" His trembling voice is barely louder than a hiss.

"Mine weren't." I stop the video. After ejecting the thumb drive, I toss it at him. "Keep it. There are more where that came from."

"You...*bitch!*" He rushes toward me.

I'm prepared for him. I pull a travel perfume spritzer from my pocket and spray his eyes.

Smarting from the sting, he shouts a litany of curses.

Hearing him, Julia and a Secret Service agent open different doors.

Realizing this, Edmonton shouts, *"Get out!* We're... discussing...*something!"*

With lightning speed, the doors close.

Edmonton glares at me through squinting eyes.

I smile back.

"Well played, Mrs. Craig." He straightens his back in an attempt to regain his composure. "What do you want?"

"Frankly, I want a permanent truce. Let Jack off the hook for *your* sanctioned extermination of Congresswoman Elle Grisham, and he—and I, and our family—go on our merry way."

He thinks about that for a moment. "Is that all?"

"This isn't blackmail, Bradley. As I said, it's exoneration. A pardon. A truce. Call it what you will, but take it or leave it. However, I warn you: should you choose the latter, the contents of this thumb drive will not only be sent to House and Senate leaders, but transmitted to every media outlet and streamed on all social media. If the outrage of watching you kill a woman in cold blood doesn't oust you from office, the subsequent investigation will."

Edmonton attempts a smile, but it fades in the heat of his anger. He growls, "You'll have my answer in an hour, by courier."

I have to go back to the Watergate.

Shit.

"EDMONTON MAY BITE." IN HINDSIGHT, I REALIZE THAT COULD mean literally, from what we witnessed of his treatment of Khrystyna. "On the truce, I mean."

"When will you know?" Jack is concerned.

"For sure, in an hour."

"Good! That means I can be close at hand." Jack's relief mirrors mine. "'Milo' isn't sending Edmonton the rendezvous coordinates until Mad Hacker cracks his bank account. She doesn't anticipate that happening for a few hours yet. Perhaps as late as tonight."

"Edmonton is sending a courier to the Watergate with his answer."

"I don't like it."

"Why? Do you think he's setting me up for a hit?"

"I wouldn't doubt it. You're no longer his gofer or play-thing, which makes you a loose end." Jack goes silent. Then: "Abu, Dominic, and I will be next door, just in case. That way, we can monitor the building's interior and exterior security feeds. I'll leave Henry on the street for exterior surveillance. When you get to the Watergate, instruct the lobby concierge to ask the courier to leave the package there. She can deliver it to you herself."

"I don't know…I mean… Can we trust her?"

"Why do you ask?"

"She seems a little off to me."

"In what way?" Jack asks.

"Too nosy, I guess."

"I'll tell her to calm it down."

"Why would you do that? I'll never see her again."

"You might. I'm her boss." Jack adds hesitantly. "Truth be told, Poppy's got a bad case of hero-worship."

"Oh?" I stifle a snicker. "Egad! A crush on the boss? Of course, who wouldn't be mesmerized by such a handsome devil! Looks. Power. That impish grin. You're a human resources director's nightmare—"

"Silly woman! I was talking about *you*. She worships you! A lot of the female operatives do. You're a legend in your own time." He's laughing hard enough to bust a gut. "Hey, I told you I had you covered."

By noon, I still haven't heard from Edmonton.

A little before one, I get a call from Trisha.

"Hi, sweet girl. How are you?" I steel myself for the worst.

"Mom! You'll never believe what just happened!" It's been a while since I've heard her so happy.

It can only mean one thing: "Did you make up with Janie?"

Trisha snickers. "No! Like *that* will ever happen."

My heart sinks. "So, tell me."

"Riley dumped her! *For me!*"

"*What?...But...why?*"

"Riley told me she felt so bad about all those awful things Janie said to me on the phone. She sees now she made the wrong choice. Mom, she asked if I'd ever forgive her."

"Can you?"

"I suppose so...I mean, isn't that what you'd hope I'd do?"

"Yes...But... Are you sure Riley is sincere?"

"What do you mean by that?" Trisha mutters.

"She was the reason Janie dropped you in the first place.

And she certainly didn't care about your feelings when she made that kiss-off video with Janie."

"What are you saying, Mom?" she mutters.

"I just don't know if you should trust someone who can be mean, cruel, and manipulative. And not only to you but to the person she just announced to the world was her best friend—and who dumped you for the dubious honor of being it! Tell the truth, Trisha: doesn't that bother you?"

"Why do you care about Janie's feelings more than mine?" she sulks.

"Because you have a history together."

"Isn't it really because Mr. Chiffray is your best friend?"

Annoyed, I counter, "What makes you think that?"

"It's true, isn't it? That's why you want me to like Janie—despite the horrible thing she did to me!"

"Lee is a close, dear friend, Trisha. *To both me and Dad.* And it is nice when one's parents actually like the parents of their friends." I'm trying hard to keep the anger out of my voice, but it's not easy. "I haven't even met the Trents yet."

"That's not their fault! You haven't been here to meet with them. Remember?"

Guilt mutes my tongue.

"Mrs. Trent was over this morning, in fact. She wanted to meet you, but since you weren't here, she left a gift with Aunt Phyllis."

"What is it?"

"A pie. She felt it was the least she could do for all the bad blood between Janie and me."

"Well...that was nice of her," I admit.

"Then you won't mind if I go camping with them?"

"What?... *Camping?*"

"Yes! In Angeles National Park. They'd planned the trip anyway because the teacher's workday gives us a three-day weekend. They felt the least they could do was ask me to join them and Riley, considering her contest got me suspended."

"Well...that is very lovely of Mrs. Trent..." I sigh. "And you say Aunt Phyllis met her?"

"*Yes,* Mom!" Trisha's exasperation grates on me.

"If it's okay with Aunt Phyllis...then...it's okay with me."

"I love you, Mom! Thanks!" She throws several loud kisses before signing off.

I guess I should appreciate that the Trents have owned up to Riley's role in Trisha's suspension. If something goes wrong here, at least Trisha will remember me fondly for cutting her some slack for her stupid trick on Janie.

She's right, though. Had I been home, none of this would have happened.

EDMONTON KEEPS ME ON TENTERHOOKS UNTIL FOUR IN THE afternoon, at which time the message is delivered by my sweet sunny acolyte. It comes in a box that looks like it may hold two dozen long-stemmed red roses, but its weight is much more substantial.

I open it to find a Sig Sauer P226 wrapped in plastic.

The box also contains two photos.

One is of Trisha.

She stands against a plain white wall. She is wearing her favorite jeans and sweater. Trisha's hands are behind her back, and her mouth is set in a frown. On the table beside her is an *LA Times* dated today.

The other photo is of Milo Cathcart.

Oh. Shit.

There is also a notecard in the box:

Mrs. Craig,
You still owe me one more task. This should incentivize you
to take it on.
Expect a courier later this evening with more details.

With shaking hands, I call Jack. As calmly as I can, I say: "Edmonton has Trisha."

22

Situation Room

THERE IS A MANSION-SIZED ROOM LOCATED IN THE BASEMENT OF the West Wing. There, the President and his national security directors monitor and deal with every crisis, both at home and abroad.

When such a crisis occurs, the "Situation Room" becomes command central.

Boasting the most advanced communications equipment, from there POTUS can give orders to every military force at his disposal without interference from enemy states.

It's the same thing you do from your cell phone in your own "situation room," a.k.a., your mommy-mobile, as you move from one carpool assignment to another.

Granted, it would be much more convenient to have multiple screens on at all times to monitor the hotspots causing angst in your life—especially during high-traffic hours. Knowing the best detour routes may actually be the answer to getting your carload of kiddies to their after-school practices on time.

Mention this imperative to your car dealer. If enough harried mothers do so, the "Mobile Situation Room" may become Car & Driver's next "Vehicle of the Year."

"So, Edmonton wants you to exterminate Milo?" Jack snickers.

For some reason, he finds that hilarious. Not me. Not while my daughter and husband's lives are on the line.

"This is no laughing matter! I'm assigned to shoot the messenger—*you!*" I chide him. "Where is 'Milo' meeting Edmonton?"

"He doesn't know it yet, but it'll be at the same abandoned factory where we cremated Khrystyna's body." He shrugs. "Now that we know there's a target on Milo's back and you've been contracted to do the hit, I doubt Edmonton will come himself." Jack guffaws. "In hindsight, I wish I'd brought the real Milo with me."

"*Why?*"

"It would have made it easier to fake the hit. You could have taken your thumbs-up photo with his body and then tossed him in the furnace."

"Ha! Great idea…" A thought comes to me. "Jack, we can still do that if you send George back for Milo right now!"

"But…that's nearly six hours to LA, and another five hours coming back!"

I look at my watch. "Timing 'Milo's' meeting with Edmonton so that it's the middle of the night is ideal! You've said Edmonton is already on tenterhooks about it, as is. And besides, Milo can thaw out on the way over." I'm pacing the room now as I think out loud. "With all the moving parts, the tech component is a two-person job. Have Arnie hop on the plane so that Abu has on-site tech assistance. And Dominic wants to go back to LA to help find Trisha. He's had a soft spot for her ever since we moved in with him while we waited for our house to be rebuilt."

"Good idea," Jack agrees. "We can't have you actually being seen on the video making the hit, and Arnie is the best tech we have."

"Don't worry about anyone ID'ing me. I'll be hooded, masked, and catsuited, and they can angle the camera so that it's over my shoulder," I remind him. "Also, I'll be using blanks. In any event, you'll be wearing body armor, so only the real Milo will shed something that appears to be blood. Arnie can bring a couple of pints of the fake stuff with him."

"And if Abu can prop up and manipulate Milo during the 'hit,' I may not be needed for the video at all," Jack points out.

"Well, then, let's pray Abu is as good at puppetry arts as he is with makeup." I shrug.

Jack puts his arms around me. "In any case, you'll have my back."

Of course, I will.

A cool calm drifts over me.

"I'll put in a call to George while you get an update from Emma on Trisha's kidnappers." Jack grabs his phone.

I do the same. But my first call is to Aunt Phyllis.

AUNT PHYLLIS SNORTS. "WHAT DO YOU MEAN, TRISHA HAS BEEN kidnapped! She's on a camping trip with the Trents!"

"We've been contacted about it by the kidnappers—*who are the Trents!*" I'm trying to keep calm. "They sent a timed photo and *a demand.*"

"But...why would they do it?... Oh my God! They're grifters! They want her for—"

"Please, Phyllis! We've got to stay calm!"

"But I should have said no! I was the adult in charge. I

should have trusted my instincts instead of trying so hard to be the fun, cool aunt!"

"You mean, you felt something was off about Mrs. Trent?"

Phyllis sighs. "Well…yes."

"Like what?"

"For one thing, she tried to pawn off that stupid pie as homemade. She'd even warmed it up before bringing it over. But the crust was machine-made. As if I wouldn't have noticed! Heck, I've used that trick myself." Aunt Phyllis snorts indignantly. "I let her little white lie slide. It's the thought that counts, right? And I've been calling that woman's number—what's her name again? Oh yeah: Heidi! I've called it every few minutes since they left with Trisha, but the phone goes into some sort of mechanical voice mail."

"Why were you calling? What else tipped you off that they were shady?"

Aunt Phyllis sighs. "Don't get mad, but Trisha didn't pack her retainer, and I know you're a stickler about that sort of thing. So, my bad."

"You're right! You should have trusted your instincts," I mutter.

The second I say this, I regret it. Aunt Phyllis bursts into tears.

"Me? You're blaming *me*?" Aunt Phyllis sputters. "Listen here, Mommy Dearest—if you were home more often, maybe your self-proclaimed 'spidey sense' would have picked up on the fact that Heidi Trent is a con artist!" Aunt Phyllis's voice trembles as she shouts. "But *no*! You'd much rather gallivant around the world, doing who knows what!"

I slam down the phone. I'm too angry to talk further.

In truth, I'm angry at myself, because she's right. Mary almost got raped by an older boy while on a working vacation for Jack and me. I was chosen as the prom committee chair at Jeff's school. But because I was training my mission replacements, I was kowtowed into letting Hilldale's meanest mommy, Penelope Bing, choose the hotel where the prom was to be held. There, Jeff was held hostage by a terrorist.

Now Trisha's life is in danger.

Aunt Phyllis is right. I'm a crappy mom.

I allow myself a good cry before I pick up the phone and call Lee.

"Trisha...*kidnapped*?" Lee can't believe his ears. "Are you sure?"

"Yes! The Trents are working for Edmonton!" I explain. "He had them take Trisha as leverage for me to kill 'Milo.'"

"Oh...*Hell!*"

The next thing I know, Lee is barking on the intercom for Eve to find Porter and send him in.

When he comes back on the line, I add: "Trisha mentioned that Riley Trent dumped Janie for her. Do you know anything about that?"

"I know that Janie was distraught over it. She cried all last night. I was concerned when Porter divulged that things got competitive between Janie and Trisha. When that Trent kid proclaimed Janie her BFF, I tried to remind Janie how close she and Trisha had been their whole lives; how Trisha had been with her through thick and thin."

"I did the same," I assure him. "When Janie came into Trisha's school, I'd hoped that Trisha would be a big enough person to share Janie's friendship with others. Pretty much, she rose to the occasion."

"I totally agree," Lee replies. "Ever since she was a little girl, Janie saw how her—the whole family's—celebrity was a double-edged sword. Trisha was her compass, always nudging her in the right direction, toward the right friends and activities. They're like…well, sisters."

"Thank you for that, Lee." I hesitate, then add: "Now, knowing what we do about the Trents, Jack thinks their original endgame was to do to Janie what they've done to Trisha. Edmonton must want intel that he never got from you."

"You're right. But…it's a discussion to have on a different day." Lee sighs heavily. "I assume you and Jack have devised some sort of back-up plan to simulate an extermination without actually pulling the trigger."

"I may be pulling the trigger anyway," I mutter. "But not on Edmonton's desired target."

"I'll pretend I didn't hear that." He's not joking.

Neither am I.

"Such irony, considering that Milo is already dead," Lee muses.

"But what he holds over Edmonton is in Acme's hands," I remind him.

"All the more reason we need to assure Trisha's safety. Porter just walked in. Do you mind if I put us on speakerphone?"

"Go for it."

A moment later, Porter says, "Donna, I'm so sorry this has happened."

"Thank you for your concern, Porter. I assume you know where the Trents live?"

"On Camellia Court," he replies, "Number 946. The house is dead center at the end of the cul-de-sac."

I envision Hilldale. Camellia Court is at the back end of our gated community. Behind the Trents' home is a four-lane road leading to the expressway.

I pull it up on GPS and see that I'm right. I also notice that their driveway runs to a gate in their back fence, so that they can leave Hilldale without being caught on any of the community's webcams.

Damn it.

"Did you ever meet Mr. Trent?" I ask.

"Only the wife, Heidi. I was with Janie at all times, but usually, the girls went to a movie or met at the park. Neither she nor I went into their home."

My last question: "Anything out of the ordinary that sticks out?"

Porter takes a moment to think. Finally: "One thing, now that I think about it. Even before preschool, Janie was taught to say specific phrases in different languages. It was something Babette insisted on. She felt it was a show of respect to at least know how to say 'hello' in the native tongues of the various dignitaries who came to the White House."

I'm surprised. Diplomacy wasn't one of Babette's strengths. "Go on."

"Well, Janie was taught that the word 'hello' in Russian is *'privet.'* It is, but that's an informal greeting," Porter explains. "Riley corrected her with the formal word, which is *'Zdrastvuyte.'*"

That nails it.

"That's a big help, Porter. Thank you."

My next call is to Emma.

"Marcus and I just got off the phone with Jack!" she declares.

"I take it, he told you about Trisha?"

"Yes! I'm so sorry, Donna! If it had happened to my little guy..." Emma's voice trails off.

"Thank you." I'm trying hard not to tear up.

"But, of course, my dearest friend." Emma is choking on her words. "In fact, I've been researching Heidi and her husband, Bill Trent, but their backgrounds aren't all that deep."

"What do you mean?"

"As you already know, they moved into Hilldale within the past month. And to tell you the truth, Donna, there is not much on them prior to fifteen years ago. In Heidi's case, if her maiden name and SSI are any indication, she graduated from high school but never held a job in her life."

"Sounds like they stole their identities," I reason. "Conduct a nationwide search of her maiden name with birth certificates within a five-year window of her claimed age."

"Already on it," Emma responds. "As for Bill, he's listed as self-employed, so there's no employer to question about him."

"How does he make his living?"

"As a landscaper."

"Interesting." Emma is right. There won't be much intel to show there unless he aggressively promotes his client referrals. My guess is that he doesn't. "They live on Camellia Drive in Hilldale," I inform her. "The Hilldale police force archives a month's worth of traffic video footage. Hack into it to see if you can trace either Heidi or Bill's vehicles going in and out of the neighborhood over the past twenty-four hours. By the way, I've got the cell phone numbers they gave the school. But they may be using burners now."

"It's still worth putting traces on all the Trents' phones, including Riley's number. I've got a pen to write it down, so shoot."

I read her the cell phone numbers. "Emma, if you find anything at all, be sure to relay it to both Jack and me."

"Will do. Oh, and by the way, Arnie hacked into Edmonton's secure cloud! We were able to erase evidence of his relationship with you."

"That's not exactly what I'd call it, but thank him for me," I mutter.

"I will. Really, though, you can thank Mad Hacker. She always inspires him to up his game. I guess that's one upside to his adoring a woman other than me—and you."

"You're just saying that to raise my spirits."

"No, it's true. How can I blame him? I do too." Emma jumps off the call.

I'm glad she wasn't here to see me blush at her compliments.

Now the only thing left to do is wait for news.

And to hear that my baby has survived this ordeal.

I drop to my knees and say a prayer.

FOR THE PAST HOUR, I'VE BEEN PACING THROUGH MY APARTMENT while Jack and Abu work out the logistics on Milo's rendezvous with Edmonton.

When they're ready, they call me over to Abu's side of the closet to see if I can punch holes in the plan.

It won't be as satisfying as punching a hole in Edmonton's face. Still, I welcome the distraction.

"There are three scenarios," Abu explains. "We've prepared for each of them."

I nod. "Go on."

"'Milo' will instruct Edmonton to come alone. He'll inform POTUS he already has a written copy of his pardon for Edmonton's signature. It'll be the only way Edmonton will learn where his money is now parked."

I nod.

"The most ideal scenario is that Edmonton pulls a no-show because he's got you doing his dirty work," Jack admits. "In that case, he'll want proof of the kill. If he asks for it, we take it from your Acme lenses, so that you're never seen on video. You can haul the real Milo into the furnace so that you can record the cremation."

Abu rolls out a schematic of the warehouse. "I'll install enough cameras to cover every angle of the warehouse." He points to possible locations. "Arnie will be situated in this empty building next door, monitoring the action, both inside the warehouse and outside, within a ten-block radius. Jack, as Milo, will be waiting inside, in front of the furnace."

He points to a six-feet by six-foot-square steel box centered on the far side of the first floor.

A long rectangle is drawn in front of it. I assume it's the assembly belt that drops the clay pots into the furnace.

"Next to the furnace is an exit door." Abu points to it. "I'll leave it unlocked. That way, you can enter and shoot Milo in the back. Jack will hear the 'shot'—which, in fact, is just an ammo blank—and fall forward onto the assembly belt. We'll alter the video so that the real Milo can be substituted before the point where you walk up to take a picture of him. While you're doing this, Jack takes off. Final step: You shove Milo onto the conveyor belt, start the furnace, and the body is gone."

"Got it," I reply. "But, what happens if Edmonton wants to be there for the kill?"

"That's a definite possibility," Jack replies. "Let's not forget, Edmonton is a spy, first and foremost. The scuttlebutt in the IC is that he regularly shakes his Secret Service detail when visiting one of his regular mistresses. Apparently, the full-block building in which her penthouse is located has garage exits on all four streets. Edmonton puts on a disguise, takes a car he keeps there, and off he goes."

"I'll bet he does it anytime he wants to meet with one of the handlers Putin has assigned to him," Abu retorts.

"If it's that easy for him to do, he may come for the sole purpose that he'll get his jollies watching Milo's assassination," I add.

"If so, we'll need to alter the sting. Which brings us to Scenario Number Two," Abu replies. "Again, Donna you'll shoot Jack from the back. When Jack hears the sound, he'll pop a fake blood balloon via remote. Then, Donna, you'll lug him into the furnace, which has a large ash door. Jack will crawl out of it. As for the real Milo, he will have already been placed inside the furnace when Donna turns it on."

"Which brings us to Scenario Three," Jack says. "There is always the possibility that Edmonton will have a small army trailing him."

Abu points to a building next to the warehouse. "Remember, Arnie and I will also be monitoring and controlling security cameras within a ten-block radius of the warehouse. If Edmonton brings an entourage, Henry and a few other Acme assets will create detours to separate them from Edmonton's vehicle."

"What if he shows up with his driver and a couple of Secret Service agents?"

"Last spring, Acme's lab came up with a new trick that might help. We used it when we were trying to oust a Mexican drug lord from his safe house." Out of his pocket, Abu pulls out something the size of a gumball.

I stare at it, aghast. "Is it a bomb?"

"No, a sleeping gas pellet. After Edmonton drives up and parks, 'Milo' will call and remind him that he's got eyes and ears on him. If POTUS doesn't get out of the car alone, the meeting won't happen. However, the moment he leaves the vehicle, I'll detonate it remotely through the tailpipe, via drone. Immediately, Edmonton's security detail will curl up and snore like babies for a few hours."

Jack nods, impressed. "And then we pull Scenario Two!"

"Exactly." Abu pats my hand. "Donna, I know you're worried about the little one. But you've also got a big night in front of you. Try to take a nap. If Emma calls with any news—good or bad—I'll wake you. I promise."

Good or bad.

I nod.

When the door closes after him, Jack looks down at me. "Now, tell me about Trisha."

"THIS HAPPENED TO TRISHA BECAUSE OF ME." MY VOICE IS barely a whisper.

"Don't blame yourself," Jack insists.

"Who else can I blame? Aunt Phyllis? She's...just living her life! Which is continually interrupted by mine!"

"She loves you like a daughter!" Jack counters.

"I know that! She's always been there for me—since my own mother died!" My words stick in my throat. "And since Carl pretended to be dead! She's always put her life on hold—for me! I was the one whose mother hid her cancer and then died on us, not her! I was the one with the alcoholic father, not Phyllis! I was the one who married a son-of-a-bitch narcissist killer, not her! I was the one who had three children—again, not her! I'm the one who thinks I can save the world, but Phyllis is the one who has spent her life keeping my world together! And yet, I dared to blame her for not being vigilant on

Trisha's behalf?" I fall down on the bed. "It's my fault, not hers!"

"It's no one's fault, Donna! We were just...we're doing our jobs."

"Our main job is being Mary, Jeff, and Trisha's parents," I retort. "You signed on for that too. Remember?"

"Yes—I remember!" Jack scowls. "Look, I'm just as upset at this turn of events as you are. But that doesn't bring us any closer to finding Trisha. Completing this mission will, however. Try to hold it together, okay? *For all of us.*"

When Trisha was three, she admitted that, before she fell asleep each night, she'd say out loud the things she didn't want to dream about. Doing this, she believed, would keep them from popping up later as nightmares.

So, now I must voice my biggest fear: "Jack...what if she dies?"

In a flash, he is beside me. Jack holds me close. His touch revitalizes the hope extinguished by my fear for our child's safety. It strengthens my resolve.

We stay like that until his cell buzzes, bringing us back to the real world.

Jack stares down at his phone. "It's Emma." He puts it on speakerphone. "I'm here with Donna."

"Perfect," she replies. "I've got some encouraging news. By looking at the Hilldale security cameras, we were able to pinpoint the time at which the Trents left their home this morning. Trisha was with them."

My heart pounds hard in my chest. "Where did they go?"

"We tracked them going south on CA-1, but...unfortunately, we lost them at the 107 junction. They pulled into the Ikea store's multi-story parking lot. We assume they had a second car parked there for that very purpose. At that point, they could have either gone north again, through Torrance, via the four-oh-five. Or they could have continued south on CA-1 and ended up going east."

In other words, we've reached a dead end.

"We're pulling footage from the Ikea security feeds to see where they parked, and what car they may have taken instead," Emma assures us. "Boss Man, unless you've got something else for me, I think I'll get back to testing the hearing device on the new Milo mask coming your way."

"Do your thing," Jack insists.

Now, all we can do is wait until the plane gets back here with Arnie, Milo, and the mask.

At Jack's behest, I take a nap.

As I fall asleep, I feel his body curling around mine.

"Wake up, sleeping beauties." Abu nudges us awake.

I open my eyes to find it's dark outside.

I sit straight up. Beside me, Jack does the same.

Arnie stands beside him. He glances around the room, then gives us a thumbs-up. "Classy digs you've got here, Craigs."

"Where's Milo?" I ask.

"Thawing out in Dominic's old bedroom," Abu replies. "One good stiff deserves another." He raises his lips into a tepid smile.

I've sorely missed his wry sense of humor.

Arnie flops down on the bed beside us. "Craigs, you'll want to hear this."

Is it bad news—about Trisha?

Jack must be thinking this too because he growls, "Don't leave us in suspense."

"Mad Hacker did it!" Arnie exclaimed.

"She got into Edmonton's bank account?" I practically fall out of the bed. "How much was in there?"

"I'm glad you're sitting down because it will knock you off your feet. Pretend you hear a drum roll." Arnie takes a deep breath: *"Three billion dollars was recently deposited!"*

The thought is dizzying. I whistle long and low.

"Can you tell who made the deposit?" Jack asks.

"Marcus' sources have identified it as an account controlled by Putin that *wasn't* published in the Panama Papers," Arnie explains.

"Meaning the transfer Edmonton received came from Putin's personal stash," I reason. "What could Edmonton have given Putin that he felt was worth that much money?"

"Great question," Jack replies. "My guess: something he feels will bring our country to its knees, so we better find out —and quickly."

"By the way, per Emma's instruction, Mad Hacker moved it into a new Acme account—minus her commission, of course," Arnie adds. "It was a pittance, considering the amount now in Acme's coffers."

"Do we get to hold onto it?" Abu asks.

"I'm sure Acme will take a very generous finder's fee," Jack assures me. "I'll let the Three Amigos decide its highest and best use."

"So, what's next?" I ask.

Abu nods toward Arnie and then Jack. "Now that Joker has landed, it's time to suit up, Batman."

Jack shrugs himself awake. "Let's get this show on the road."

23

Full Powers

"F*ull* P*owers*" *is a term used in international law to describe the authority of a person to sign a treaty or convention on behalf of a sovereign state.*

Before signing, diplomats who themselves are not the head of state, head of government, or foreign minister of the state are obligated to show what is known as a "full-powers document."

During your next negotiation, remember this: you don't need no stinkin' piece of paper to represent your own best interests.

All you need are nerves of steel.

Just stand your ground and you'll get what you want on your terms.

O*nce again*, J*ack is* M*ilo*.

His goodbye kiss comes with too many regrets.

I regret that, thanks to my confirming Edmonton's suspicion that Jack killed Elle, we are in this mess.

And I regret that Jack now has to put his life on the line to get us out of it.

And I regret that his life is in my hands. Should I fail, I'll have no one to blame but myself.

I also regret that we fell asleep instead of making love. Who knows? Should something go wrong, it may have been our last chance.

~

JACK RINGS ME FROM THE WAREHOUSE.

I listen in as 'Milo,' with the voice alteration app turned on, makes an untraceable call to Edmonton.

He tells POTUS that he's drained his bank account. But never fear! He's got an offer Edmonton can't refuse: he'll release the funds for a letter giving him a full pardon.

"You are to hand it off to me, personally. And, by the way, I'll be keeping a billion for myself," 'Milo' informs him. "For all my time and effort. If you don't come alone, intel on your double-dealings with Putin will be released to every major news organization in the country. The same goes if you're a no-show."

"Where...and...when?" Anger seethes from each of Edmonton's syllables.

"Right now. So, hop over to your mistress's place and grab that car you use for joyriding. *But come alone.* And remember: I'm watching your every move."

"Milo" reads him the meeting location and then hangs up.

Now it's up to me to make "Milo's" death look real and save our daughter.

~

Ten minutes later, Jack calls back. "Edmonton is on his way to his mistress's place. Abu and Henry are conducting continual visual surveillance of the area surrounding the factory. As of yet, they haven't identified any shadow surveillance teams. At the same time, Arnie has looped all local CCTV with dead air. Leave as soon as you can."

I put blanks in the Sig Sauer before slipping it into my appendix holster. Then I tuck a small serrated knife, sheathed, into a hidden pocket. After slipping on my coat, I pocket my pullover mask along with my gloves. Just as I grab my key fob—

The doorbell rings. That should be Poppy with the address provided by Edmonton's courier.

But when I look out the peephole, I see Mario.

What the hell is he doing here?

Cautiously, I open the door but I leave the security bar in place. "Haven't you heard? I've quit the Administration."

Mario shrugs. "I'm spitballing when I say it wasn't a great fit. Am I right?"

I smile despite my anxiety of finding him on my doorstep.

"POTUS is to meet Milo—now, in fact." Mario hands me a small sheet of paper. "I'm to take you there."

Nonchalantly, I shrug. "Oh... Okay."

Shit! Shit! Shit!

Mario is here to escort me to my own execution, which undoubtedly will take place the moment after "Milo" is put out of his misery.

We shall see about that.

～

249

MARIO AND I DON'T SPEAK AS HE DRIVES US TO THE DESIGNATED location. My mind is racing as I devise ways to rid myself of him in order to save my husband's life.

Since the gun shoots blanks, it's useless. I'm sure he'll stand close enough that I can cut his throat. But, hey, that'll tip off Edmonton that something is very, very wrong.

If it comes to that, I'll deal with it then.

I now have no doubt at all that Edmonton is probably armed and may attempt to kill 'Milo' himself, and me too.

At least I know Abu and Arnie will see us enter together, and they'll warn Jack.

Finally, Mario pulls up a block from the factory. "POTUS is still a few minutes away. He'll wait until we're positioned before going inside."

"But the target is already here, right?" I ask.

"Yes. At least, he says he is."

Time to play dumb. "Other than the fact he's a complete sadist, why would Edmonton show up at a hit?"

Mario shrugs. "He's got to, or else the target won't give him something he wants." He holds out his hand. "Let me see your gun."

My heart drops into my gut. "Why?"

"Just hand it over, Donna." His steely tone means business.

Reluctantly, I release it from its holster.

He grabs the gun from me. It takes only a quick moment for him to eject the mag and replace it with another.

I'll be killing Jack.

He nods at the door. "Shall we go inside and set up?"

≈

MARIO AGREES WITH ME THAT USING THE FRONT DOOR WOULD BE what Milo expects. I take my time, checking the building's other doors and windows. As Abu promised, they are locked.

Eventually, we come upon the back door that Abu left open for me. It opens silently.

Mario is so close behind me that I feel his breath on my neck.

We inch our way onto the factory floor.

As we'd discussed, "Milo" is positioned beside the assembly belt in front of the furnace. He stares straight ahead, at the front door—

In time to see Edmonton walking through it.

EDMONTON AND JACK ARE TALKING AND I SHOULD BE LISTENING but I can't because my mind is moving furiously through all the scenarios that could go so wrong in the next few seconds.

I'll shoot Mario first, then do the same to Edmonton. It's the worst-case scenario, but at least Jack and I can run.

But who knows how far we'll get? There's the rub.

Edmonton looks around, nervously—

Waiting for me to make my move.

"Take the damn shot," Mario hisses.

I can't...

I won't.

I swing the gun around in Mario's direction—

But he's close enough to yank my arm and swings it back behind me, to the breaking point—

And snatches the gun out of my hand.

Before I can move, he's got me in a choke hold. His shooting hand is free to take the shot—which he does.

Jack falls forward.

A river of blood seeps out from the hole in the back of his jacket.

I break away from Mario and run to him.

"WELL PLAYED, MRS. CRAIG." EDMONTON CLAPS AS IF HE'S SEEN the finale of a great piece of theater.

If only that were the case.

"Clean up this mess," he snarls. "Then we'll finish our transaction involving your daughter and your husband." Edmonton smirks as he stares down at "Milo."

My Jack.

Fuck you.

I break away from Mario—but just far enough away to hit him with a snap kick to his solar plexus. When he drops the gun, I grab it and point it at Edmonton. I finger the trigger—

But stop, awed, when Jack rises from the floor.

Edmonton follows my gaze.

His eyes bulge as "Milo" stands before him. Edmonton takes a step backward—

But then he stops suddenly—

And falls forward.

When his head hits the concrete, an arc of blood sprays the floor beyond him. Much more blood seeps out around his head.

I drop to his side and turn him over.

Edmonton's eyes are open in a glazed stare.

I feel for a pulse, but there isn't one.

His lips have puckered into a smirk as if mocking death.

I look at Jack. "He's dead! I guess he thought you were a ghost!"

Still on the floor, Mario groans, "But you're not because I put blanks in your gun. *You're welcome.*"

"DONNA'S GUN ALREADY HAD BLANKS," JACK RETORTS.

Hearing this, Mario laughs through his pain.

"No...because took out my mag and replaced it with another," I explain. "So, yeah, apparently the one he loaded into my gun had blanks too."

As Jack rips off his mask, Mario laughs even harder. "This just keeps getting better," he sputters.

Not amused, Jack jerks him to his feet and puts him into a choke hold. "Shut up and start talking sense."

"Sure, okay. Let me start by saying, Mrs. Craig, that I also let Edmonton assume I'd cleaned up the mess he made from your supposed death," Mario bows in my direction. "For that matter, thanks for saving me the trouble." He ventures a grin. "By the way, when you showed up in his office, you gave Edmonton quite a jolt. His doctor has been hiding the fact of his heart condition for years. You almost killed him right then and there." Mario shrugs. "I wish you had. It would have saved everyone a lot of time and trouble."

"By 'everyone,' who exactly do you mean?" I ask.

"The whole intelligence community," Mario retorts.

Jack stares hard at Mario. "You're working *for us*?"

"Yes and no. I'm working *with* you, but under the orders and auspices of the Director of National Intelligence, and with the blessing of all four leaders of the Intelligence Committees and the current DNI. The past one knew, too, by the way."

Jack and I stare at each other, then back to him. "Ryan and Marcus knew this all along?"

"Yes. In fact, Marcus's very last order as DNI was to assign me as Donna's shadow. And although he's no longer a government employee, for obvious reasons he was not at liberty to divulge his knowledge of any government-sanctioned operation, including this one."

"Marcus is confirming this." Abu's voice echoes through the factory from its overhead speakers.

"And when Ryan hinted he had me shadowed, he meant you," I murmur.

"Aren't you glad it wasn't Mildred?"

I shrug. So, he knows about that too.

"I was the one who planted the bug on Mildred's keepsake to Edmonton. She was getting suspicious of me, so I felt it was a good use of one of Edmonton's tasks for you—taking out yet another Russian mole."

"Smart move." I clap slowly.

"Thank you. I return the compliment by saying you make a very cute mermaid." He grins when I blush.

"How long have the Powers That Be known about Edmonton's illicit actions?" I mutter.

"Some while now. I mean, let's face it: since the day Edmonton took office, he's been decimating years of US intelligence work—first as a senator, and then with his influence as Veep. Despite what the IC suspected, after President Chiffray stepped down and Edmonton became POTUS, there was nothing it could do—until Acme back-channeled evidence to Marcus that Edmonton was a Russian mole known to his handlers as 'Scorpio.'" Mario bows to us. "It's thanks to your success with the Horoscope mission that the Director of National Intelligence, Marcus, was given the clearance to, as the Congressional intelligence committees delicately put it, 'clear POTUS, or bring evidence to the contrary.'"

"And as Edmonton's Chief of Staff, you've been collecting evidence from the inside!" I exclaim.

Mario nods. "Including a video of Edmonton threatening you with Jack's arrest for Edmonton's sanctioned hit on Congresswoman Elle Grisham."

I turn white. "So...you also have evidence of the other tasks I agreed to do to clear Jack's record."

"Frankly, no. For some reason, there are gaps in those recordings, so you lucked out—including his request that you terminate Mildred for her disloyalty." His smile comes with a subtle wink.

"When you came to my apartment to tell Edmonton that Jamison had left Russia's file on Edmonton in the wallet after all, was that true?" I ask.

Mario shakes his head. "Jamison took it with him. But once he handed it over to Acme to be back-channeled to the Congressional committee chairs and entered it into evidence, a duplicate was created, which I quote-unquote conveniently found in the wallet. By the way, at Ryan's behest, I also let it slip to Edmonton I'd overheard that Central Security Service had created a new SigInt codebook, which Mankoff had removed from the Pentagon for safekeeping, now that there was a suspected mole in the White House."

"When you ratcheted up the pressure on Edmonton, he did the same to me," I mutter.

Mario grimaces. "Donna, I'm so sorry it couldn't have happened more quickly to spare you from Edmonton's beating."

"Something tells me Jamison's disappearance was reason enough for that sadistic bastard."

"And for the record, I didn't delete Edmonton's request to exterminate Director Clancy," Mario adds. "Because he was Edmonton's appointment, the Intelligence Committee chairs were reluctant to tell him about the investigation into Edmonton. But when Edmonton ordered you to take him out, the Committees had what they needed to clear Ryan." Mario chuckles. "I informed Ryan of this when he attempted to turn in his resignation. I insisted that he hold off. As we can all agree, Edmonton's paranoia was a blessing in disguise."

"Not for my sex surrogate," I mutter.

Mario's smile fades. "No. Sadly, not for her. Trust me, Khrystyna Vashchenko's role in this operation will not be forgotten. For several years she was a tremendous asset for the CIA."

"Mario, why did you show up at Davos?" I ask.

"Edmonton trusted me enough to send me to witness Milo's brush pass to Volkov. And, frankly, it dovetailed with my mission in shadowing you."

Of course, Marcus would have let him know I was there, and for what purpose.

"But you had Coquette Rambert's room key," Jack points out. "Did you kill her? And if so, why?"

Angrily, Mario shakes his head. "Hell, no! Our friendship goes back...well, several years."

"You were lovers," I murmur.

His eyes deepen with pain. "Yes, a long time ago. Seeing her there...I had to say something to her."

Coquette's words come back to me:

"There is only one happiness in life: to love and be loved...It is as rare as life is fleeting—especially for those who must lie and kill for their country..."

I touch his shoulder. "I know she was happy you did."

Nodding stoically, he mutters, "I may have blown her cover."

"Do you think Volkov had her murdered?"

Mario shrugs helplessly. "I speak Russian. When he was looking her way, he used the word '*grokhnut*' with one of his goons."

"'Assassinate,'" Jack acknowledges. "I remember she couldn't wait to get out of there. But then, when I saw her talking to you, suddenly her whole demeanor changed."

"It's why I had her hotel room key," Mario explains. "She said she had to take care of something and asked me to meet her there."

"But she never showed up." I shiver as the memory of her body floating lifeless in the mermaid tank comes to me.

"Later that night, I found out why. I should have never left her side." Mario hangs his head. When he raises his head, it is to vow: "I'll get her killer."

"If there's any way we can help, let us know," I promise.

Mario's smile is both sweet and bitter. "I may take you up on that." He stares around the factory. "Everyone involved will be relieved that Edmonton died of natural causes. Acme's video of Edmonton's heart attack would go a long way towards clearing you, and me, of any suspicions around his death."

"I would hope so!" I exclaim. Then I laugh. And laugh, until I hurt.

And then I remember my baby, Trisha, and I'm crying again.

24

Exfiltration

In espionage terms, an "exfiltration" is a clandestine rescue operation designed to get an operative, asset, defector, or refugee out of harm's way.

You conduct exfiltrations all the time! Like, when your child is in danger of being bullied or taunted, you swoop in to stop those who wish to harm him.

(You are right to keep doing so, despite your child's insistence that he fight his own battles or else he'll be viewed as a sissy.)

Another example: When your spouse is cornered by the neighborhood slut at a party, you will untangle him from her grasp with the excuse that he's needed for some chore that requires him to wear an apron.

(Again: Keep doing so, no matter how many times he insists that wearing one emasculates him. Pointing out that it will cover up his hard-on should shut him up about it once and for all.)

"Donna, it's just past eleven at night on the West Coast. I understand your wanting to call Mary and Jeff, just to hear their voices. But remember: they don't yet know about Trisha's predicament," Jack warns me. "If you mention it, you'll only make them upset too. Even if you don't and start crying, they'll worry about you."

"We've just now cleared DC air space! We won't be there for another six hours! I know I'm sounding irrational, but I need to hear their voices." I take his hand in mine. "I'll keep my cool. I promise!"

Jack purses his lips. "Go ahead, then. And please pass them over to me too."

He also misses them terribly.

Mary picks up quickly. "Oh! Thank God you called!"

Oh no—does she know about her sister?

"What is it, honey?" I hope I'm keeping any dread out of my voice.

"It's Aunt Phyllis. Mom, I think she's finally lost it! I can tell she's been crying all day. When Penelope Bing came down on her because she forgot to pick up Jeff, Cheever, and Morton from their basketball game, she almost clocked her! Mrs. Bing is threatening to have her arrested for assault and battery."

"Aunt Phyllis hit her?" Suddenly, I feel guilty. Not for Penelope but for making Phyllis upset.

"No, not really." Mary sighs. "She backed Mrs. Bing against a wall, at which point Mrs. Bing chipped a nail."

"That's not assault or battery. It's just a bad gel job," I mutter. "Listen Mary, after I talk to you and your brother, please ask Aunt Phyllis if she'll come to the phone and speak to me too."

"I will, promise. On another note, I got accepted to UCLA, so I have my safety school."

"Congratulations, honey!" I'm doing my best to hold back my tears. Suddenly, it hits me that in seven years' time, I'll be having this same conversation with Trisha...

If she gets out of her ordeal alive.

Even if she does, it may take years for her to get over the emotional trauma of a kidnapping.

We have to find her.

I pray to God she's alive...

"— so sad about President Edmonton!" Mary is saying.

"Yeah, well, life happens." Or doesn't, in his case.

May he rest in Hell...

"—US Diplomatic Services. I've always had an interest in international relations, and my French is superb, although I could do better with Spanish. Berkeley has a great Russian program—"

"Wait... What did you just say '*Diplomatic Service*'?"

Oh no...

They'll want to recruit her as a spy.

"Yes! Wouldn't it be a great way to see the world? I'm not counting my chickens to get into Berkeley, although Mario says that it's a fast track into the Diplomatic Service. But he also says I should consider Middlebury in Monterey Bay—"

"Mario...*Martinez?*"

I can't believe it. He's recruiting my daughter!

Why, that son of a bitch...

"He was so kind while touring us through the White House. He was really impressed with my French literacy."

I'll bet he was.

"Although President Edmonton died, I know Mario will follow through on his boss's promise to be a good reference for an internship there—"

"Honey, I understand your desire to travel, to gain new experiences. But International Studies is so...*vague!* You'd be better off with a Business major. You know, like Finance. It's a better paycheck and you can be based in any country you want—"

"I'll take it under advisement." Whenever Mary uses that phrase, it means she's tuned me out.

I can't wait to tell Jack what our new friend has been up to...

"Mom, Jeff is dying to talk to you."

"Sure, put him on. I love you."

"I love you too, Mom—always and forever." Any dismissiveness in Mary's tone is replaced with loving sincerity.

I swallow hard to rid myself of the lump forming in my throat.

And just in time since the first sentence out of Jeff's mouth demands an immediate and unequivocal response: "Mom! Is it true? Are you coming home for good?"

"Yes...but how did you know?"

"Aunt Phyllis. She says you missed us too much."

"She's right," I readily admit. "Hey, did you win your game?"

"Hell yeah! I was the highest scorer too!"

"*Language*, kiddo!"

"Sorry, Mom. Hey, can Dad take me to the game tomorrow? It's not that I mind Aunt Phyllis going too, but with her driving—well, hell!—I mean, *heck*—I'll be green around the gills before I even get there!"

"We both will." My tone says it all: *don't fight me on this.*

Although, none of us will be going if the worst has happened to Trisha.

The family will be in mourning for the rest of our lives...

Please, God! Keep my baby safe, so that I may hold her in my arms again...

"Okay, I hear you loud and clear," Jeff mutters. "To tell you the truth, I think Cheever's theory is all bunk anyway.

Frankly, it's Trisha and her friends who are the biggest distraction. Thank goodness they won't be around for tomorrow's game. Janie is annoying, but that Riley girl downright gives me the creeps!"

I bite my lip to keep from telling him why he may regret what he just said…

But then it dawns on me that he has reasons of his own to hate Riley.

"Why would it matter if she showed up?" I try to sound nonchalant, but I don't think I'm succeeding.

"Our game is against the Palos Verdes team. It used to be the school Riley went to, when they lived with her grandmother."

Palos Verdes is just off CA-107 where CA-1 cuts in.

I've got to call Emma now, and tell her…

"Can I speak to Dad now?" Jeff begs me. "I want to tell him about my score."

"Of course! I love you, my sweet son."

"Ditto, Mama." The casualness with which Jeff accepts my love is not taken for granted. Be it for the next hour or a lifetime, I will maintain some sense of normalcy for him.

He's already been through hell and back. I can't have him worry over Trisha's plight. Not yet, if ever.

I motion Jack over to take the phone.

My next call is to Emma.

"YOUR TIMING COULDN'T BE BETTER!" EMMA EXCLAIMS. "JACK was right. The Trents changed vehicles inside the Ikea garage. But the store's lousy video feed makes it hard for us to see which car they drove out—"

"Follow cars headed for Palos Verdes," I declare.

Emma guffaws. "Sure! But...why?"

"Riley mentioned to Jeff that she had a grandmother with a house there. See if you can pick up any pings off any towers between Hilldale and Palos Verdes."

"Got it! At the same time, we'll cross-reference anyone living in Palos Verdes named Trent or using Heidi's supposed maiden name—Josephson. We'll also track any cars by satellite that left Ikea within an hour after the Trents pulled into the garage that took any of the roads into Palos Verdes. I'll call back as soon as we've identified a vehicle and have tracked it to its final location."

"Thank you, Emma."

THE HOURS CRAWL BY.

It's only when we're two hours from landing in LGB—Long Beach International Airport—that we hear from Emma: "The house sits on a cliff overlooking the ocean. Dominic's team is ready to go in. Through their earbuds and video lenses, we'll have eyes and ears on the operation. Craigs, I assume you want to see the live feed?"

"Yes!" Jack and I shout in unison.

HERE'S HOW THE OPERATION GOES DOWN:

The sun is just now peeking up over the horizon.

From different entrances leading into the posh community known as Palos Verdes, three Acme vehicles slowly roll up onto a street of grand stuccos with nice big back yards and incomparable ocean views.

Two of the cars park a block or two away from the target's

property. These Acme operatives are paired in twos: a male and a female who look like couples out for a stroll. But from the bulk beneath their jackets, I imagine they are wearing ballistic gear.

One couple takes a public path to the cliff. They leap over a neighbor's fence next to the targets' house.

The other couple breaks apart as they reach the targets' home. They split up, each taking a side of the house, positioning themselves to cover anyone who may jump out a side door or window.

Dominic pulls up in a postal delivery van. He's dressed the part, navy shorts and all. Three boxes are stacked in his hands. Knowing Acme, the boxes hide the fact that his hand is positioned on a gun that will kill whomever answers the door.

He rings the bell.

No response.

Then again.

Still, nothing.

And again.

Nothing.

We see Dominic mutter some command. At the same time, the two operatives crouching low at the back door kick it open and go into the house in perfectly stacked SWAT formation.

Dominic, still holding the boxes, does the same through the front door.

Their lenses show them going room by room.

No one.

Anywhere.

Except in a small back bedroom.

A body is on the floor.

A blanket has been tossed over it.

265

Stealthily, Dominic approaches it. He pulls the blanket away.

It is Trisha.

Her eyes are closed. She looks...

At peace.

Is she dead?

Dominic checks for a pulse.

Stroking her hair lovingly, he cradles her in his arms before lifting her up.

Oh no. No, please, God! Not my baby...

He gives us a thumbs up, exclaiming. "She fine, but she's been drugged."

Jack and I collapse in each other's arms.

NINETY MINUTES LATER, WE TOUCH DOWN ON LGB'S TARMAC.

Dominic is waiting in the van he used for Trisha's exfiltration. Jack, Arnie, and Abu climb in with their gear.

But before I follow suit, I hug Dominic for so long that he mutters, "Mustn't allow yer ol' man to reconsider those rumors about us that have been floating about all these years."

I pull back and raise a brow. "Oh? What rumors are those?"

"That you sneak over to my place every now and again for a right proper snog—"

"Dominic Fleming, you are as mad as a bag of ferrets!" Miffed, I throw up my hands—

But then I give him a full-mouth kiss.

My surprise tactic has the desired effect. Dominic's blush has crept down his cheeks and under his collar.

He now realizes what he's been missing out on all these years.

As I climb into the van, no one dares look me in the eye.

Except for Jack. He gives me an appreciative hug. "I'd kiss him myself, but he might read too much into it."

"Understandable. You are irresistible." To prove it, I lean in and kiss him too.

∾

ON THE DRIVE HOME, DOMINIC FILLS US IN ON THE FOLLOW-UP after the exfiltration.

"The Trents cleaned out the place," he explains. "We couldn't lift nary a print."

"I take it Trisha didn't wake up on the way home?" I ask.

Dominic nods. "Donna, I wouldn't be at all surprised if they'd kept her drugged since the moment she got into the car."

"In a way, that would be a smart play. An eleven-year-old is old enough to get suspicious. It's the easiest way to keep someone that age quiet."

Dominic sighs. "Perhaps when she wakes up, it will all seem like a faraway dream."

That is my hope as well.

As we pull into Hilldale, Dominic says, "Today, though, we'll send some operatives back there to do reconnaissance through the neighbors. You can't live in a community for that long and fool everyone you meet. Someone must have had their suspicions."

I think of my first five years with Acme. My neighbors may have felt superior to a woman raising three children while her road warrior husband traipsed around the world in search of new clients with deep pockets. But as long as I kept the yard mowed, the flowerbeds neat, and followed our planned community's homeowner's manual to the letter, no one paid much attention to me.

Should the Trents' neighbors ever discover their real identities, tongues will wag for years to come.

~

ONLY AUNT PHYLLIS IS AWAKE WHEN WE PULL INTO THE driveway.

She runs out the front door and wraps us in a hug and holds on for dear life. "I…I'm so sorry!" she whispers into my ear. "Will you ever forgive me?"

I wipe a fallen tear from her cheek. "I'm sorry too. I was wrong to blame you for something you could never have imagined would happen."

"And, frankly, Donna and I didn't see this coming either," Jack adds.

"I hope you don't mind that I cried on Porter's shoulder about it." Phyllis blushes.

"Not at all," I reply. "I hope you didn't make me out to be the worst niece ever."

"No!… Well, maybe a little." Phyllis shrugs. "But when he told me all the sick stuff people have tried to do to get close to Janie—and for all the wrong reasons—it made me realize I'm just a babe in the woods about…well, about what kind of evil people are out there. So, thank you for all you've done so that the rest of us can stay oblivious to all the dangers we face."

It's great to be appreciated.

Reluctantly, Aunt Phyllis releases us so that we can run upstairs and check on Trisha.

~

Trisha lies in bed, but her eyes are open.

As Jack and I throw our arms around her, we realize she is still in a stupor.

"Why are you home?" Her drug-fogged whisper can barely be heard. Trisha tries to focus her eyes as she glances around the room. "Why…why am I here?"

"What do you remember?" Jack asks.

"We…Riley and her family and me…we were going camping. But on the drive, I got dizzy…and sick, and… sleepy." She sighs. "Did they call you to pick me up?"

"Do you want to sleep some more?" I ask.

Impatiently, Trisha shakes her head. "I'm feeling better now. I want to talk to Janie."

"It's just seven now. She may still be asleep," I remind her.

"Oh… Well, maybe I'll text her to call me when she wakes up."

"Great idea," I reply.

"Dad, Mom…may I invite her to come with me to Jeff's tournament game?"

Jack nods. "If it's fine with her father, it's fine with us."

"Thanks! I…I need to do something nice to make up for being such a jerk when Riley dumped her for me." Shamed, Trisha bows her head. "What a stupid thing to do—for so many reasons!"

"What do you mean?" Jack asks.

"Janie is my closest friend since…well, since forever! And Riley can be cruel for no reason at all."

I shake my head. "Trisha, sweetie, then why did you allow her to play those head games?"

"Believe me, Mom—there were times Janie and I wanted to just tell her to jump in a lake…or something worse." Trisha blushes. "But then, she'd say something so sweet to us, and we'd forgive her." She shrugs. "When she chose Janie first and then made her drop me, I was really hurt. But then, when she dropped Janie for me, I felt special again. And I wanted Janie to feel like an outsider, for once in her life."

"She pitted you against each other," I point out.

Trisha nods. "I realize that now. Even before, maybe. I almost backed out of going on the camping trip. I knew how much it would hurt Janie, because I could hear them talking about it in class before they broke up. But when I tried to cancel on Riley, she started to cry. She said her parents would think she made a mess of their lives here. I felt sorry for her, so I said I'd go."

"I wish you hadn't," I murmur.

"Me too!" Trisha rolls her eyes. "From the moment I got in the car with her and her parents, I could tell she was cross with them. But when I asked her why, she screamed at me to shut up. That hurt my feelings."

"Did her parents say anything?" Jack asks.

"They tried to laugh it off! That upset me too."

"Trisha, you said you felt carsick and fell asleep. Did the Trents stop somewhere to get food, or something to drink?" I ask.

Trisha shakes her head. "No...but we had snacks in the car. Trail mix, granola bars, flavored water." She shrugged. "Come to think of it, I'm starving!"

"When you're ready, come down and I'll make you anything you want for breakfast," I promise.

Trisha kisses my cheek. "So happy to have you home." Faking a pout, she adds, "Now, stay here for a while."

"Cross my heart," I vow.

Trisha waves me away as she reaches for her phone to text Janie.

270

25

Final Act

IN DIPLOMATIC CIRCLES, THE "FINAL ACT" IS A FORMAL SUMMARY statement drawn up after a conference or a negotiation.

In your life, there is no need for a written summary, a "Final Act." The proof is found in your happiness for the success of your children, in your beautiful home, and through your most memorable experiences.

Your final act is a life well-lived.

WHILE I'VE BEEN AWAY, THE ORANGE TREE IN THE BACKYARD HAS been neglected. Proof of this is the rotting fruit around its base.

While Jack plucks a few of the ripest oranges from its limbs, I assess the fridge for breakfast provisions. I should never send Aunt Phyllis to Costco with my credit card. We have enough eggs, cheese, and milk to feed a small army.

I'm pulling a loaf of bread from the pantry when my cell rings:

It's Lee.

"Act surprised when Janie and I show up at your doorstep for breakfast," he warns me.

I laugh. "I promise that my performance will be Academy-award worthy. Let me guess: Trisha and Janie are besties again?"

"Thank goodness—yes!" Lee sighs. "Janie moped around enough to make even Porter worry about her."

"Worrying is what he does for a living," I point out.

"True—but I give him credit. He took the liberty of scolding her for having dumped Trisha first," Lee replies. "Donna, I'm glad Trisha is home, safe and sound."

"Me too, Lee. It could have played out so horribly..." At that moment, a chill runs through me. "I can't for the life of me figure out why they left her as opposed to taking her with them. Or, worse yet..."

"Don't let your mind go there, Donna. Everything happens for a reason." Lee's voice is low and terse. "Janie is shoving me out the door. We'll talk when we get there."

LEE, JANIE, AND PORTER DON'T COME ALONE. RYAN AND Marcus are with them.

At the same time, Evan is getting out of a Lyft.

Mary screams as she runs out to greet him. As she jumps into Evan's arms, Lee's Secret Service detail takes its defensive stance.

I shout, "Stand down! *He's our son!*"

Everyone's heads whip around to me—

But it's Mary and Evan who look at me in loving jubilation.

I am now very grateful that Aunt Phyllis bought three dozen eggs and an extra slab of bacon.

THE ADULTS LET THE KIDS TAKE THE FIRST TABLE SHIFT. JEFF FUELS up fast for two reasons. For one, his coach is picking him up so that he can go to the tournament with the rest of the team. The Craig family will follow later. And secondly, he wants to get out of Trisha and Janie's crosshairs.

Aunt Phyllis and Porter are eating now as well. I notice that they've toned down their flirtation. They still make goo-goo eyes at each other and find some reason for their hands to touch. I'm sure they're playing footsie under the table, but I'm not brave enough to look.

I can't say that I blame her. From the look in Aunt Phyllis' eyes, he's tastier than my crisp bacon. Besides, anyone who can read Aunt Phyllis the riot act when it comes to her own safety—let alone that of the rest of us—is fine by me.

Suddenly Mary squeals. Looking up from her phone screen, she exclaims, "Mom! Dad! I just got the admissions email from Berkeley! I've been accepted!"

Evan throws his arms around her. Their hug is long—

As is their kiss.

Janie sighs, entranced.

Jeff slaps his forehead. "*AGHHHH!* Get a room already!" He stomps off.

Ah, young love.

While Jack cracks eggs and I flip the bacon for the second shift, the murmured conversation between Lee, Ryan, and Marcus suddenly comes to a standstill. I follow their stare to the television on the breakfast bar:

Messages are crawling across the screen:

PRESIDENT EDMONTON DEAD OF A HEART ATTACK
Died peacefully in his sleep. State funeral imminent. Full details to come.
VICE PRESIDENT LIBBY KENTFIELD HAS TAKEN THE OATH OF OFFICE

Relief hits me so hard that I don't realize the bacon is burning until Jack reaches over to pull the griddle off the stove and gets burned for his trouble. Once again, he's forgotten to grab a mitt first.

When it comes to doing stupid things, history has a tendency of repeating itself.

IT'S ONLY AFTER JEFF LEAVES IN HIS COACH'S VAN, MARY AND Evan go out for a walk, Aunt Phyllis and Porter are comfortable on the porch swing, and Trisha and Janie hang out upstairs (hopefully, not in Jeff's room) that we make our final mission report to the Three Amigos.

We don't leave out the unsung heroes:

Tom Jamison, the operative from the CIA's Russia Bureau, who personally delivered Edmonton's GRV file, then had to run for his life. Without it, Edmonton's long association with our enemy state could not have been validated;

The intern, Olivia Quinn, who risked her life to blow the whistle on Edmonton's conversation with Putin;

George, who spent too much time in the air to get us where we needed to go, as safely as we'd allow;

Mad Hacker, who cracked the security codes on Edmonton's offshore slush fund for us;

Emma and Arnie, always at the ready to hack, crack, decrypt, and exploit whatever was needed for our mission;

Henry, Dominic, and Abu's roles in shadowing Jack's and my actions and monitoring the danger around us;

And Dominic's efforts in retrieving Trisha.

We are sure to mention our comrades in arms who gave their lives for this mission. Coquette Rambert and Khrystyna Vashchenko will receive stars on Acme's memorial wall.

"Abu is coordinating the joint ceremony. It will take place tomorrow. Mario is flying in to attend it," Ryan tells us. "It's my first act as Acme Industry's new—or I should say, returning CEO."

I chuckle. "Is that your way of saying Jack cracked under the pressure of the position?"

"Very funny!" Jack retorts. "Hey, I know my limits. For the sake of Acme's longevity, the second Ryan's resignation was accepted by our new POTUS I begged him to take back the reins. Hell, we all know I'm not cut out to be a desk jockey. I need the travel, the intrigue, the suspense—"

"*Yada, yada yada.*" I roll my eyes. "We get the picture. Ryan's shoes were too big to fill."

In truth, I'm glad Jack will be at my side—in life and in the field.

If, in fact, we're going back on our vow to get out of the business altogether.

Shit…

Is that what he's saying?

"I'll make no bones about it. I felt exactly the same way about the DNI gig," Ryan admits. "So, Marcus, when President Kentfield asks you to take it back, do us all a favor and just say yes."

"She made the call this morning. I told her I'd start next week since Lee is in no rush to get Muriel and me out of his guest house." Longingly, he sighs. "I'll certainly miss all of this California sunshine."

"You're welcome to come back anytime," Lee declares.

As I hand Lee his bacon and eggs, I remind him: "You told me you knew something about Trisha's ordeal with the Trents. Care to elaborate?"

Lee's smile fades. "When Trisha went missing, I reached the Russian ambassador, Stanislav Chernov. He confirmed my suspicions: Riley's parents and her so-called grandmother are Russian assets. The one acting as her grandmother—an operative whose real name is Natalya Novikova—was once Edmonton's handler. And yes, Janie was the initial target. Edmonton had wanted to blackmail me into giving away state secrets. At the last minute, Edmonton told the Trents to kidnap Trisha instead. It's why Riley broke it off with Janie and invited Trisha to go on the family camping trip in her place." Lee pauses then adds, "Ambassador Chernov also admitted that Edmonton was one of their stateside operatives."

"Jesus! Why would the ambassador do that?" Jack asked.

"Because Putin was incensed at Edmonton's numerous requests for financial quid pro quo. In fact, he intimated that they would be happy if we took care of the 'Edmonton prob- lem' for them and that they'd reciprocate in other ways. I told them that there was one urgent thing they'd have to arrange: to contact Natalya immediately and tell her not to harm a hair on Trisha's head."

Stunned, I drop a plate of toast on the floor.

Our dogs, Lassie and Rin Tin Tin, have been waiting patiently for just such a moment. They snatch the slices in mid-air before leaping through the dog door with their ill- gotten gains.

When I find my voice again, I stutter, "*Wait!*... So, what

you're telling me is that I was supposed to do *Putin's wet work*?"

"Yes...and no." Lee shrugs. "Since they wouldn't have yet known that Edmonton had already died of a heart attack, I figured, 'no harm, no foul.' Just chalk it up to a mutually beneficial collaboration between two great nations. On the one hand, Putin's most successful mole is gone from where he could do the US the most harm. On the other, Putin gets his revenge."

"If it wasn't so ludicrous, it would actually be funny..." Marcus stops mid-sentence. "Donna, are you okay?"

Maybe he's asking because I'm laughing like a deranged hyena.

So, I guess he's got my answer.

Hell yeah, I'm okay.

"Of course, Putin would like to get his money back, too..."

Lee's voice fades as my cackle fills the room.

Except for Mad Hacker's commission of five million dollars and Acme's usual five percent, as of this morning the rest of it was transferred into Ukraine's war chest, courtesy of their deceased countrywoman: Khrystyna Vashchenko.

The menfolk take the hint: *Edmonton's blackmail booty is long gone.*

It's great to be home.

Or, in this case, courtside at one of my children's sports events.

Especially in times of unrest, the pursuit of normalcy is how humankind enjoys life to the fullest.

For Mary, it means resting her head on Evan's shoulder

and knowing that his love for her is just as rock-solid as hers is for him. Even if Mary forgoes joining him at Berkeley, I don't think distance, circumstance, or others whose paths they cross will sever their precious bond. They have already weathered traumatic events that could have broken hearts and lives forever. Both lost a father. And in Evan's case, a mother as well: one whose infamy will shadow him forever, no matter his own accomplishments and good deeds, of which I've no doubt there will be many.

No matter what path Mary takes, she too will go far. I just pray she doesn't follow in her parents' footsteps.

I watch as Jeff uses his physical strength, well-honed athletic skills, and controlled emotions to eviscerate his on-court opponents. Whereas my son's brush with death could have left him with emotional scars that never healed, it has only made him stronger and more determined to make a difference in the world around him.

Now that Trisha and Janie have made up, my younger daughter's naturally sunny disposition—warmed by her melodic giggle and her welcoming smile—bathes those in her presence in a happy glow. It is a parent's instinct to protect and defend those who and that which are dearest to us.

At any age, dire situations test our strengths. Will I ever tell Trisha how close she was to death? Will I use it as a warning as to how fate can change the course of our lives in the blink of an eye?

Yes. But not today.

Instead, I will take a day—maybe even a whole week—to revel in this moment of bliss with those I love most.

At least, that's what I think until Jack whispers in my ear, "Something's come up, hon. We need to talk."

I sigh. "Can you give me a hint?"

He turns my head so that we're eye to eye. "Ryan discovered what Edmonton sold the Russians for his big payday."

Okay, now I'm worried.

THE END

Next Up for Donna!

The Housewife Assassin's Assassination Vacation Planner

(Book 20)

The clock is ticking as housewife assassin Donna Craig and her husband-mission partner, Jack, race across the world to stop the assassinations of seven world leaders.

Other Books by Josie Brown

The Extracurricular Series

Books 1, 2, and 3

The Totlandia Series

The Onesies - Book 1 (Fall)

The Onesies - Book 2 (Winter)

The Onesies - Book 3 (Spring)

The Onesies - Book 4 (Summer)

The Twosies - Book 5 (Fall)

The Twosies – Book 6 (Winter)

The Twosies - Book 7 (Spring)

The Twosies - Book 8 (Summer)

The True Hollywood Lies Series

Hollywood Hunk

Hollywood Whore

More Josie Brown Novels

The Candidate

Secret Lives of Husbands and Wives

The Baby Planner

How to Reach Josie

To write Josie, go to:
mailfromjosie@gmail.com

To find out more about Josie, or to get on her eLetter list for
book launch announcements, go to her website:
www.JosieBrown.com

You can also find her at:

www.AuthorProvocateur.com

twitter.com/JosieBrownCA

facebook.com/josiebrownauthor

pinterest.com/josiebrownca

instagram.com/josiebrownnovels

Lightning Source UK Ltd.
Milton Keynes UK
UKHW022101250822
407860UK00010BA/312/J